'Of course!'

'So we must have our chronicle ready,' Eleanor observed, 'about how Prince Henry Tudor, born on the Feast of St Agnes at Pembroke Castle, was replaced by a changeling.'

DARK QUEEN WARY

DARK QUEEN WARY

Paul Doherty

SEVERN
HOUSE

First world edition published in Great Britain and the USA in 2023
by Severn House, an imprint of Canongate Books Ltd,
14 High Street, Edinburgh EH1 1TE.

Trade paperback edition first published in Great Britain and the USA in 2023
by Severn House, an imprint of Canongate Books Ltd.

severnhouse.com

British Library Cataloguing-in-Publication Data
A CIP catalogue record for this title is available from the British Library.

ISBN-13: 978-1-4483-0864-4 (cased)
ISBN-13: 978-1-4483-1030-2 (trade paper)
ISBN-13: 978-1-4483-1021-0 (e-book)

All Severn House titles are printed on acid-free paper.

MIX
Paper from
responsible sources
FSC® C013056

Typeset by Palimpsest Book Production Ltd.,
Falkirk, Stirlingshire, Scotland.
Printed and bound in Great Britain by
TJ Books Ltd, Padstow, Cornwall.

HISTORICAL NOTE

By 1472 Edward IV, the 'Glorious Son of York', was triumphant. He and his entourage had annihilated their rivals the Lancastrians. Only one true claimant was left to challenge Edward's supremacy: the young Henry Tudor, son of Margaret Beaufort, Countess of Richmond and Lord Edmund Tudor, a Welsh lord who could also claim descent from kings. Edward of York revelled in his triumph. The previous year he had brought to battle, and utterly destroyed, the armies of Lancaster at Barnet, north of London, and Tewkesbury in the West Country. The Battle of Barnet particularly was a gruesome, bitter conflict where both armies were hampered by the thickest mist which, one chronicle maintained, had never been seen before in England.

Once the battle was over, Edward marched back into London. He brought with him the corpses of two of Lancaster's champions: Richard Neville, Earl of Warwick, and his brother John, Marquess of Montagu. Edward, surrounded by his henchmen, was committed to enjoying his victories, yet the Wars of the Roses were not truly over. The ghosts of the dead haunted the living. Memories were sharp and fresh about treachery, treason, and the hideous bloodshed these had caused. More importantly, Edward and his two brothers, George of Clarence and Richard of Gloucester, were still troubled by the continued existence of young Henry Tudor. Shakespeare wrote, 'uneasy lies the head which wears the crown': this certainly applied to Edward of York. If Tudor went into the dark then the 'Game of Kings' would finally be over. No one would be left to challenge York's supremacy and monopoly of power.

The Wars of the Roses had been characterised by subterfuge, intrigue and betrayal: these poisonous weeds flourished vigorously in Edward's court. The Yorkist lords dreamed of clearing the chessboard of all opposition and, especially, Henry Tudor. York's minions worked hard to make this dream a reality, whatever the cost . . .

The Author's Note at the end of the novel creates the context for the remarkable events this novel is based on. The quotations at the beginning of each section are from *The Chronicles of the White Rose of York*.

HISTORICAL CHARACTERS

House of York

Richard Duke of York and his wife Cecily, Duchess of York, 'The Rose of Raby'.
Parents of:
Edward (later King Edward IV),
George of Clarence,
Richard Duke of Gloucester (later King Richard III).

House of Lancaster

John of Gaunt: son of Edward III, founder of the Lancastrian dynasty.
Henry VI, Henry's wife Margaret of Anjou and their son Prince Edward.

House of Tudor

Edmund Tudor, first husband of Margaret Beaufort, Countess of Richmond, and half-brother to Henry VI of England.
Edmund's father Owain had married Katherine of Valois, French princess and widow of King Henry V, father of Henry VI.
Jasper Tudor, Edmund's brother, kinsman to Henry Tudor (later Henry VII).

House of Beaufort

Margaret Beaufort, Countess of Richmond, married first to Edmund Tudor, then Sir Henry Stafford and finally Lord Thomas Stanley.

John Beaufort, first Duke of Somerset and Margaret's father.
Christopher Urswicke, Margaret Beaufort's personal clerk and leading henchman.
Reginald Bray, Margaret's principal steward and controller of her household.

House of Neville

Richard Neville, Earl of Warwick.
John Neville, Marquess of Montague, brother of Richard Neville.
George Neville, Archbishop of York, brother to Richard and John.

House of Oxford

John de Vere, 13th Earl of Oxford.

Others

Sir Thomas Urswicke, Recorder of London, father of the aforementioned Christopher Urswicke.
Sir Henry Stafford, Margaret Beaufort's second husband.
Lord Thomas Stanley, Countess Margaret's betrothed.

THE PROLOGUES

'And there was such a great mist, neither side could even see each other'

His world was dying. The day of judgement, Easter Sunday, 14 April, the year of Our Lord 1471. Dawn had broken, yet heaven hid the rising sun under the thickest, cloying mist. Such a mist had never been seen before and, after the battle, when tales were told, the common consensus was that the mist had been boiled in hell. Richard Neville, Earl of Warwick – self-styled kingmaker, the shatterer of crowns, the arbiter of power – realized all of this was now lost. This day of judgement truly was his time of reckoning. He had taken off his helmet and cast it to one side and let the freezing mist catch his bruised, battered face. He tried to stagger forward, to be immersed in that violent, bloody surf of weapons as the last of Lancaster's battle lines buckled under the ferocious assault of Edward of York and his minions. All was lost! Warwick's banners, displaying the ragged staff and bear, and all the other insignia had long disappeared. John Neville, Marquess of Montagu, Richard's brother, had been cut down, hacked to the ground by a Yorkist battle group. Warwick, wild eyed, gazed around. Men were fleeing for their lives, running to the left and right of him. Warwick's sweaty body began to cool, his mailed shirt and armour clasping him with icy clamps, the freezing beckoning of the grave. The harsh, strident din of battle was drawing closer. Warwick's own array was falling back in utter confusion, though a few of his captains strove to hold their battle groups against the enemy. In truth, what an enemy! Edward of York, golden-haired and blue-eyed, had moved like the magnificent leopard he was. Breaking out of London with his brothers, pale-faced, narrow-souled Richard of Gloucester, and that Judas incarnate George of Clarence. They

had caught Warwick's army by surprise. John de Vere, Earl of
Oxford, had tried to hold the left wing of Warwick's force, but
his men had been lured away, good for nothing. Warwick peered
into the gathering mist. For a brief breath it parted and Warwick
glimpsed the golden sun of York. Edward, surrounded by his
household bodyguard, hand-picked knights, who were carving
and hacking their way through their opponents. A constant club-
bing and cutting to spray the mist with a deep, bloody tinge.
Trumpets brayed. Horns howled. The war cries grew stronger.
All was lost, it was time to flee. Desperate, Warwick turned,
looking for his own battle group, The Five Wounds, a group of
skilful swordsmen who had vowed loyalty to their master, body
and soul, to the death. Warwick quietly cursed. He had taken the
advice of Matthew Poppleton, the captain of The Five Wounds
to dispense with his warhorse, to reassure the common foot that
Warwick and his captains would not flee the field. They would
not leave them to the not-so-tender mercies of York. Warwick
thought he heard his name called. He glanced over his shoulder
and thought he glimpsed the tabards of his battle group, The Five
Wounds, close to a copse. The strident call of trumpets and the
harsh song of the battle horns cut above the din, the agreed sign
to retreat. Warwick glanced around: his own battle line was
writhing about, falling apart; all was lost. Warwick turned, heavy-
hearted, stumbling as he ripped off his heavy armour, desperate
to reach that copse. Perhaps his battle group waited there. They
had horses fresh to ride. They would escape. Warwick would
fight again. He paused to breathe, sucking the icy air through his
lips. He had failed because he had been betrayed. He sensed
this. Something had gone terribly wrong. Was it the work of the
damnable Achitophel, that dark spirit who moved between
the warring factions of England, offering information, selling his
service, which always meant disruption and betrayal? Had this
happened here? After all, why had he been left like this, alone
and forsaken? He was Richard Neville, Earl of Warwick, Europe's
premier warrior, once this kingdom's ruler, yet now he was alone
in this muddy, bloody, mist-hung field. For a brief moment the
great earl thought of what he was leaving: his hapless brother
George and the Lady Grace. How would they fare when
confronted by the power of York? He just thanked God that he

had not brought the Secretum with him but hidden it away at The Moor for others to use. So many wanted that document, but it had always been his and his only. Now, if he was going to die, he could rejoice in that one thought. The truth could still spill out to trap and shatter his enemies. For they were all there: false, conniving George of Clarence, treacherous Thomas Urswicke, and all the other canting crew. But time was passing. Warwick hastened on but then he slipped, his armoured foot catching a gore-soaked clump of harsh grass. Warwick crashed to the ground. He rolled, staring up into the blankness of heaven. He struggled to rise but he was abruptly pushed back by a hooded figure whose tabard displayed the suns of York. Warwick gargled in fear. He fought to speak. He wanted to explain who he was, what he could do. He tried to plead but his gorget was ripped off and the dagger blade sank deep into his exposed throat.

A courier, carrying one of King Edward's bloody, battered gauntlets, thundered through Bishopsgate into the city. He presented the gauntlet to Edward's beautiful queen, Elizabeth, as a token of her husband's resounding victory at Barnet a few hours earlier. He brought news, startling news. Warwick was dead. Gone to judgement. Montagu, Richard's brother, also slain, together with a long array of Lancastrian captains.

News of Edward's outstanding, blood-soaked victory soon swept the city. George Neville, Archbishop of York and Warwick's beloved brother, made an immediate submission to York, personally prostrating himself before the King. He also handed to Edward the keys of the city, as well as the hapless Lancastrian King Henry, for whom Warwick had so vainly fought. Archbishop Neville was now in comfortable confinement in the Tower, where Henry, the King whom George Neville had sworn to protect, soon joined him. In the meantime, the Brothers York revelled in their great triumph.

Late that same afternoon, Edward entered London with standards displayed, banners billowing, horns and trumpets braying, as every bell in the city rang out their joyous welcome. Edward led his army straight from the battlefield and the good citizens shivered as they looked at the wounded soldiers, their faces and noses hacked, squashed, bloodied and sliced, a gruesome testimony to the ferocious hand-to-hand fighting at Barnet, where helmets were discarded and visors raised, as man became wolf to man. Edward led his bloodied host in formal procession into St Paul's, through the sprawling graveyard, past its famous wooden pulpit and soaring cross. He entered the church through its main door, riding up the nave to be formally greeted and congratulated by the mayor, leading citizens and masters of the guilds. Once he had reached the sanctuary, Edward, accompanied only by his henchmen, set up his battle standards and war pennants, shredded and tattered by cannon, culverin and fire arrows. They were displayed in the sanctuary as the choir chanted the Easter hymn, 'How joyfully is this day celebrated'. The choir celebrated God's victory over hell, which in this case was the House of Lancaster.

Early next morning, shortly after the dawn mass, a more sombre and macabre procession arrived at St Paul's. An open coffin, escorted by six Friars of the Sack, their black pointed hoods pulled forward to conceal both head and face. The good brothers, three on either side, each held a lighted taper. They walked slowly, preceded by a ragged boy beating a tambour. They reached the trestles specially erected just outside the entrance to the rood screen where they deposited the coffin, little more than a battered weapons chest. Once they had done so, they intoned psalms of mourning for the two corpses crammed in the coffin like slabs of meat. The two cadavers lay face to face, naked as they were born except for a dirty cloth covering their genitals. This was the final humiliation for Richard Neville, Earl of Warwick, self-styled kingmaker, and his brother John, Marquess of Montagu. Nailed to each side of the coffin was a proclamation which declared that these were 'the mortal remains of two traitors, Richard Neville and his brother John, displayed openly so as to counter any subtle and malicious rumour that Warwick might have survived the hellish, brutal slaughter at Barnet, to cause fresh mischief, new murmurs, insurrection and rebellion'. The corpses, the proclamation continued, would lie until the following Friday evening, when they would be removed before compline to the Neville mausoleum at Bisham Priory.

On that same day, after thousands had filed past the coffin, a dark garbed figure, dressed in heavy widow weeds, slipped in through the corpse door of St Pauls. The church lay deserted. The good citizens of London had slaked their morbid curiosity. More important, a vicious, violent windstorm had racked the city. According to the warlocks and wizards who plied their trade in St Paul's gloomy graveyard, this storm was really a veritable host of demons sweeping into the west in preparation for another great bloodletting. A fresh Lancastrian army had landed in the West Country. Old King Henry's warlike queen, Margaret of Anjou, had secured safe harbour at Weymouth and was now eager to entice York to fresh battle.

Such news had dampened rejoicings in London. People were no longer interested in the remains of the Barnet struggle, which had really resolved nothing. People also realized they should be careful. Lancastrian corpses, naked and bloodied, might soon be replaced by those of York. However, the dark, shrouded figure who'd come to pay its respects was not concerned with such news. Moving as soft and swift as a ghost, the mysterious pilgrim was not interested in the living but the dead. More specifically, the two corpses who lay like ghastly twins in their makeshift coffin casket. The figure bent over the corpses and stared at the bruised, battered remains. Richard Neville's death wound was to the throat; John's was a deep thrust through the right eye and to the left side. The figure pressed a delicately gloved hand against each of the dead men's heads and silently swore bloody retribution.

Almost a year later Achitophel, that professional Judas man, that wraith of the night who'd gleefully assumed the name ascribed to him, sat in the darkest corner of The Mercy Pew, a sombre, ill-lit tavern not far from the precincts of Westminster. He had journeyed into London on some fictitious reason, but in truth he wanted to think, reflect, and to plot for the future. He favoured The Mercy Pew: it was an ideal place to meet strangers who wanted to do business with Achitophel. The tavern's taproom had its own original sinister arrangement. The opposite walls of the long dining hall boasted self-contained closets sealed by a door with a trellised screen running down the middle of each of these narrow chambers, a sure way to protect oneself. On occasions such as this, Achitophel would sit, like a priest at the mercy pew, and listen to what his client had to say but, of course, there was no shriving, no forgiveness, nothing of the mercy of God or man. Indeed, the opposite. Achitophel dabbled in the deepest treachery, but now he realized his time was passing. He had to accept that. The deadly struggle between York and Lancaster had drawn to an end. Almost a year had lapsed since the Yorkist victories at Tewkesbury and, above all, Barnet. The Brothers York were, and would be, triumphant. Old Henry, Lancaster's King, witless as a pigeon, had been lodged in the Tower where, of course, he suddenly died, and his corpse had been dressed and carted off to Chertsey. His warlike queen, Margaret of Anjou, had also grievously suffered: captured after Tewkesbury, she had to witness her only son, Prince Edward, being stabbed to death by Yorkist warlords in a tavern overlooking Tewkesbury market-place. Afterwards, Margaret had been thrown into some prison where she would linger until the Brothers York decided to send her home to Anjou. The war was truly ended. The fighting had faded away and the armies dispersed. Time would pass. Times would change. There would be fewer opportunities for Achitophel to dabble in, though one attractive possibility remained which might still yield a rich harvest.

Achitophel unfurled the piece of parchment, smoothing it out on the tabletop. He stared at the five names listed there. Matthew Poppleton. 'Oh what a man.' He breathed. 'You'll have to die; you will have to disappear.' He glanced at the other names. Mark Chadwick, Luke Colworth, John Forester and Simon Fladgate; all members of the battle group known as The Five Wounds. Each of these warriors had sworn to defend their master, Richard, Earl of Warwick. They had certainly failed, thanks to Achitophel. But could he now exploit that further? Could he ruthlessly slaughter The Five Wounds? Silence their mouths and be lavishly rewarded for doing so? He had seen Warwick's bloodied white corpse sprawled on the ground at Barnet, with that dreadful mist curling about like a host of night wraiths, gathering to collect the great earl's sinful soul. Achitophel picked up his goblet of wine and sipped slowly. He had heard such a poetic reference given by one of the many tale-tellers who used to throng Westminster with this news or that. They would describe the great battles between York and Lancaster, Barnet in particular.

In truth, that is where it all truly ended. Achitophel placed his goblet back on the table and half closed his eyes, his mind teeming with all sorts of possibilities. 'I wonder,' Achitophel whispered to himself. 'Was Warwick, when he was cut down, carrying the Secretum? A most valuable manuscript in which, according to rumour, Warwick had clearly described the constant intrigue and treachery which swirled during that hurling time. Men who fought for Lancaster on Monday would, by the end of the week, have entered York's camp. Fervent adherents to one house would, overnight, become avid supporters of the other.' Achitophel shook his head, opened his eyes and took another sip of wine. Warwick, he thought, was too astute, too cunning for that. He would keep the Secretum hidden. But where? In one of his great fortresses? Or would he entrust it to Warwick's own feckless brother, George, Archbishop of York? Now that might be a possibility. Or had it been handed over to Warwick's lithesome sister, the Lady Grace? Oh yes, there were a number of people who would love to get their hands on the Secretum. The Brothers York, Clarence in particular, and even some of their loyal adherents such as Thomas Urswicke, Recorder of the City. Achitophel had been asked, when he had approached individuals with an offer to do something on their behalf, if he could also seize the Secretum? Of course, he could not. Achitophel was no fool. He dabbled in dealings with souls, setting one person off against another. He did this for profit, and the season for that was swiftly disappearing. He might lack custom, but searching for the Secretum would, he concluded, make him little profit.

Times were changing and so must he. In the Old Testament, the original Achitophel betrayed King David and, racked by remorse, hanged himself. Well, in a way, that might happen again. He would finish one more task, the one he was plotting, then disappear before re-emerging in a completely new guise.

Achitophel pulled his hood closer and raised the muffler across his mouth. He liked it that way, so no one could even glimpse his face. He rose, left the closet, and walked into the tavern yard to relieve himself. When he returned to the taproom, he abruptly stopped, his gaze caught by a small shrine within the doorway: a copy of the cross of San Damiano, before which Francis of Assisi had prayed for God's guidance. The small crucifix was bathed in the light of a votive candle placed in a glass jar next to it.

Achitophel studied it carefully. In truth and in fact, such depictions meant nothing to Achitophel. He had lost all and any faith on the many battlefields he'd scoured. Man was a savage beast. No God reigned in heaven and, if he did, he couldn't give a fig about the creatures of the dark who thronged the earth. Men were no more than wolves who sloped through the dark and, on their death, disappeared into oblivion. Nonetheless, works of art fascinated Achitophel, and this one in particular, with its emphasis on the five wounds of Christ. Achitophel studied these and quietly marvelled at the prospect they provoked. He would remember all this when the time came. Nevertheless, such an idea would only prove fruitful if the offer he'd so recently made, was accepted.

According to the chroniclers of the era, the year of Our Lord 1473 was a most dangerous time. Conspiracy and betrayal were the flavour of the day, and the spirit of Judas moved merrily amongst the children of men. Palaces, manors, and even self-proclaimed houses of religion were not free of this spiritual malignancy. The Benedictine convent of St Ursula on Leetehoven Street, close to the great market of Ghent, was a fine example of this, thanks to the arrival of two nuns from the Convent of Valle Crucis close to Neath Abbey in South Wales. Sisters Eleanor and Matilda Patmore had, in full chapter at the convent, petitioned to move from Valle Crucis to St Ursula's before Maundy Thursday. They claimed that they wished to do so for deeply spiritual reasons which they could only share with their father confessor and, of course, he could not say a word on the matter. In fact, Mother Superior at Valle Crucis had only been too willing to let both nuns go. She and her principal officers did not like the two sisters at all. Both Matilda and Eleanor had been given prebends at Valle Crucis at the instigation of Margaret, the now widowed Countess of Richmond. Countess Margaret, being the only daughter of the powerful John Beaufort, Duke of Somerset, now deceased, could not be ignored.

The Patmore sisters had entered Valle Crucis a few years after Margaret had given birth to her son Henry, her only child by Lord Edmund Tudor. Once in Valle Crucis, both sisters had assumed the air of great ladies, constantly hinting at their powerful friends and the excellent service they had provided the countess when, at only fourteen years of age, she had given birth to Prince Henry. Oh, the two ladies were certainly haughty enough, and this was reflected in their white, sharp-featured faces and the way they talked and sang through their noses with a rather nasty disdain which was difficult to brook. Oh yes, Eleanor and Matilda Patmore were very much the grand ladies, with all their airs and graces and the constant half-formed allusions to knowing the secret counsels of their former mistress, Countess Margaret.

In the end, Mother Superior had joyfully bade them a swift farewell from Valle Crucis and, after a pleasant sea voyage to Dordrecht, the two nuns had safely reached the convent of St Ursula. Once they had been given comfortable cells, both sisters had prowled the sacred precincts and discovered a small, enclosed rose garden. With its sheer thick walls and narrow postern gate, the garden was probably the best place to plot their great enterprise: the scheme they had discussed and devised with Eleanor's son, Thomas Patmore. Of course, they waited for weeks before they began to talk in detail about their secret design, and it was best done here in the rose garden. No eaves-dropper could loiter, clinging like a shadow to the keyhole, the squint or the gap, which always attracted the mischievous as well as the curious. God knows there were enough of these in St Ursula's. Since their arrival at the convent, Eleanor and Matilda had lost no time in informing people how important they were and, as candleflame lures the moths, Eleanor and Matilda attracted those gossips who plague so-called houses of prayer. Both Eleanor and Matilda had even, on occasion, stumbled on these furtive listeners, but that couldn't happen here amongst the roses. Confident of this, both sisters gathered in the garden, on the Feast of St Remier, to discuss a recent letter Eleanor had received from her son.

'Thomas is now in London,' Eleanor declared, 'and those who patronise him will make good use of who he is and what he does.'

'And when his work is finished, he will slip away here,'

Matilda replied. 'To Ghent, beyond the reach of the King of England and Margaret, Countess of Richmond. We shall be ready. We shall make that petty princess, that self-proclaimed great lady, repent of her arrogance to us. Remember how it was when her boy was born? January, the weather was freezing cold and the same was true of the castle. A truly sorrowful time and place. Pembroke was in deep mourning over the death of Lord Edmund, the boy's father, who died only two months before his birth. Margaret was no more than fourteen, a puppy yelping as she gave birth. Remember Eleanor, the only people in that birth chamber were you, me, and the wise woman who has, thankfully, gone to her eternal reward. Lord Jasper, Edmund's brother, was outside waiting in the stairwell, desperate for news. Prince Henry was born, wrapped in swaddling clothes and taken to Jasper by your good self. We entrusted the Prince to him. Of course, and that is where our story diverts. We believe that soon afterwards, the same Lord Jasper, to protect the baby Prince from his enemies . . .'

'Who were and who are, Matilda?'

'Well, those who also have a claim to the English Throne. Whatever we think of her, Margaret Beaufort is a direct descendant of John of Gaunt, the root and source of the Lancastrian claim to the Crown. Countess Margaret often reminded us and others of that. Anyway, to protect her son, Lord Jasper made an exchange. He placed the true Prince with the nuns at Valle Crucis, whilst the boy named Owain was slipped into the royal cradle at Pembroke.

'So, this is the time of reckoning.' Matilda whispered excitedly. 'When truth is out?'

'Be patient,' Eleanor warned, 'we cannot move until Thomas is finished in England and comes hurrying to us. I just worry about him,' she glanced quickly at her sister who nodded knowingly, 'he places himself in great danger. I just hope he is prudent, watchful.'

'And what shall we do with all we know?' Matilda asked, eager to change the conversation.

'We shall wait for Thomas and then publish and print a chronicle which the courts of Europe, and everyone else, will want to buy.'

PART ONE

'And one of Kind Edward's men came upon him and killed him and despoiled him naked.'

Margaret, Countess of Richmond, fought to control the rage seething within her. She sat in the council chamber of the White Tower and glared at the couple seated opposite. Edward the King, his brothers Clarence and Gloucester, together with Thomas Urswicke, Recorder of London and principal clerk in the Secret Chancery, had been most cunning. They had arranged the table in a horseshoe fashion. Margaret and her two henchmen on one side and Thomas Patmore and the young man claiming to be Henry Tudor on the other. The stage was now ready for their mummery, a vicious tournament was set to begin. A cruel and insidious game about to unfurl.

'Your Grace.' Christopher Urswicke forced a smile, turning to nod respectfully at the King before shifting his gaze to his most insidious father who, Christopher believed, was the true cause for them being here. Sir Thomas Urswicke, despite his smiling face and gentle eyes, housed a truly sinister spirit. The Recorder could carefully coif his auburn hair and neatly trim his moustache and beard. He could grin with his friendly green eyes, but all this was a mere mask for his most malicious soul.

'Your Grace,' Christopher repeated, because protocol dictated that he could not continue to address Edward without the King's permission. Edward, however, just sat head down, as if deeply interested in the document before him, apparently most reluctant to allow Christopher to continue. Countess Margaret moved slightly in her chair and gently tapped Christopher's arm. He turned; his smooth, pale, shaven face creased into a knowing smile. Margaret sighed with relief. Christopher would not lose his temper. Indeed, with his unruly auburn hair, soft eyes and full, generous lips, Christopher reminded Margaret of a painting she'd seen of an angel. In truth, however, Christopher was as cunning and wily as his father, perhaps even more so. Christopher's antipathy to Sir Thomas sprang from Christopher's fervent belief that his father had, through his constant dalliance with a veritable stable of willing ladies, driven his beloved mother, Margaret's closest friend, to an early grave. The countess leaned closer and quickly whispered that Christopher should wait for His Grace the King to reply. She then turned to the man on her left, Reginald Bray, her principal receiver and steward. If Christopher reflected the light, Bray, with his sallow face, raven-black hair and deep-set eyes, reflected the dark. Christopher, she knew from his childhood, but Bray? Did a man like Reginald have a childhood, a true one? Margaret was concerned. Christopher knew all the cunning games of the English court and chancery, but Bray had a violent temper; easily taunted, he would rise to the bait. Margaret stretched out and squeezed Bray's arm warningly. She recognized the game being played. Edward and his coven wanted this silence. They rejoiced in the fact that she had to sit and stare at the young man opposite, introduced as the countess's one and only beloved son, Henry Tudor.

Margaret shifted her gaze, staring up at a triptych celebrating the martyrdom of St Sebastian, a beautiful young man transfixed by arrows. Margaret closed her eyes and quietly prayed for the strength to sustain this martyrdom. She recalled her beloved Edmund, Henry's father. On one most memorable occasion he had taken her out to lie beneath a massive spreading oak in a nearby wood. He did this as he laughingly assured her, to pay humble court and true devotion to his beloved lady. Months later, a violent windstorm swept the same wood, overturning that ancient oak standing at the centre of a shadow-filled glade. Edmund had taken her out to see what had happened and she recalled staring down into the black tangled roots which circled and snaked against the darkness. Edmund, all serious, declared it was an entrance into another kingdom: a place of shifting spirit-shapes which lurked beneath the ground and preyed on humankind. Well, Margaret opened her eyes, this was no different.

Her Yorkist masters seated at the top of the table truly were lords of hell, some more than others. Richard, Edward's younger

brother, sat quietly, his white, peaked face the mask of an inscru-
table prince. Clarence, seated on the other side of his kingly
brother, was a most malignant creature. Edward of England,
standing over six feet tall and possessed of the finest figure, with
the face and golden hair to match, was a truly handsome man.
George of Clarence, sprawled in his chair, was the total opposite,
with his bloated, rubicund drunken face. He truly was a parody
of his elder brother, for he also lacked any of York's charm and
bonhomie. Moreover, Margaret knew that Clarence, who was
now glaring bleary-eyed at her, hated Lancaster, the Beauforts,
and herself in particular.

'Ah yes Master Urswicke.' Edward now pretended to have
finished reading, pushing away the sheet of parchment on the
table before him.

'Well Master Urswicke?' Clarence bawled.

'Your Grace.' Christopher chose to ignore Clarence. 'I swear
to God,' Christopher pointed across at the young man, 'he is not
Henry Tudor. He is not the son of my mistress the countess of
Richmond. He is a mammet; an Imposter.'

'I agree.' Bray grated, pulling himself up in his chair.

'How can you be so sure?' Sir Thomas silkily intervened.
'When was the last time you met Henry Tudor?'

'Years ago.' Countess Margaret swiftly intervened, fearful Bray
might reveal that young Henry had in fact secretly visited his
mother at least twice since the great bloodbath at Barnet and
Tewkesbury almost a year ago. 'More importantly,' she added,
'I know that young man, whoever he is and from wherever he
has sprung, is not my son. True,' she continued sharply, 'he has
the same look, the dark hair, the eyes, nose and long face of my
beloved Edmund. He is, I am also sure, of the same year as
Henry Tudor, some sixteen summers.' Margaret then abruptly
lapsed into Welsh. The Imposter, as Urswicke had now labelled
him, smiled, and fluently answered in the same tongue. Margaret
sighed, shook her head and sat back in her chair.

'You have taught him well, Master Patmore.'

'Not taught, madam,' Patmore replied. 'He has his birthright
as he has his native tongue.'

Margaret didn't deign to answer. She glanced away, opened
her purse and drew out a set of ivory ave beads, a wedding gift

from her first husband. Urswicke realized that his mistress was on the verge of tears at this cruel baiting, but she would not break down, not here, not in front of her mortal enemies, this gaggle of Yorkist lords.

Urswicke stared hard at Patmore. Of course, he had heard the name before and was more than aware that Thomas Patmore had been Henry Tudor's principal tutor at Pembroke and elsewhere. Patmore was a skinny man with thinning, reddish hair. He sat sour-faced, his heavy-lidded eyes never still, lips slightly twisted, as if he found constant fault with everything and everyone around him.

'Your Grace.' Christopher was determined to close the meeting and extricate his mistress as swiftly as possible. They were trapped, being baited and taunted beyond belief.

'Yes, Master Urswicke?' Clarence rasped testily.

'What is all this? When did this Imposter, this claimant appear?'

'Five days ago.' Sir Thomas replied. 'Five days ago,' he repeated. 'This young man and Master Thomas Patmore disembarked at Queenhithe from the two-masted cog, *The Lantern*, out of Brest. Its captain, who knew of their identity, which they didn't try to hide, immediately informed the harbour master, who of course sent swift scurriers to my chambers in both the Guildhall and the Secret Chancery at Westminster. I hastened down to Queenhithe and collected both our guests. Since then, they have been here in the Tower, in comfortable rooms along the first gallery of the King's lodgings. They had considerable baggage, all of which is now safely stored away, as well as letters and licences from Duke Francis of Brittany, who had given them safe shelter at Rennes. Here, do take a look at these.' Sir Thomas pushed across a selection of parchment which his son, a trained clerk, quickly sifted. All bore the personal seal of Duke Francis, signed at Rennes a month earlier. All the documents decreed that 'Henry Tudor and Master Patmore be given safe passage through Brittany to Brest and beyond.' The script was executed in a clerkly hand; the seals looked genuine, displaying the duke's arms. Urswicke sighed deeply. He thrust the documents back towards his father. Sir Thomas leaned forward, his eyes dancing with malicious glee as he collected the parchments.

'All in order, my son, and, I am pleased to inform you, Henry Tudor has made full submission to the King. He has renounced all treasons and declared he will take an oath of fealty to Edward King of England and his heirs.' Sir Thomas's smile widened. 'Let us rejoice at such good news.'

'Peace and harmony are God's own gift,' Christopher evasively replied, even as he quietly conceded to himself that this truly was a deepening nightmare. The Imposter was a cruel, subtle device to taunt the countess and all she stood for and, at this moment, what could she do? Try to question a young man steeped deeply in all that was known about the real Henry Tudor? No. That must not happen. It was time to leave. He nodded at the King then turned to whisper to the countess. Sir Thomas, now all hard-eyed, rapped the table then paused as a horrific, heart-rending scream echoed up from below. Christopher pushed back his chair in alarm until he remembered it was execution day on Tower Green. A gibbet and execution table had been set up so the constable could punish a cohort of malefactors judged and sentenced by special courts sitting in the Tower.

'What I was going to say,' Sir Thomas declared, 'is that His Grace the King in his deep wisdom, now confident of Henry Tudor's loyalty, be safely lodged, my Lady, in your townhouse, as a specially honoured guest . . .'

'No!' The countess, clutching her ave beads, leaned against the table. 'Why? What is this? It is too much to bear!'

'Silence.' Edward the King thumped the table with a bejewelled fist. 'Silence!' he thundered, his voice rising to a shout.

Margaret turned back in her chair. She realised the trap she'd walked into. Edward may be England's golden boy. He could, and often did, charm everyone, especially the ladies, his own special delight. But not now! Edwards's face was twisted in rage, his eyes mere slits, mouth half open to help his breathing.

'You, madam,' Edward jabbed a finger at Margaret, 'you are a Beaufort, the kin of great traitors to this kingdom, a descendant of malignants, utterly opposed to me and mine. Your father, uncle and all that ilk have gone into the dark. Many now argue that you should follow them. You and this.' Edward pointed at the Imposter. 'Your so-called beloved son, no longer sheltering in

Brittany. I have shown you woman and your familiars.' The King lowered his hand and smiled icily at Christopher. 'Yes, you and all your coven have been shown great mercy and favour. Now, madam, you test me sorely.'

'True, true,' Clarence echoed, beating the table with his fingers. Sir Thomas also murmured his agreement, though Richard of Gloucester just gazed stonily into the middle distance.

'Of course.' Christopher hastily intervened, putting a restraining hand on his mistress's arm. 'Of course, my lady will make you,' he gestured across the table, 'will provide you,' he corrected himself, 'with suitable quarters.'

'Truly comfortable,' Clarence snarled.

'Of course, Your Grace.'

'Warm lodgings and meals becoming his status.' Clarence couldn't keep the sneer out of his voice.

'Of course, Your Grace.'

Christopher pleaded with his eyes that both the countess and Bray remain silent.

'Good, good.' Edward now became his other self, the genial, benevolent prince.

'In which case.' He abruptly rose, compelling everyone else to do likewise. 'In three days . . .' The King picked up his cloak from the back of his chair. 'In three days, my Lady, our guests will arrive by barge at your riverside mansion. Make sure you welcome them.'

'Come, come.' Sir Thomas gestured to the Imposter. 'We need to discuss matters further.'

The royal party then swept out of the chamber, with little courtesy or deference towards the countess. Once they'd gone, she sat down in her chair, putting her face in her hands. Christopher stood listening to the King and his entourage, including the Imposter and his mentor, clatter down the stone spiral staircase. He heard the King shouting for his guards, then the door to Tower Green slammed shut. Christopher gestured with his head for Bray to go down and ensure that they had not left some eavesdropper lurking in that shadow-filled staircase. Bray, hardly concealing his furious temper, hurried out, clattering down the steps. Christopher gently stroked the countess's shoulder. Bray returned.

'None,' he rasped. 'All the bast . . .' He drew a deep breath. 'Edward and his minions have left.'

'Then come,' Christopher urged. He helped his pale-faced mistress to stand up. For a while she just leaned against the table as if gasping for breath. She then crossed herself and made ready to leave. Christopher drew comfort from the change in the countess, her petite, narrow face was now determinedly set, eyes clear, lips slightly compressed.

'Let us be gone,' she murmured, 'from this House of the Red Slayer; this domain of demons. Let us not say one further word about what has happened here until we have shaken off the devil's dust from this deadly place.'

Christopher offered his arm; she took it and smiled bleakly up at him then at Bray standing slightly behind.

'My two angels,' she whispered. 'My brave warriors who fly on eagles' wings. Let us be gone.'

They left the White Tower, a knight banneret, his tabard displaying the suns of York, returned their warbelts. Urswicke strapped his on, bracing himself against the chilling breeze before turning away in disgust at the dreadful stench wafting from the makeshift gallows close to the sombre chapel of St Peter in Chains. Six felons had been executed. Archers stood on guard to ensure the corpses would hang there till dusk, when relatives and friends could collect them for burial. Until then, those who waited could do nothing but stare up into the contorted, twisted faces of the hanged. Or, if they were so inclined, join the two Friars of the Sack reciting psalms of mourning, though their voices were almost drowned by the roars and growls from the animal pens in the royal bestiary. She smiled at Christopher then pointed at the thickening mist swirling about. 'In the end,' she whispered, 'such are our enemies. Here for the moment but soon gone, like tears in the rain.'

One hand resting on Urswicke's arm, with Bray showing the way, they hastened down the runnels leading to the magnificent Lion Gate. Urswicke remained on his guard. The Tower was still busy, with stalls on either side offering everything from bloodied chunks of meat to clothing, some of these being the effects of the recently hanged. Different noises dinned the air. All kinds of smells and odours curled above the people pushing and shoving their way through the narrow gullies, dominated either side by the soaring walls of different towers. Due to the King's arrival, archers and men-at-arms stood in groups watching the crowd, ready to curb and crush any mischief. At last, they reached the gate. They showed licences and passed through on to the long, broad Tower quayside, which was just recovering from a period of chaos. A tinker explained how a huge sow had broken loose from its pen and forced its bulky way through the gateway on to the quayside. Lumbering about there, the sow soon attracted the attention of the ferocious, feral dogs which roamed the quayside and the derelict common land to the north of the Tower. Carnage ensued. The dogs attacked and the sow fought back, drenching the cobbles in blood, until a cohort of archers killed both prey and predator. The quayside still glistened red as the light caught the rivulets of blood snaking between the cobbles.

With her henchmen either side, the countess walked carefully to the river steps where her barge was waiting, a long, high-prowed craft with a canopied stern for the countess and her companions to shelter in. Once they were settled, the rudder man ordered his oarsmen to cast off, then he and his crew skilfully guided the barge away from the quayside. They were soon caught up in the narrow, surging gullies of turbulent river water, which pounded and thundered their way down to the narrow arches which supported London Bridge.

Urswicke stared up as they approached. He glimpsed the houses built along the side of the bridge and, above these, the poled, severed heads of traitors; black balls against the clear sky. Urswicke closed his eyes and murmured a prayer for safety, pleading for the protection of St Thomas Beckett, whose chapel dominated the centre of the bridge. Now free of the quayside, the barge moved swiftly. The river thundered fast and furious; a torrent of turbulent water which could have easily dashed them against the starlings built around the struts of the bridge. The light dimmed. The noise was now infernal, as if the river had become a roaring beast, set on smashing everything in its path. Spray, thick and heavy, poured over the barge. Bray just sat head down. Urswicke wondered if he was praying, though he suspected that Bray believed in nothing but the power of his right arm. The countess threaded her ave beads. Urswicke recited one last prayer then they were through, under the bridge into calmer waters.

Once there, the rudder man kept the barge as close as possible to the north bank of the Thames. They passed busy quaysides where stout, full-bellied cogs and an array of fishing smacks delivered their cargoes and received fresh loads for the next voyage. The sun was still strong. The breeze even shifting to waft a myriad of smells across the choppy waters: fish, salt, tar, pitch, as well as the different odours from the countless stoves and kitchens which fed the busy, frenetic world of the river people.

Urswicke narrowed his eyes against the light as he reflected on the nonsense he had witnessed earlier at the Tower – it was nonsense, yet very dangerous nonsense. More importantly, what could be done about it? Urswicke broke from his reverie as the prow boy sang out how they should now turn in. The barge did so, almost creeping along the riverside to the water-gate of the countess's town mansion. The barge was safely berthed. The countess and her party disembarked. She and her henchmen maintained their silence. The countess's retainers were, in the main, loyal and devoted, though – undoubtedly – weeds had been cleverly sown amongst the flowers. Sir Thomas Urswicke had a veritable legion of spies, Judas men and informants. Some of these must have been placed in the countess's household. Indeed, at Urswicke's insistence, they never talked of matters politic until they were safely ensconced in the countess's private chamber. Urswicke had searched that room from floor to ceiling in order to establish there were no squints, gaps or cracks for any eavesdropper to prey on the countess's secret affairs.

Urswicke heaved a sigh of relief as Bray locked the door to this safe chamber. He then hurried to place a few small logs on the fire. Spring was in full bloom, Easter had just come and gone, yet there was still a touch of frost and the night breezes could turn bitter. Christopher helped the countess take off her cloak and made sure she was comfortable in her high-backed chair before the fire. He served goblets of posset from the jug placed in the inglenook, then glanced at Bray who stood close to the door. Bray gestured silently that both he and Urswicke needed to leave. The countess turned quickly and caught the glance between her two henchmen.

'Go, leave me,' she murmured. 'I know full well what you must do. We are caught up in a sharp, cruel blizzard. We must weather this storm. Once you return, we shall sit in close and secret council.'

Urswicke and Bray made their farewells and left the house, striding up Knight Rider Street towards Carter Lane and the soaring, sombre mass of St Paul's. The streets were busy. Citizens flooding out to greet the pleasant weather and strengthening sun. The crowds surged and shifted in a bright array of colours and strident noise. Urswicke and Bray shoved their way through, vigilant against the hordes of naps and foists who hunted for prey amongst the droves of citizens.

'Look out for the street swallows,' Urswicke murmured. 'Especially one of their captains.'

Bray agreed, glancing to the left and right, searching for that red rag which distinguished a leader of the heralds of the alleyways. These rumour-mongers proclaimed whatever news reached the city. Some of it was false though, in the main, the street swallows were often the first to learn of genuine news from the city, the surrounding shires, and even from across the Narrow Seas.

Both men pressed on, passing the dung carts emptying the jakes cupboards and lay stalls, brimming with human filth, as well as the corpses of dogs and cats – most of these crushed beneath the carts trundling up and down the narrow streets. Coffin parties jostled with wedding revellers. Priests and friars led their procession to this shrine or that. Whores clustered together whilst their masked pimps touted for business, darting in and out of doorways. Bray and Urswicke paused outside a tavern, where a storyteller stood on a makeshift pulpit; a battered barrel the taverner had placed outside his main door so that itinerant chanteurs could proclaim their fabulous stories. The barrel also served as a podium for the street swallows and two of these, one displaying the scarlet rag, were impatiently waiting for the storyteller to finish, heckling him loudly, much to the enjoyment of other street people. Urswicke and Bray waited. The heckling grew more strident, pieces of horse dung and other rubbish were flung at the would-be troubadour. An acting troupe also appeared, attracted by the small gathering around the barrel. Eager to earn a crust, the mummers began to stage their own offering; a fire-eater waved a flaming torch whilst a counterfeit man began to twirl a coin which would disappear from one hand and reappear in the other. A casement window above the tavern door was flung open and, to a cry of cackled laughter, two full jakes pots were emptied out on to the street. The spectators screamed their protests, the would-be troubadour gave up in disgust and climbed down.

Urswicke and Bray moved to exploit the chaos which now blocked the entrance to the tavern. They quickly crossed the street, Urswicke producing a coin which he waved before the sharp-eyed street swallows.

'What is it?' the captain demanded in a sing-song voice.

'Your news!'

'Wait and you'll hear!'

'If I wait then you and yours get no coin.'

The dirty-faced street swallow shrugged, glanced at his companion, and led Bray and Urswicke into the tavern's taproom. Once they were seated on upturned barrels around a grease-covered table, Bray introduced himself and his companion. Both swallows abruptly changed their attitude.

'We did not know,' the captain murmured, peering closer at Bray and Urswicke. 'So you are the countess's henchmen. Good.' He rubbed his hands. 'Perhaps we'll have some ale.'

'And perhaps not,' Urswicke retorted, putting a coin down on the table.

'Tell us your news,' Urswicke demanded.

'I urge you to do so,' Bray declared. 'Lord Nightshade, your master, is my close and bosom friend. Indeed,' Bray added warningly, 'I am the lawyer who saved your master from at least two hangings.'

Both street swallows gaped in astonishment.

'Apologies, master,' the captain stammered. 'We did not know. Lord Nightshade despatched us down to St Paul's just after the Jesus Mass.'

'Which I am sure you did not attend.'

'Of course, master, we were too busy. We reached St Paul's

and went straight across to the Cross and there it was. A herald's proclamation, pinned to its wood. I was once,' the captain gabbled on, 'a pupil in the schools. I can read and write my own name.'

'Very interesting, and . . .?'

'News out of Brittany,' the captain intoned as he closed his eyes, speaking by rote like a scholar conjugating a Latin verb.

'Henry Tudor,' he declared. 'Son of the traitor Edmund.'

'No reference to the countess,' Urswicke warned.

The captain, eyes still shut, nodded in agreement.

'Just bear with me masters,' he declared. 'Let me finish.'

'Continue.'

'Son of the traitor Edmund Tudor and close kin of Jasper Tudor, his uncle, who has recently died of a fever and lies buried in the chapel at Rennes.'

'What?' Bray exclaimed.

Urswicke gripped his companion by the arm, urging him to stay silent.

'Henry Tudor,' the street swallow continued merrily, 'has now returned to this kingdom. He has openly confessed that his opposition to his sovereign lord, King Edward of York, must cease. He has in truth made full submission to our King. He has confessed and renounced all treasons and been accepted into the King's love. A full and free pardon has been issued to him and any of his coven who wish to be admitted into the King's peace.' The street swallow opened his eyes. 'And that, masters, is what we've learnt. Oh!' He held a hand up. 'The message closed with the following: that Henry Tudor and his escort, now pardoned, lodge comfortably and safely with his mother, Margaret Countess of Richmond, at her house in the city.'

'Bastards!' Bray exclaimed.

'That's the truth, good sirs or,' the street swallow grinned, 'is what we've been told.'

'By whom, where, when?'

'Oh, the news has been published in the usual places. Proclamations have been posted at St Paul's Cross, the Standard in Cheapside, the approaches to London Bridge, as well as at different gates in the city.'

'By whom?'

'By Sir Thomas Urswicke, Recorder of this City . . .'

'And principal clerk of the Secret Chancery.' Urswicke finished the sentence.

'Masters, we have told you what we know. Lord Nightshade first heard of these rumours. He believes they are true.'

'Oh, they're true.' Urswicke whispered. 'Edward of England has spun his web and whoever's caught there will be devoured.'

Master Brasenose, former priest, defrocked cleric, mercenary, and now one of Sir Thomas Urswicke's principal henchmen, rubbed his scarred face where his nose had once been until it was severed during the vicious hand-to-hand combat at Barnet almost a year ago. Brasenose closed his eyes as he recalled that bloody, violent struggle, with that damnable mist swirling round, the ragged fluttering banners of York and Lancaster. Brasenose, with Rutger his henchman, had slithered and slipped on that gore-soaked ground, gasping and cursing as they forced their path through a world of swinging, razor-sharp steel. They had hacked and slaughtered their way towards the Lancastrian commanders. Both men were eager, desperate to be the ones who would be proclaimed royal champions, the loyal retainers of York who'd cut down the high and mighty in the House of Lancaster. Warwick they could not find; Brasenose thought he'd withdrawn, defended by his personal bodyguard. Warwick's brother John Neville, Marquis of Montagu, however, was a different matter. He and a few loyal stalwarts had been surrounded and the ring of steel was locking fast around the Lancastrian lord. Helmet off, gorget hanging loose, John Neville fought for his life. Brasenose had closed with him in a bloody, murderous embrace, both cutting and slicing each other with their daggers. At last Neville broke free with a slashing stroke which severed most of his enemy's nose. Neville then slipped, crashing in a tangle of armour to the ground, tormented by the pain, almost blinded by spurting blood, Brasenose had fallen on Neville and drove his dagger deep into his enemy's exposed face, digging deep until Rutger pulled him away.

Brasenose's exploit had been lauded by York and proclaimed as a mighty act. Brasenose had been favoured and fawned upon. In the months following Barnet, he had risen high in the service of York to become Sir Thomas Urswicke's principal henchman,

known to all as Brasenose the Valiant. He'd almost forgotten his
real name, the one given to him by his father and mother over
the baptismal font in a small chapel outside Whitby. In fact, he
didn't really care. He was now Urswicke's man in peace and war
and that included this, the splendid mansion known as The Moor,
a residence of the man he'd so brutally slain.

Brasenose stood in the shade of a gnarled oak. He stared across
the broad sward of grass; it swept up to a white, pebble-dashed
pathway which fronted the majestic entrance. The Moor truly
was palatial, built over an ancient Templar manor. Archbishop
George Neville had used the same eye-catching Cotswold
stone of the Templar architects to fashion a most luxurious
residence. The mansion rose three storeys high with a sloping,
blood-red-tiled roof. Some of the top-floor windows were sealed
with horn, though most of the others were filled with glass, a
few of which had been delicately painted with dazzling, heraldic
devices which now shimmered brilliantly in the late afternoon
sunshine. The gleaming oak front door was definitely the work
of a city craftsman. Indeed the glass, the cornices, the corbels
and other decorations must have been fashioned by the masters
of their individual guilds: glaziers, carpenters and masons, all
specially hired from London. A rounded turret rose at each end
of the main building; from these, two three-storey extensions ran
parallel to each other to meet the rear curtain wall. The space
this great enclosure formed housed all the necessary work places,
stores and outhouses, be they kitchen, bakery, forge, washhouse,
smithy and the rest. To the left of the mansion stretched orchards
of plum, apple and cherry, together with spice plots, flower
beds and a richly stocked herb garden. Brasenose, shielding his
eyes against the light, looked to the right from where he stood
and stared hard at the massive greenery, the soaring hedges which
formed the great maze, allegedly one of the finest in the kingdom.

'Master.'

Brasenose, one hand falling to the hilt of his dagger, spun
round as his henchman Rutger came out of the shadows, pulling
back the hood of his fustian jacket.

'I've been walking, master.' He gestured with his hand towards
the mansion. 'Meadow after meadow, cow byres, piggeries, hen
coops and carp ponds.'

'Certainly a place of wealth,' Brasenose agreed.

'And then this.' Rutger nodded towards the manor house. 'What is the story behind such a place? I've heard rumours, whispers.'

Rutger joined his master beneath the stout entwined branches of the oak.

'Oh, a haunting, blood-thirsty tale,' Brasenose replied. 'Let me tell you. The Saxons lived here, they built a chapel, but that was eventually swept away by time and war. Then it was handed over to the Templar Order. You've heard of them?'

'Monk knights. They owned a palace in London; it still bears their name.'

'Correct. Yes, they were once powerful in the city but eventually they were dissolved. Their lands and buildings were seized and, in this part of the shire, handed over to the Fitzallens. Lord Henry Fitzallen built a fair dwelling here for the lady he loved, the light of his life.'

'Did he construct the maze?'

'No, he did not. He preserved and strengthened it but the maze was the work of the Templars. They were founded to protect pilgrims and the holy places of Outremer. They failed. Their great fortress at Acre fell to the armies of Islam and the Templars were pushed out of the Holy Land.'

'And the maze?'

'The Templars returned here. They brought with them a Greek, Daedalus, a master of horticulture who had worked in the rich, varied gardens of the East. He planted and cultivated that maze, a perfect square of twenty yards by twenty yards, with a cross on a plinth in the centre. The Templars used this to creep to the cross, especially at noon on Fridays, the hour of Christ's passion. They regarded this as an act of reparation for their loss of the holy places in Outremer. And so it is.'

'And Fitzallen preserved the maze?'

'Oh yes. Why destroy such a mysterious sea of greenery with its winding tunnels and flowery arbours?'

Rutger almost replied how the maze must host an array of sweet fragrances but stopped short just in time. Rutger's master was, understandably, extremely sensitive about any mention of smelling or savouring with the nose. Indeed, there was certain amusement amongst the Recorder's coven about Brasenose's hideous disfigurement. However, this was not the time nor the place for such macabre humour.

'Lord Fitzallen had two passions, his wife and that maze. Yet,' Brasenose sighed, 'it all ended in tragedy. Lord Fitzallen journeyed across the Narrow Seas to fight in the royal array. On his return he discovered that, in his absence, his lovely wife had been playing the two-backed beast with his steward.' Brasenose shrugged. 'To cut to the end: Lord Fitzallen executed the steward at the entrance to the maze. He severed the man's head and pickled it in a barrel of brine.'

'And his wife?'

'Imprisoned for life in a cage kept at the centre of the maze. Every night, whatever the weather, Lord Fitzallen, under a canopied cover, processed by torchlight to that cage. Manservants carried platters of food beside him, while Lord Fitzallen held the severed head of his lady's paramour in a shallow silver bowl. He would enter the cage and force his wife to dine with that gruesome head on the table between them.' Brasenose paused to adjust the mask across his ravaged face.

'And how did it end?'

'As with all such incidents, an even deeper tragedy. Fitzallen's wife managed to get hold of some cord and she hanged herself. Her husband buried her somewhere in that maze with a stake driven through her heart and her lover's severed head wedged between her thighs.'

'And Lord Fitzallen?'

'He survived a few years. He died during the great pestilence and his manor, The Moor, became a lonely ruin avoided by the local peasantry. They claim a host of ghosts haunted the place, swarming through it like a horde of malignant bats.'

'Strange.' Rutger gestured towards the great maze, its greenery glistening under the late afternoon sun. 'It's so beautiful,' he exclaimed.

'Perhaps that's only a mask!' Brasenose replied wiping the sweat from his double chin. 'I reckon the place is certainly haunted.'

'Master?'

'That's what brought me down here. I was at a window along the gallery on the first floor. The manor lay quiet. The

Angelus bell had sounded. His Grace the Archbishop had, as usual, gathered his household in the main chapel for noonday prayers. After that he and his minions would rest. Anyway, I peered through a glass window and, I am sure, I glimpsed a woman, a mere flitting shadow, like a swallow, a flurry of colour, then it was gone. Yet I am sure something or someone had entered that maze.'

'A ghost?' Rutger joked, yet he repressed a shiver, a premonition of something malignant lurking in that apparently rich, green, leafy maze.

Brasenose patted the pommel of his sword and adjusted his warbelt.

'I am curious. I intend to go in.'

'Master, you could become lost.'

'I can thread my way. The good archbishop,' Brasenose's voice was rich with sarcasm, 'has graciously informed me that he has laid out a guide rope which runs from the main entrance of the maze to the cross at the centre. I fully intend to inspect this mysterious place. Who knows?' He patted his bulging belly. 'Perhaps I might meet our lady the ghost and dine with her.'

'Should I go with you?'

'No, Rutger, walk once more this glorious mansion, discover what you can and we'll meet when the vespers bell tolls.'

'Master?' Rutger asked tentatively. 'Why are we really here?'

'To spy out the lie of the land, to ensure all is well before our masters arrive.'

'And to discover if Achitophel lurks here? I heard Sir Thomas mention that name.'

'I am here, as I said, to walk this place. I have a crude map to assist me as I have of the other place. I have met the Nevilles and had, on more than one occasion, sharp words with members of The Five Wounds: they are restless, eager to break out of here.'

'And Achitophel?' Rutger insisted.

'Oh yes, that most perfidious of names,' Brasenose retorted. 'That elusive, spying spirit, that most subtle of deceivers, moving from camp to camp, from this great lord to that, offering to arrange matters for whoever hired him. Oh yes, Sir Thomas would dearly love to unmask and confront such a malignant, murderous mummer. However,' Brasenose smacked his lips, 'the discovery of Achitophel is, I believe, only one part of Sir Thomas's subtle scheme.'

'Which is?'

'To put it bluntly, the total and utter destruction of the House of Lancaster, or what is left of it.'

Rutger watched his master walk across the grass, then disappear as he turned on to the path which skirted the maze. Rutger then left, walking across to the manor and its well-furnished buttery where he could slake his thirst with tankards of home-brewed ale. Eventually he felt sleepy and went up to his own narrow chamber on the top gallery of the main mansion. He stood by a window, staring down at the maze which, despite its green glory, exuded, or so Rutger thought, a brooding malevolence.

Rutger, also a former priest, had encountered evil in so many ways, and he truly believed The Moor was a place of darkness. Agitated by his worries, yet heavy-eyed after the ale, Rutger lay down on his cot bed and fell into a deep sleep till he was roused by the tolling vespers bell. Recalling Brasenose's order, Rutger pulled himself up, hastily donning cloak, boots and warbelt. Once ready, he hurried out down the stairs. Servants milled about along the gallery which housed the main dining hall, solar and kitchen. Rutger stopped servants, asking them if they had seen the royal clerk, Brasenose? All he received in reply were shrugs and blunt denials. Brasenose and Rutger may well be royal clerks, but their presence was deeply resented in this Lancastrian stronghold. Rutger searched both manor and gardens but he could find no trace of his master.

'The maze!' Rutger whispered. 'God save us!' The clerk hastened back into the mansion and forced a servitor to take a lantern and accompany him. Rutger, sword drawn, followed the retainer around to the main entrance into the maze. Dusk was gathering, the hour of the screeching bat and the mournful, lonely hymn of the owls. The sky was still clear but the breeze had quickened, rustling the hedges which soared above them as if these walls of greenery housed their own sharp and sinister spirits. Rutger, the guide rope in one hand, sword in the other, forced the servant on, snarling at him to play the man and cease from his constant moaning. They followed the snaking, pebble-dashed path, the lantern light dancing like a golden

circle before them. Now and again Rutger would curse as a
bird screeched, bursting out of the hedge in a flutter of wings.
The maze now seemed like a living thing, overshadowing the
path, watching them, waiting for them to make a mistake.
Sometimes the trackway narrowed, no broader than an arrow
path. At other times it spread out only to close in again. They
rounded a corner and almost tripped over the corpse lying
there. Rutger snatched the lantern from the terrified servant
and knelt beside the corpse of his master. Brasenose lay
sprawled out, head slightly turned, the mask across his disfigured face had slipped to reveal the horrid scar where his
nose had once been. One glassy eye stared emptily. Rutger
immediately searched his master's body; pockets, purses and
wallet. He emptied the contents, coins, seals and other items,
including a bracelet and a ring.

'So, this was not robbery.' Rutger murmured, slipping the
items into his own wallet. He then turned the corpse over
and loosened his master's warbelt, noting that both sword and
dagger were still sheathed. He tried to ignore his master's dead
eyes, the gaping, blood-encrusted mouth. He scrutinised the
front of the corpse, then turned it over and, in the light of
the lantern, examined the stab wounds to the back. There were
at least five, the blood long dried. Rutger glanced up at the
shivering servant.

'Five wounds,' he exclaimed. 'And all to the back. Dagger
blows, but how eh? How?' Rutger clambered to his feet and
rubbed a booted foot across the pebbles. 'This assassin,' he
declared, 'struck from behind. But how?' He once again tapped
his boot against the ground. 'My master's hearing was sharp
enough. The pebbles on the path would betray any footfall. Yet
he never turned. He didn't even draw his dagger or sword. There
is no sign of any defence, or . . .' he glanced around, 'the slightest
struggle. Master Brasenose was a mailed clerk, skilled as any
dagger boy along London's alleys, yet he never turned! Never
defended himself. No clash of steel. No shout or cry.'

The servant just gazed fearfully back as Rutger recalled the
stories about The Moor and the ghosts which undoubtedly
haunted it.

*　　*　　*

Countess Margaret sat at the head of the polished oval table in
the chancery office of her town mansion. To her right sat Urswicke,
with Bray on her left. The countess's mood had hardened, her
pale, aesthetic face now a mask of determination as she stared at
the man sitting opposite.

'Welcome.' Margaret declared, lifting her goblet of posset.
'Welcome Autolycos, my most treasured and loyal spy, truly a
soul devoted to my cause.' Margaret gestured around the warm,
comfortable chamber which smelled so fragrantly of beeswax,
herbs and spices. 'You are safe here, Autolycos,' she added, 'this
is my holy of holies.'

'Welcome indeed.' Urswicke declared, lifting his own goblet
in toast as did Bray. 'But what,' Urswicke continued, 'has brought
you here so agitated at such an early hour?'

Autolycos, thin-faced and sharp-eyed, gratefully accepted the
toast and then sipped from his own goblet.

'What indeed?' Bray declared. 'Though we can guess the
reasons. We have discovered that the news about the Imposter
has been voiced and proclaimed throughout this city.'

'Aye and so it has,' Autolycos responded sombrely. 'My Lady,
you know how I sell parchment, wax, and . . .' he gestured
around, 'all the needs of a chancery. I can wander where I wish,
be it here or across the Narrow Seas. On your behalf I collect
and deliver information.'

'And now?' Bray testily demanded.

'And now, my friend, all this confusion, which is deepening
and spreading like some foul fog from the river. God knows,
Master Bray, how it goes. Has Henry Tudor truly arrived from
Brittany? Has he accepted the King's peace? Has he renounced
his claims? Is he going to deliver the names of those who
supported him? Has Jasper Tudor, his uncle, really died of a
fever? Have you, my Lady, accepted this person as your son? Do
you still need, require, the services of others such as myself?
How vulnerable are we? Will we be taken up for questioning?
Could we be indicted before King's Bench? Do we try to
communicate with Henry Tudor?'

'No, no.' The Countess shook her head. 'On that last point
my answer is definitely no. We are dealing with an Imposter
surrounded by a host of lies. I doubt very much whether Jasper

Tudor is dead, as I do that Duke Francis has accepted this Imposter as my son. We must be careful that they do not use this lie to trap your good self. You and your legion of informants form an integral part of a tapestry we've spun so expertly over the years, and it includes only the trusted. So be careful, be prudent. Who knows,' she added bitterly, 'why all this has been plotted. Was it so people would betray themselves? Or is it, as it would appear, to cause absolute chaos and confusion for me and mine? My advice at this stage is to do nothing. Give all your company the same message. Stay silent, stay still so you stay safe.' She paused. 'One favour, one great favour I do ask you.'

'Mistress?'

'Journey with all speed to Rennes. Meet Lord Jasper, I am certain he is hale and hearty. Inform him about what has happened.'

'In truth he must already know,' Urswicke interjected. 'Edward would want this mayhem to be bruited abroad. Mistress, we learned about all this what, two days ago? God only knows when King Edward began to disseminate it to Paris, Cologne and all the great cities of Europe. I am certain professional rumour-mongers have been hired to sing the same damnable hymn.'

'That is why, Autolycos,' the countess declared, 'you must meet with my son to ensure all is well. Plead with him and Lord Jasper to watch and wait.'

'It may be too late,' Autolycos replied, moving uneasily in his chair. He stared down at the tabletop, tapping his fingers. 'Or at least too late for some.'

'Which means?'

'Caiaphas the courier, mistress? One of your most ardent supporters has been seized.'

'Oh no! Caiaphas has a mouth as large as his heart.'

'A merry mischief-maker,' Urswicke declared. 'Always ready to proclaim the virtues of young Henry Tudor.'

'Not so merry now,' Autolycos replied. 'Lodged in Newgate. He has been arraigned before a commission of Oyer et Terminer.'

'My father?'

'Yes, Master Christopher, before no less a person than the Recorder of London.'

'God have mercy on poor Caiaphas. He must have read
the proclamation posted at St Paul's.'

'Oh yes, Master Christopher. He read it, then he committed
treason by tearing it down. He loudly declared that it was all a
blatant lie and those responsible were sons of Satan deeply mired
in sin.'

'Lord have mercy on him,' the countess whispered. 'Because
York will not.'

'Strange man, Caiaphas,' Autolycos mused. 'My lady, between
tearing down the proclamation and being abruptly arrested,
Caiaphas met me at our favourite tavern, The Old Serpent; it
stands on the borders of Whitefriars, where no law officer likes
to go. Anyway, Caiaphas was full of fury about the proclamation
and openly declared that it might be the work of Achitophel.'

'We have heard that name whispered,' Countess Margaret
replied. 'A meddler? A professional informant?'

'According to Caiaphas, who collects stories and rumours as
a miser does coins, Achitophel is more than that, my Lady. He
is the cause of so many troubles. He moves from camp to camp,
selling secrets and information, offering to carry out certain
tasks. He is an inciter. He urges people to take a path and promises to accompany them along it. Anyway, Caiaphas wondered
if the emergence of the Imposter could be the work of this
Achitophel, deepening the tension between you and the Brothers
York. Stirring the pot of troubles till it bubbles over.'

'Of this I can assure you,' the countess replied. 'We would
have no business with such a person. My advice, Autolycos, is
this: do not trust anyone outside our circle. Stay silent, remain
watchful, and we will all stay safe.'

'In which case, my Lady, I should go. Perhaps learn what has
happened to Caiaphas.'

'No, leave that.' The countess shook her head. 'Too dangerous,
too dangerous. I have told you what I need you to do, so be busy
about that.'

Autolycos promised he would, rose and left, Urswicke
escorting him down and out into the street. Once he had
returned, locking the door behind him, Countess Margaret
crossed herself, murmuring the open lines of the '*Veni Sancte
Spiritus*'. She then twined the ave beads around her long fingers,

staring at a crucifix nailed to the far wall. She waited for Urswicke to take his seat.

'My friends,' she breathed, 'let us begin. Let us unroll this ghastly tapestry, its threads a veritable knot of falsehoods, clever lies and subtle ploys. First, we have the Imposter, as you call him, Christopher. A young man of about fifteen or sixteen summers, very close to the age of my darling Henry. He speaks and understands fluent Welsh and has been closely instructed by Master Patmore who, in fact, was my son's principal tutor for more than a year.'

'Would Patmore know so much?'

'Reginald, Reginald. Patmore was my son's escort for years. He is himself from Welsh parents and upbringing. He is a well-educated man, a former scholar at Jesus College Oxford, who has served as a mailed clerk in my late beloved husband's battle host. Patmore,' she concluded, 'is a skilled man of war. He is also well learned in the law, attending the Inns of Court here in this city.'

'Which is probably how my father knows him. So, he was once your first husband's henchman?'

'Yes.'

'Then why has he turned his heart and his hand so cruelly against you?'

'First, Christopher, Patmore always was a distant, cold-hearted man with little or no passion for anyone.' She breathed out noisily. 'Nor must I forget his mother, Eleanor, and her sister, Matilda, two of my ladies-in-waiting when I was at Pembroke. They actually assisted in the birth of Prince Henry.' She shook her head. 'Two ladies bitter about life, openly resentful. I was only too pleased to find them safe lodgings at Valle Crucis Nunnery.'

'They became nuns?'

'Yes, Reginald, as so many ladies do if they are in the widowed state.' The countess picked up her goblet and sipped carefully at the mulled wine. 'As for why Patmore has become the Judas, from what I gather, many in the Principality have done likewise. The petty chieftains of South Wales regard our cause as finished. Remember how Prince Henry and Lord Jasper had to flee for their lives after the disasters at Tewkesbury and Barnet. Those battles truly shattered the House of Lancaster. They annihilated most of our leaders; those who were not slaughtered in the bloody massacres that followed were summarily executed. Lord Jasper and Henry were blessed by God. They escaped, hiding out in Raglan, Pembroke, and other isolated places. People like Patmore saw first-hand how the winds of fortune had changed and so they did likewise.'

'Yes, and my father Sir Thomas would watch and, like the fox he is, pounce on his prey.'

'One thing more,' the countess replied. 'Yes,' she murmured to herself as she swilled the dregs around her goblet, 'one more thing,' she repeated as the tears started in her eyes, 'my first husband, Edmund Tudor, truly was a Jack of the Greenwood, a roaring boy who loved the ladies, a merry soul with the heart of a troubadour. Some would call him wild and wanton . . .'

The countess paused and Urswicke steeled himself, suspecting full well what was coming.

'To be blunt,' the countess breathed, 'the Imposter may well be Edmund's illegitimate son, begotten on some wench he ardently fell in love with for a day, or even less. True? Possibly! The Imposter does have an uncanny resemblance to Prince Henry.'

Bray and Urswicke simply nodded. They had also heard stories about young Edmund Tudor and his love for the ladies. They could comment, but both men realised it was best to stay silent. The countess was murmuring to herself. Urswicke noted that she was conversing in Welsh, talking to herself or the spirit of her dead husband. She did so for a while and then lapsed into silence. Eventually, she sat up straight, her face all schooled, betraying nothing of the emotions surging within her. Urswicke knew full well that his mistress's relationship with Edmund was a sacred place where he dared not tread. Countess Margaret had loved Edmund with a passion beyond all understanding. Prince Henry was a manifestation of that love. For as long as she lived and as long as she breathed, Henry and his claims to the throne of England were the very stuff of Margaret's existence. Urswicke glanced quickly at Bray, shaking his head and putting his finger to his lips. This was not the time to question Margaret Beaufort about the life and loves of her first husband.

The countess abruptly asserted herself.

'So,' she declared in a loud voice, 'we know now who the Imposter really is. A bastard born of my beloved Edmund. A secret which Edmund could not reveal to me before our marriage. I understand that. Edmund confessed that he was a ladies' man but only I was his true lady. He nursed this secret and, I suspect, shared it with Patmore. Indeed, the more I reflect, the more I suspect that Edmund entrusted his bastard boy to the care of Patmore.'

'True, true,' Urswicke agreed. 'So, we now know who the Imposter probably is, as we do that Patmore is the moving spirit in this great deception, though one patronised, protected and privileged by York and his coven. In particular by my father and that other limb of Satan, Clarence. Secondly, we all acknowledge how this news will cause deep confusion and chaos amongst the ranks of our own adherents. They will ask what is the truth? If it's a lie, then why is the Imposter lodged with the countess? Should they approach him? What would be the response from Brittany? Oh Lord.' Urswicke raised a hand. 'This is a most wicked web and we are really caught fast. We cannot break free, yet the more we flounder, the deeper we are enmeshed.'

'So, what should we do?' Bray demanded.

'Well, we could kill Patmore and the Imposter.'

'No, Christopher,' the countess interjected. 'Christopher, Reginald, I would willingly see Patmore go to judgement, whatever that may be. But not the Imposter, not the boy, not the possible son of my beloved Edmund. I cannot do that and, if I did, I would be cursed by God. I studied that young man when we met in the Tower. He is as much a prisoner as we all are. In many ways he is innocent. Someone born at the wrong time. Someone to be used by the men of power. He should be silenced but not killed.'

'True,' Bray replied. 'And there are other dangers. If we kill Patmore, York would hold us responsible for any assault on the Imposter.'

'Accordingly, we must reject such a proposal,' the countess murmured. 'Indeed, what could really be achieved by murder? It would only deepen our troubles. King Edward has insisted that both Patmore and his protégé should lodge with me. I will be held responsible for their well-being. On the other hand, if I refuse to cooperate, that could be construed as rebellion, rank disobedience or even treason. I certainly don't want to be lodged in some bleak chamber in the Tower. Once locked up, I doubt very much if I would ever escape. The Brothers York are determined to clear the board, to remove all challenges, and that includes me. My reply is this. Let us relax, let us wait and, above all, let us watch. And,' Margaret sniffed, 'let us finish the business in hand.'

For a while the countess and her two henchmen pondered on how to manage the Imposter and his familiar; where the couple would lodge, eat and sleep. The countess then dictated a summary of what they knew about the present danger and the conclusions they had reached to deal with it. The evening drew on, the light now fading. A mist had swirled in just as dusk fell. Lamps, lanterns and candles were lit as the bells of the city churches greeted the gathering night.

They were just bringing the business of the day to an end when the sound of running footsteps echoed along the gallery outside, followed by a furious knocking on the door. This was flung open and the countess's house steward, gasping for breath, pointed back at the way he'd come.

'Mistress, I am sorry but, but, but . . .'

'But what?' Bray shouted.

'*Pax et bonum*,' Urswicke soothed, grabbing his warbelt. He strapped this on before he seized the house steward's arm and forced him into a chair. 'What is happening, man?'

'The Shadow of Death.' The man gasped. 'Newgate's executioner, the city's principal hangman?'

'What on earth . . .?'

'They have brought a scaffold,' the steward replied, wiping the sweat from his face. 'Gallows set up in a death cart.'

'Caiaphas,' Urswicke exclaimed. 'They brought him here. They intend to execute him as both an example and a threat to us all. *No!*' He gestured at the countess. 'No, my Lady, you stay here. Reginald, remain with her. Lock the door behind me.'

'Mauclerc's in charge,' the steward bleated fearfully. 'Clarence's man . . .'

'Of course, he is never far from wickedness. He revels in it. Come my friend,' Urswicke beckoned. 'Let us go down.'

Both men left, Urswicke only staying to ensure the door behind him was locked before he clattered down the stairs. The hall entrance was empty, the servants, all fearful, fleeing deep back into the house. Urswicke told the steward to stand at the foot of the stairs. He then opened the front door and stared out at the hideous spectacle confronting him. The Shadow of Death, garbed in black except for a blood-red mask, sat on the seat of the execution cart, twitching the reins restraining the great dray horses which pulled the garishly decorated death cart. This contained a one-branched gibbet which rose at least four yards high, with two narrow siege ladders leaning against it. Beside the gibbet, a gaggle of the executioner's apprentices gathered around the condemned man, a short, plump individual with a white hood pulled fast over his head. Some of the apprentices carried cressets, flaming torches, as did the city bailiffs, who'd escorted the cart from Newgate. The curious had gathered but they were roughly pushed back. A Friar of the Sack thrust his way through and began to dolefully chant a death psalm. A hooded figure came from behind the cart and walked to stand on the bottom step. He pulled back his hood and Urswicke stared down at a man who truly hated him: Clarence's henchman, a killer to the very marrow of his being. Mauclerc looked what he truly was – a wolf in sheep's clothing. He had scrawny hair, his narrow, high-cheekboned face pitted with the pox, his eyes slightly slanted, his nose as sharp as any quill above bloodless lips. Mauclerc always reminded Urswicke of a ravenous, sloping wolf.

'Good evening, Master Christopher.' Mauclerc's voice was surprisingly modulated. 'So, you have come to see justice done.'

'I doubt very much if it is justice.'

'It is the King's justice.'

'As you say,' Urswicke countered. 'But who . . .'

'Caiaphas the courier. The mischief-maker. A mountebank.' Mauclerc's powerful voice cut the air, silencing the clamour around the death cart; even the friar paused in his chanting. 'Condemned before the King's justiciar and sentenced to death by hanging.' Mauclerc pressed on. 'So,' he turned, 'tried, indicted, convicted; let punishment be carried out now.'

'Why? Why now?' Urswicke shouted. 'Why here?'

'Because,' Mauclerc turned, grinning like a dog baring his teeth, 'he dared to malign the Countess of Richmond's beloved son, who is soon to lodge here. Indeed, I wonder if the countess should witness justice being done.'

'She has every confidence in His Grace the King. She need not witness this!'

'True, true,' Mauclerc agreed. 'But this nonsense should be drawn to an end.' He turned back to face the cart, arms extended. 'Now,' he bellowed, 'is the hour of judgement.'

Urswicke watched as the macabre ceremony unfurled. The Shadow of Death moved swiftly and skilfully. He seized the hapless prisoner and forced him up one of the ladders leaning against the scaffold. Then, nimble as a squirrel, the executioner climbed the second ladder to stand alongside the prisoner, who desperately clutched the step above him. Two of the apprentices began to beat on tambours, a mournful sound which blended with the psalm of mourning that the Friar of the Sack intoned. The grotesquely garbed hangman turned to the trembling prisoner and slipped the noose, fastened by Mauclerc, over the condemned man's head. The executioner tightened the knot just behind the prisoner's left ear then slid, swift as a snake, down the ladder. He stood staring at Mauclerc, who lifted his right hand. The tambour beat quickened. The Friar of the Sack began the '*De Profundis*' – 'Out of the depths do I cry to thee, O Lord.' The night breeze quickened sharply, sending the flames of the hand-held cressets darting like devils, waiting for the prisoner's soul. The drumbeat grew incessantly louder, then abruptly paused as Mauclerc dropped his hand. The executioner swiftly turned the ladder. The condemned man dropped like a stone, the sheer fall tightening the noose to choke off his breath.

Urswicke watched the poor man dance and twist, but eventually turned away to whisper one requiem after another. Anything to distract him from the gruesome gurgling of a man slowly choking to death. At last, it was over. Urswicke opened his eyes. Mauclerc was now ordering the corpse to be cut down and laid in the cart. The Friar of the Sack climbed in to recite the final prayers. Urswicke followed. Mauclerc shouted that Christopher was welcome to view the corpse. Urswicke did so in the light of a lanternhorn. He peeled back the mask. The hanged man's face was truly hideous, with his popping eyes, the tongue twisting between yellowing teeth, the skin an eerie colouring. Despite all the horrors, Urswicke recognized Caiaphas but kept his peace. He drew his dagger and went to slice the noose cord wrapped so tightly around the dead man's throat. The knot of the noose was intricately looped and fastened to form a cluster of twine, hard as an iron ball.

'My handiwork,' Mauclerc, standing at the tail of the cart, boasted.

'Is it indeed.' Urswicke sheathed his knife, rose and got out of the cart to stand as close as he could to this prince amongst bully boys. 'Is it indeed?' Urswicke repeated, hand on the hilt of his sword. He stepped even closer so he could smell Mauclerc's wine-laden breath.

'You're certainly skilled in the art of inflicting brutal death.'

'I have been to places; I have seen things, Urswicke, that you could not even imagine in your most heart-chilling nightmares. I have served at sea well beyond the Pillars of Hercules. Never forget that.'

Mauclerc turned away, then abruptly strode back.

'I'll see to the corpse. Our friar here has a wheelbarrow. He can take the remains to the great charnel house, The Paradisium, the public mortuary near St Mary-le-Bow. He can ask the Harrower of the Dead to provide a coffin sheath to bury the poor bastard in. So, Master Urswicke, in the words of the Gospel, let's leave the dead to bury the dead. Now, as for the living: Master Henry, together with myself and Patmore, will arrive here the day after tomorrow.'

'You?'

'Yes, Master Urswicke, me. I am to be their escort, their guardian, their protector.'

Urswicke steeled himself against the spurt of anger which surged through him.

'I will,' Urswicke grated, holding Mauclerc's gaze, 'make you as comfortable as you deserve.'

'Very good. In which case, Master Urswicke,' Mauclerc waggled his fingers, 'I am finished with you.'

Urswicke turned on the top step.

'Mauclerc.'

'Yes, my dear?'

'We are never finished.'

PART TWO

'King Edward commanded the body of Warwick and the Marquess be thrown into a cart.'

The battle group, the Company of the Five Wounds, were relaxing, as they always did at the end of the day. They gathered in the small buttery to drink deep of The Moors' home-brewed ale; full-bodied, rich to the taste, yet soft and mellowing on both tongue and throat. Five warriors, war-hardened veterans, the former personal bodyguard of the once great Earl of Warwick.

'All of us.' Matthew Poppleton, their grey-haired, grizzle-faced leader, clapped his hands gently to attract their attention. 'Let us give a toast,' he murmured, 'to our dead Lord's brother, His Grace George Neville, Archbishop of York, and his illustrious sister Lady Grace.'

Murmurs of approval greeted this declaration, followed by more raucous toasts, tankards clinking, ale slopping on the table and floor. Poppleton again demanded silence.

'Listen,' he urged. 'Barnet and Tewkesbury are now locked in the past. The bloody harvest is over, those we followed have also gone. Our own master lies buried with his kinsmen at Bisham. We have been pardoned, admitted to the King's peace. We have also signed indentures to be the archbishop's men in peace and war and yet . . .' Poppleton drank deep from his blackjack. 'And yet,' he repeated, 'violence seems to have followed us here.'

'Brasenose's murder has nothing to do with us,' Luke Colworth replied. The balding, hard-faced Scotsman tapped his tankard against the table.

'Brother,' Poppleton retorted, 'I am not too sure. The war may have ended but the vengeful ghosts still gather and we, especially us, the Brotherhood of the Five Wounds, must never forget that.'

'How can we? I still have dreams, sweat-drenched nightmares.' John Forester, the youngest of the group, fair-haired, smooth-faced, and garbed in a long black tunic. Many mistook him for a priest. 'What we did . . .' he stammered.

'What we did, we had to. To survive,' Poppleton snapped. 'And as for Brasenose. His henchman Rutger is equally mystified by his master's murder. Killed in a maze, wounded only in the back. No sign that he even confronted or resisted his killer.'

'That maze is a mystery in itself,' Chadwick warned.

'The entire house is a hall of ghosts,' Poppleton added. The stories about Fitzallen and his wretched spouse; the murder of his wife and her lover; the cruelty inflicted upon them both. Then we have the Templars, who cursed all those who dispossessed them. So, despite all its beauty, be careful, be prudent,' Poppleton advised. 'And remember, this is now our home. We are the henchmen of George, Archbishop of York, as we were once . . .' He paused, stumbling over the words, '. . . as we were once,' he added wearily, 'of his brother, the great Earl of Warwick. Comrades, the world has changed. Men we fought so ruthlessly against are now, apparently, our friends and allies. Look at Brasenose, he fought resolutely against us at Barnet yet he is also a guest here.'

'Until he was murdered,' Forester replied. 'So, who did that? Why? One of us? Or some servant of the archbishop? God knows, this is a truly luxurious manor, but it houses a killer, an assassin.'

'But that should not trouble us,' Poppleton asserted. 'In the end, I believe Brasenose's death cannot be laid at our door. And now,' he continued, 'we have other matters to deal with. His Grace the Archbishop and his sister have invited Edward of York, his brothers and their henchmen to splendid festivities here at The Moor to celebrate the Feast of St George. His Grace wishes to cement his friendship with the King and show his support for the House of York.'

'We still haven't mentioned it,' Forester blurted out. He fished into his wallet and plucked out scraps of parchment. 'We haven't mentioned this, the threat pinned to the chapel door.' Forester, all agitated, leaned across the table to pull the candelabra closer so its pool of golden light bathed the tattered pieces of parchment and its doggerel message. 'Company of the Five Wounds,'

Forester intoned, touching each word with a stubby forefinger. 'Company of the Five Wounds,' he repeated, as if he was chanting a death psalm.

'For the love of God,' Poppleton snarled, 'we've been through this before. Read out the message, an empty threat. Should we really even be bothered?'

'Oh, read it again,' Colworth declared.

'Company of the Five Wounds, ride not so bold, for your treachery and treason will be told.' Forester's sombre voice stilled all noise in the small buttery. Two of the company shouted for more ale. Poppleton yawned noisily, stretched and stamped his booted feet.

'It's all a nonsense,' he grumbled. 'No one knows the truth, I mean the real truth.'

'We should retire,' Colworth declared. 'Tomorrow beckons. His Grace has to prepare for York's visit.' His voice trailed away, the others weren't really listening, lost in their own memories and regrets. The gathering then broke up, the comrades wishing each other '*pax et bonum*' and a good night's sleep.

They all left the buttery except, as usual, for Fladgate, the ever-taciturn Fladgate. He had sat through the entire meeting drinking quickly, cradling his tankard. Now, as he always did, he'd stay for one last blackjack of ale: a time of great silence when he could reflect and prepare for the night. He sat listening to the sound of his departing comrades fade away. He refilled his tankard from the small tun at the end of the table and returned to his seat. Try as he might, Fladgate, like the rest, could not forget that last bloody, ferocious affray at Barnet. What he and the others had done or, in truth, failed to do. Nor had they mentioned tonight what they had discussed with Brasenose – their freedom. The wars were ended. The Company of the Five Wounds should disband; leave this place and go where they wanted. Fladgate was sure of that: he and his comrades wanted their freedom and Brasenose hadn't been very helpful on this issue.

An owl hooted long and mournfully from a copse of trees beyond the walls. Fladgate recalled the ancient saying that 'if you were to die soon, an owl would call your name'. Fladgate shivered and pulled his cloak closer about him. Had that owl called his name? Was he being summoned to judgement?

Fladgate leaned back on the wall bench, tilting his head as different memories caught his sombre mood; Brasenose's cadaver being brought out of that sinister maze, the corpse sprawled face down on a makeshift stretcher, those horrid wounds to Brasenose's back. The sheer mystery of how this cunning fighting man had been so cleverly and secretly slain was all so startling. 'Ah well.' Fladgate lurched to his feet. 'The ghosts are closing in,' he murmured to himself. 'The hour candle burns fiercely, time is passing.'

Wrapping his cloak about him, Fladgate left the small buttery, going across the cobbled yard to the guest chambers. Night had fallen. The air had turned cold. Again, a clammy spurt of fear as that owl hooted, to be answered by the harsh howling of a war dog in its pen beyond the manor house. Fladgate's hand fell to the hilt of his dagger. He heard a sound and whirled round, but it was only the door to the jakes shed built against an outside wall. The door swung backwards and forwards. Fladgate caught the faint glow of a candle under its cap on a ledge in the jakes cupboard. Intrigued, wondering if one of his company had gone to relieve himself and fallen asleep, Fladgate walked across. He opened the door and gasped in horror. Rutger, his hose around his ankles, sat slumped, head back to reveal the long, deep scarlet gash which had opened Rutger's throat to create a second gaping, blood-soaked mouth. The dead man's eyes had rolled back in a dreadful gaze. The corpse was a pathetic sight, yet also terrifying. Fladgate could only stand and stare. He felt a hand gently tap his right shoulder. Fladgate turned to face the night wraith before him.

'What . . .?' He stuttered.

'Vengeance!' The wraith lifted the arbalest and released a barbed bolt to shatter Fladgate's skull.

The days following Caiaphas's hanging were subdued enough. The countess kept to her chambers. Bray prepared the guestrooms for their expected but most unwelcome guests, whilst Urswicke searched the city, dispensing silver in exchange for information; anything about the Imposter and his familiar, Patmore. Despite his best efforts, Urswicke could discover nothing of substance. He returned, dispirited, to the countess's household, and waited with the rest for the inevitable.

Patmore and the Imposter eventually arrived under the careful watch of Mauclerc. The sight of all three, as Urswicke confided in Bray, reminded him of the story about a fox herding two ducklings. Countess Margaret refused to meet them, keeping to her quarters, whilst Bray and Urswicke showed their self-proclaimed guests to the chambers allocated to them. Nothing had changed. Patmore still acted the guardian tutor, while the Imposter remained impassive, though Urswicke was genuinely surprised by the burgeoning relationship between the Imposter and Mauclerc. When Clarence's henchman was in attendance, the young man seemed to come to life, teasing and laughing with Mauclerc.

Urswicke had no illusions about Clarence's man, a true killer, yet he seemed to have taken a strong liking to the boy. Urswicke once caught him ruffling the Imposter's hair and, on more than one occasion, heard Mauclerc regaling his young admirer with stories about his heroic exploits against the Mamelukes in the Middle Sea. Mauclerc, however, continued to maintain his watching malevolence towards both the countess and Urswicke. Two days after he had taken up lodgings, Mauclerc confronted Urswicke in the hallway, poking the clerk repeatedly in the chest as he hissed that no less a person than Sir Thomas, Christopher's father, would be visiting the house to have urgent words with the countess.

'Be there with her,' Mauclerc whispered hoarsely.

Christopher grasped Mauclerc's wrist tightly, forcing his arm down.

'And when,' Christopher demanded, 'does my beloved father arrive?'

'Tomorrow,' Mauclerc gasped, 'between the Jesus Mass and the Angelus bell.'

Urswicke let go of Mauclerc's wrist and hurried to inform the countess, who was busy at her chancery desk, Bray sitting next to her. She leaned across and gently squeezed Christopher's hand.

'Christopher, my son, believe me the masque is about to begin. My good servant, Malkin the Moonman, wanders the face of God's earth, acting all fey-witted. He crosses the City into Southwark and then on into the towns and villages of Essex. He can act slack-jawed, as if lost in another world. However, believe me, Christopher, he can sit in a tavern, listen and memorise what he hears. He has done so recently for me. He slipped in and out of this house like a shadow – no one saw him – but the news he brought was not good. People believe that Henry Tudor has returned to be admitted to the King's peace. Common rumour has it that the wars are well and truly ended. York is supreme and will remain so.'

'And what can we do about that, mistress?' Bray demanded. 'If we sent the likes of the Moonman with a different message, he'd end up being strangled like poor Caiaphas.'

'What we do,' the countess replied, 'is nothing. As I have said before, we simply wait and watch. Every masque has its beginning, the story unfolds and then hurries to a conclusion. We have yet to discover what York and Sir Thomas are preparing for us. In the meantime, let us keep good order here,' she tapped the side of her nose, 'be careful what we say. Be prudent about what we do, where we go and whom we meet. We must do nothing which Sir Thomas could use to draw up an indictment. In fact, the opposite. We are loyal subjects of the King. We acknowledge the power of York and are obedient to the royal command. Now Patmore and Mauclerc are on the prowl here in this house, or will be soon, we must be ever so prudent and keep our own designs very secret.'

Sir Thomas arrived late the next morning. Apart from an escort of two Tower archers, who waited outside, he came alone. As soon as the Recorder was ushered into the countess's council chamber, Christopher realised that his grim-faced father was deeply troubled. Christopher watched intently as Sir Thomas prepared himself for the meeting, doffing cloak, hood and ornamental sword belt. Servants milled around him to take this or to offer that. Eventually Bray cleared the chamber. Urswicke just sat, watched and wondered, as he always did, why he resented his father so much? And he came to the usual conclusion. Sir Thomas had, through his constant lechery, driven his wife, Christopher's mother, to an early grave. A haughty, arrogant and most devious man, Thomas Urswicke's brain teemed like a box of filthy worms. Nevertheless, at times, though only rarely, Christopher felt sorry for his father. Sometimes he would catch a glance, a look of deep sadness, as if Sir Thomas was mourning what could have been.

Christopher recalled the words of an ancient Franciscan who had listened to Christopher's confession at the mercy pew. Christopher had spilled out the hatred he felt for his father. How was he to cope with it and what forgiveness could he offer? The Franciscan had not been harsh but had given him good advice: 'It is easier for a father to have children than children to have a real father.' Christopher closed his eyes. He wondered what kind of father he himself would make, but then broke from his reverie when the countess coughed and Sir Thomas settled into his chair. Mauclerc appeared, breathing insincere apologies for keeping them waiting. The countess, barely concealing her irritation, asked her guests if they wanted any refreshment. Both men refused.

'So,' the countess declared, 'what is this, Sir Thomas?'

'What is what, madam? Nothing short of murder and treason.'

'But why come here to tell us that?'

'To put it bluntly, madam, I need your help. Or, to be more precise, that of my son.' Sir Thomas flicked his fingers at Christopher. Bray he ignored, as he always did.

'Why?'

'Because someone we know, a mutual acquaintance, has been seized and taken up. Master Haddon?'

Christopher just blinked and glanced away. The countess stiffened.

'Why, who . . .?' Bray stammered.

Sir Thomas didn't even deign to look at Bray and totally ignored his question.

'Come, come,' Mauclerc patronised. 'Master Haddon. You must know him? You must have heard about the scrivener Haddon? He's a member of that tribe of ink-stains whom you patronise. He owns, or did till the Crown seized it, a shop under the sign of The Red Keg, in the shadow of St Paul's. Apparently, madam, Master Haddon is a fervent supporter of your son, a balladeer for the spurious claims of Henry Tudor. Anyway,' he glanced sideways at Sir Thomas, who nodded at Mauclerc to continue. 'Anyway, this morning,' he continued blithely, 'Haddon tried to affix a broadsheet on the Cross of St Paul's, declaring that your guest here, the noble Prince Henry—'

'Don't bait me, Mauclerc,' the countess snapped. 'If you want to vomit your filth, then vomit you must.'

'The noble Prince Henry,' Mauclerc continued, 'now lodged comfortably here, is – according to Haddon – a mummer, a mammet. Haddon thought he could post such treasonable filth and scurry away. Oh no.' Mauclerc shook his head reprovingly, imitating a schoolmaster. 'Oh no,' he repeated, 'Haddon the fool. He was soon seized and arrested and is now lodged in Newgate. From there he will be escorted through the streets to the sound of tambour, bagpipe and fife, to be hanged on the common gibbet. In fact,' Mauclerc grinned wolfishly, 'I can arrange that it will be the same one from which the traitor Caiaphas was strung to perform his last dance in the air. You must agree, madam. We cannot have such treasonable writings posted in the King's cities.' He waved a finger close to the countess's face, but then dropped his hand as Sir Thomas coughed warningly. 'Well,' Mauclerc sighed noisily, 'that's for the future. At this moment in time, Haddon is reflecting upon his sins in the death cell at Newgate.'

Christopher exhaled, fighting deeply to control the anger rising within him. Mauclerc was correct. Haddon was a parchment maker, a pamphleteer and, like many of his guild, a fervent support of the countess, who patronised them lavishly. Haddon's arrest was a severe blow.

'And?' The countess's voice cut like a whip. 'Why do you mention this man?'

'Come, come, my Lady.' Sir Thomas spread his hands. 'Let us be blunt. Haddon could well hang but, there again, depending on you and my beloved son, Haddon could still scurry scot-free from Newgate.'

'Why should we?' Christopher asked. 'Esteemed father, let us be blunt. What do you want?'

'Let me explain,' Sir Thomas continued. 'George Neville, Archbishop of York, blood-brother to the late Earl of Warwick, together with his sister the Lady Grace, have invited our noble King, his brothers and immediate entourage to a splendid festival at his opulent manor, The Moor in Hertfordshire. He would like us to arrive on the eve of the Feast of St George to celebrate one of our King's great patron saints. The King has graciously accepted, and so the court will move there, certainly within the next two weeks.'

'And we are to join you?'

'My boy, esteemed son, thank God for your keen wits.'

'I wish they were keener.'

'Madam, you will move to The Moor with your guests in the next few days. You will certainly be given comfortable lodgings.'

'But that's not the real business you've come to discuss, is it? There's something else? With you, Sir Thomas, there always is.'

'True, my Lady. A few days ago, my henchman, my stalwart retainer, Brasenose,' Sir Thomas pointed to Christopher. 'You know him?'

'Regrettably.'

'Well, no regrets now. Brasenose was foully murdered in the maze at The Moor.'

'Maze!' Bray exclaimed.

'A subtle conceit,' the countess intervened.

'How murdered?'

'Mysteriously, my son. Wounds to the back, as if someone was following him and struck swiftly.' Sir Thomas shrugged. 'That is not for now. Not all the details.'

'Brasenose had a henchman, Rutger?'

'True, my son, but Rutger has also been murdered. He and one of the Company of the Five Wounds.'

'I know of those,' the countess declared. 'Warwick's bodyguard. I thought they were included in the Act of Attainder, which listed those marked down for punishment after York's great victories.'

'For a while, for a while, they were,' Sir Thomas replied. He leaned against the table and smiled across at his son. 'I will not give you lengthy detail or provide further information. Suffice to say, I shall leave you this.' The Recorder opened the chancery satchel on the table before him. He took out, and pushed across, manuscript scrolls tightly fastened and sealed.

'Mauclerc also knows the details,' Sir Thomas declared. 'But this schedule of documents will provide you with points of interest. You will investigate these murders.'

'And Haddon?'

'Ah yes Haddon. Christopher, my esteemed son. You have the most enquiring mind.'

'My mother's legacy.'

'Quite, quite. I want you to investigate the murders at The Moor, hunt the killer and, when you apprehend him, hang him.' Sir Thomas shrugged. 'Or her or them. Christopher, I know what you are capable of. Will you accept such a commission?'

'And Haddon?'

'Ah yes. If you accept, Haddon will be a free man by vespers.'

'In which case I accept.'

'Good. As soon as you reach The Moor, and I urge you not to tarry, begin your investigation. Tonight, or tomorrow morning at the latest. Mauclerc will bring the necessary licences and commission. You will assume the role and position of a Justice of Oyer et Terminer on those matters I have described above. Now I am finished.' Sir Thomas scraped back his chair, rose and collected his belongings, Mauclerc assisting him. Both men sketched a bow towards the countess and left the chamber.

Margaret lifted a finger to her lips and they sat in silence, listening to the faint sounds from the streets: trumpets rang out, horns brayed. Church bells clanged, issuing their invitation to prayer, which was almost deafened by the crash of cartwheels, the crack of whips and the rolling surf of cries and shouts. Eventually the countess crossed herself. She then despatched Bray to ensure that their guests had truly gone and the gallery and stairs were empty and well-guarded by her retainers. Once he had, Urswicke went down to the buttery and brought up a tray of fresh food and drink. He poured the sweet wine of Alsace and, for a while, all three just sat sipping at their cups and eating comfits from the platter.

'So,' the countess declared, 'it looks as if we're going to sup with the devil. In which case we had better take long spoons.'

'My Lady?'

'My friends, pay heed! George Neville, Archbishop of York, is a man of the deepest deceit, with allegiance to no one but himself. A self-proclaimed ardent Yorkist, he turned Lancastrian.' The countess pulled a face. 'I will not bore you with a litany of his transgressions, except to say that in the end, George Neville, given to double-dealing more than any man in this kingdom, made his final choice by siding with Lancaster.' She smiled thinly and held up a hand. 'Until the very end, George had sworn to defend both London and the hapless King Henry housed here. After Barnet, he cheerfully handed both over to Edward and was rewarded with a shower of petty gifts. Now,' the countess drank from her goblet, 'George is a twin, his sister the Lady Grace is also a fervent Yorkist. Indeed, so passionately devoted to Edward is she that the lady merrily shared her bed with him and, I suggest, would cheerfully do so again.'

'I've heard such tittle-tattle,' Urswicke murmured. 'Lady Grace is woman who enjoys everything in life and doesn't give a fig for anyone else.'

'Both Nevilles,' Bray declared, 'would make you dizzy with their toing and froing. On Monday Lancastrian, on Tuesday Yorkist. They would sell themselves, and anyone else, if the price was right, Lady Grace in particular.'

'Oh yes,' the countess agreed. 'Lady Grace is as wayward as her twin brother and should be watched. They both reside at The Moor, a truly magnificent mansion of a manor, close to the village of Rickmansworth in Hertfordshire. The house, like those who dwell there, is beautiful to view, yet it houses, so they say, great evil. Stories about the maze and the manor depict a grim, gruesome, ghostly past.'

'And the others?'

The countess broke the seal and opened the schedule of documents Sir Thomas had handed over. She quickly read the elegant, clerkly script before passing them to Christopher, who swiftly scrutinised the documents whilst the countess and Bray sat in silence.

'Little we do not know already,' the countess murmured. 'Now, Reginald, you mentioned the others. Well, most of the retainers at The Moor are, or were, the most loyal adherents of the late Earl of Warwick.'

'And none more so,' Urswicke added, tapping the document, 'than the Company of the Five Wounds. Sir Thomas refers to them; they are, or were, a battle group of seasoned knights who swore to defend and protect the Earl of Warwick. You know how it is, Reginald. A commander will select a small group of the best swordsmen; in battle they group around him, mailed and armoured. They carry long kite shields and cast a ring of steel around their master. Battle groups can be for defence or attack. At Tewkesbury, Richard of Gloucester commanded his brother's battle group. They were given a list of those they should seek out and kill. It's not just revenge, but plotting the destruction of the enemy. If the captains of war are cut down, fear, panic and confusion soon spread.'

'But whatever the battle group,' the countess declared, 'and I remember my beloved Edmund talking about this, they were futile in the mist-hung valleys of Wales, where you can barely see your comrade, never mind some enemy advancing towards you. From what I understand, the battle at Barnet was no different. Everything and everyone was shrouded in a thick, cloying mist.'

'Nevertheless,' Bray declared, 'the Five Wounds failed most miserably at Barnet.'

'No, Reginald, don't judge them so harshly,' the countess replied. 'As you know, my late husband Sir Henry was at Barnet. He sustained wounds which later cost him his life. He never recovered. He spent most of the last months of his life bed-ridden and in constant pain. He declared he was finished with princes and their plotting. He did not care for either York or Lancaster and cursed both their houses. Nevertheless, and these matters have certainly stirred my memory, Sir Henry often talked about Barnet. He described it as a battle from hell. How that deadly mist I mentioned caused absolute chaos and confusion. Soldiers, entire phalanxes, blundering about, unable to distinguish friend from foe.'

'Certainly true,' Urswicke declared. 'The Lancastrians began to attack themselves, the Earl of Oxford emerged where he shouldn't have been. His allies, led by Exeter and the rest, thought Oxford standards emblazoned with stars were in fact the banners of York with their golden suns. Exeter's forces mistakenly attacked their allies who, in turn, believing they were being betrayed, fiercely resisted. Many of the fighting men were in a constant state of indecision, wondering whether they should change sides. My father told me a remarkable story. How some of the combatant wore two surcoats, one over the other, ready to change sides.'

'Chaos created in hell,' the countess declared. 'That's how Sir

Henry described it, so perhaps it's wrong to judge the Five Wounds.' She tapped the manuscript on the table before her. 'According to Sir Thomas, the Five Wounds became separated from their lord and had to fight their own way out. After the battle, when it became clear that the victory was York's, all five went into hiding. They later petitioned His Grace the Archbishop to intercede for them. He did so successfully. All five received a full pardon and were admitted into the King's Peace, George Neville standing guarantor for them. They had to lodge with him for a while to ensure their oaths of allegiance were kept, a common enough arrangement which suits all parties.'

'So,' Bray exclaimed, 'what do we have here and what do we do about it?'

'First,' Urswicke replied, 'we have the Imposter and his familiar Patmore. Heaven knows what they and those who manipulate them really want. Confusion, chaos? Possible! Poor Caiaphas and Haddon are eloquent testimony to that, but I am sure more is intended.'

'Oh, I fully agree.' The countess turned to Urswicke. 'What else, Christopher?'

'Secondly we have this invitation, or rather summons, to join the festivities at The Moor with York and his court. Again why? Why us? Why there? Why now? What is intended?'

For a while all three sat in silence.

'Thirdly,' Urswicke continued, 'we have the unexpected murders at The Moor. One of the Company of the Five Wounds has been slain, together with Brasenose and his henchman Rutger. Three sudden, bloody killings. At first sight, such deaths might well be the result of some hidden enmity, a bitter legacy of the recent wars, especially those two great battles at Tewkesbury and Barnet. However, two of those murders were of loyal Yorkists, whilst a third was a close supporter of Warwick and Lancaster. I cannot detect a pattern in these slayings, any reason for them or to what end. I mean, true, Brasenose arrived at The Moor and was killed almost immediately but the Five Wounds had been there for some time. What is apparent is that my esteemed father had not reckoned on this. He seemed genuinely mystified and, quite surprisingly, he wants me to investigate, but why? Why not some royal justiciar?'

'Because you are more skilled and swifter,' the countess retorted, 'and I suspect,' she added laughingly, 'you can be trusted. Sir Thomas certainly doesn't want any interference by some busybody justiciar. In turn this must reinforce our belief that Sir Thomas has something planned for The Moor. But, for the life of me, I cannot even guess what it is. So . . .' She drew a deep breath. 'What do you suggest, Christopher? What move should we make on the chessboard?'

'First, my Lady, let us concentrate on Patmore and the Imposter. I have reflected on what we've learnt. My father declared how both came on a cog out of Brest. Utter nonsense! Such a claim adds weight to their pretensions but in truth it's a fiction. I believe that if the precious pair had appeared in Brest, they would have been taken up by Duke Francis's men, even more so if they'd tried to negotiate their passage to England on a Breton cog. Everything about this precious pair is an illusion,' Urswicke continued, 'a sham, a masque, a make-believe.'

'What do you mean?' Bray queried.

'Well, Patmore creates the illusion of complete Breton support, a move which is strengthened by the production of letters allegedly signed and sealed by Duke Francis at La Rochelle, Brest, or some other place in Brittany. However, we all know that excellent forgeries can be produced and, like the rumour about Lord Jasper's death, it can take weeks, even months to establish the truth of any such situation. For goodness' sake,' Urswicke declared, 'Duke Francis has been our most loyal supporter. He has treated young Henry as he would his own son. Why should he suddenly change? Of course, eventually he will discover what has happened and publish the truth of all this. He will dismiss Patmore and the Imposter for what they are. But just think, how long will that take, not to mention the utter mayhem it will cause.'

'True, true,' Bray murmured. 'Sharp, Christopher, very sharp. So, what do you suggest?'

'On reflection, I believe our two mummers only boarded that cog when it docked at some port along our south coast: Southampton, Dover, or any of the ports along the Narrow Seas.'

'I agree,' Bray whispered. 'And the truth of the situation?'

'I suspect Patmore and his charge appeared out of Wales.

Patmore had studied in the halls of Oxford but he could not go there. The schools are fairly small, enclosed communities. Patmore and his mammet would find it difficult to hide there.'

'So, London was their choice?'

'Yes, Reginald, London. An army could hide in this city and sometimes has. Moreover, it's an ideal place for such plotters. Patmore studied at the Inns of Court, a busy thronging place. Think of the many taverns and hostelries he could shelter in. In short, we should begin there.'

'I agree,' the countess declared. 'So, look Christopher, you will accompany me into Hertfordshire. We have no choice; we shall lodge at The Moor. We are in fact being imprisoned in a gilded cage. We will be watched, followed and closely guarded. Oh, not up close, but from afar. I think we will find it hard to write letters or for me to leave and come back. Once there, I am sure I will have to stay until this masque has finished. They will also watch you, Christopher, but I need you there. Reginald, I want you to use all your knowledge of the city and its hidden places, especially around the Inns of Court. Patmore must have been known there and, I am sure, lodged in that ward before he and the Imposter decided to make their move. Search out Lord Nightshade and his ruffians, press them for information, speak to the street swallows. Sooner or later, you will turn a dirty stone to reveal something most precious underneath. Oh yes,' she continued, 'we will keep Master Patmore in our thoughts whilst we find the means to bring both him and the Imposter crashing down. In the meantime,' the countess rubbed her eyes, 'we must keep a sharp eye on this invitation to The Moor. Something rotten, some nasty mischief is planned.' The countess sipped from her goblet and wetted her lips. 'Reginald, I want you to stay well clear of The Moor. Only come if you have to. Let us prepare for that. If I recall the countryside around The Moor correctly, it is well cultivated, rich farmland, dotted with small hamlets. Rickmansworth is a thriving village. You will be watched, perhaps even obstructed. However, once we've left here you must seek out Wolkind, Caiaphas's brother. He must move to Rickmansworth and lodge in its most comfortable hostelry. Once there, Wolkind can act as our messenger to the outside world; I deeply suspect we are going to need one.

We must be prepared. Also, tell Wolkind to organise horses, provender and purveyance in case we have to flee. Oh yes, I do believe something truly hideous this way comes.'

John de Vere, Earl of Oxford, came out of his cabin beneath the stern of his recently refurbished two-masted war cog, *The Glory of Lancaster*. He nodded at his henchmen, grouped around the main mast, and went to stand by the taffrail, staring out into the dark at the faint outline of his favourite landfall, that stretch of lonely, windswept beach at Walton-on-the-Naze. Oxford stood gripping the rail as he fought back the tears caused by both the salty spray, as well as a profoundly heartrending homesickness. If he landed on that beach and took horse he could be on his domain within the hour. He would enter a promised land, with its lush water meadows, prosperous ploughed land, richly dense forests, woods and copses, as well as fertile orchards producing heavy ripe fruit, be it apple, pear or plum. Manor houses, vills and hamlets dotted that paradise, watered by streams and brooks teeming with all kinds of fish. It was his! That domain had been his father's! Oxford grasped the rail even tighter. One day it would be his again. De Vere stared to his left and right. The war cog rode gently at anchor. Master Corbin had predicted good sailing conditions under clear skies, except for a few fair-weather clouds. The master had been proven correct. The swell of the sea was majestic yet calm and serene. They had moved into position just before nightfall, taking advantage of the change in tide. Now they were waiting.

Oxford's ship constantly hugged the eastern coastline from the mouth of the Thames, north to Hunstanton and the other lonely ports along England's east coast. Oxford was well supported here; friends and allies were close. He could rest his crew, clean his cog, secure fresh purveyance and other supplies. Above all, he could collect the gossip of the shires and receive the reports from his spies. He had been standing off the Norfolk coast when a fisherman and his son had brought information that in two days' time, after the chimes of midnight, a messenger would be waiting in Walton cove, Oxford's favourite place, a true listening post into York's kingdom.

De Vere felt the cog move slowly beneath him. York's kingdom!

It should have been his and Lancaster's. They would have achieved success if it had not been for that bloody fateful struggle at Barnet. On that Easter Sunday, they should have carried all before them, but no, Warwick had decided to fight on foot. He had been persuaded by some poltroon that such a decision would encourage their own common soldiers, a clear demonstration that their leaders were not plotting to flee on horseback. And what then? Utter confusion and chaos, thanks to the devil's mist which had shrouded the battlefield that fateful Sunday morning. Oxford had inflicted grievous damage on York's right wing, pushing them into retreat, pursuing them with a vengeance. They had charged too far. On their return to the battlefield, Oxford's forces had been mistaken for Yorkists and the mayhem had turned to a massacre. The Lancastrian army had disintegrated and fled. If only Warwick had survived! He could have returned to hoist the Ragged Staff and continue the struggle. But no, he'd fallen and been killed. So, what really had happened to Warwick? Was it true that he had died alone? More importantly, what had happened to his bodyguard? His own small battle group, the Five Wounds?

On that doom-laden Sunday morning, the clash between York and Lancaster had boiled furiously, like an angry sea swirling backwards and forwards. Just before the Lancastrian line had finally broken, John Neville, Marquess of Montagu, had been cut down, his standard seized by the Yorkists. A sign that it truly was all over. Oxford immediately realized the battle was lost. He'd turned to flee and glimpsed the Company of the Five Wounds on the edge of the battlefield. He could not see what state they were in, and it was too frenetic to try and reach them. Their leader, Matthew Poppleton, had raised his sword in silent salute before the mist swirled back, as thick as a horse-blanket, cutting off sight and sound. Undoubtedly the Five Wounds had, like him, fled for their lives, but it still left the question: what had happened to Warwick, Lancaster's great champion? Had that sinister, sly spy; that perpetual turncoat; that dabbler in devices; that lord of lies, Achitophel, have anything to do with Warwick's downfall? Oxford had learned a little about Achitophel, an elusive, mysterious being who worked for both York and Lancaster. One of the tribe of spies and informants who thrived on the conflict which divided the kingdom. Matters had turned so dreadfully dire on that fateful Easter morning; Oxford did wonder if events had been given a helping hand by Achitophel.

De Vere wiped the salted spray from his face. The breeze had strengthened somewhat and the decks shifted sharply. De Vere steadied himself and peered through the darkness. He had received information from Archbishop George Neville that he needed to discuss urgent business with Oxford, if not personally, then through his trusted steward, Maillac, and Robin of Redesdale. Oxford closed his eyes. Maillac he trusted, but Robin of Redesdale was simply a title that so many rebel captains assumed when they lifted the red and black banners of rebellion. So, what did he want? Who was he?

'My Lord,' one of his henchmen called, 'I see it.'

Oxford followed the man's direction and sighed in relief. A fire had been lit on the beach, the flames being fed till they danced against the darkness. Oxford immediately issued a spate of orders. The bumboat was lowered. Soldiers and men-at-arms clambered down, followed by Oxford, who took a seat in the stern. The earl braced himself against the swell. The boat turned and twisted, but at last the oarsmen brought it under control and the boat aimed like an arrow towards that fire burning so merrily on the beach. Oxford turned his face into the wind, breathing in the pure, fresh air, happy to be away from the reek of the ship. Above them, seagulls whirled and screeched. Oxford kept his gaze on that fire. The boat surged forward, the tide now pushing it in. At last, the prow caught the loose sandy shale and lay rocking close to the shore. The crew climbed out, pulling the boat even further up the beach to rest on the pebble-dashed sand. Two of the men-at-arms hastened towards the fire. Oxford caught the murmured greetings.

'All well, my Lord!' one of the soldiers sang out. 'All well!'

'Come, my Lord.' Another voice cut through the dark. 'Come quickly, for the hours burn as swiftly as this fire.'

Oxford ordered his men to stay with the boat and went to squat before the fire, staring at the two hooded and visored men sitting opposite. One of these rose to a half-crouch and passed across the two seals. Oxford inspected these and handed them back.

'So,' he declared, 'you are the envoys of His Grace the Archbishop of York. What does he want? Why has he sent you, Maillac, and this?' Oxford flicked his fingers at the second man sitting so quietly.

'I am Robin of Redesdale.'

'I don't care if you call yourself the Great Cham of Tartary. Who are you? What is your name? What are you doing here?'

The second man now handed across a seal for Oxford to inspect. He did so in the light of the dancing flames and immediately recognized the royal arms and insignia of the late, hapless Henry VI, so recently murdered in the Tower.

'I was,' the stranger intoned, 'a mailed clerk high in the household of King Henry of blessed memory, and his beloved wife-queen, Margaret of Anjou. I am here, my Lord, to help. On the death of King Henry—'

'Murder!' Oxford interjected. 'Henry was foully murdered.'

'In truth yes, my Lord, and I live and work, like you do, to avenge his death. What my real name is does not matter. However, believe me, I am as fervent to the cause as you are. The House of Lancaster must return. Both I and others plot such a course, as sure and clear as you do your cog across the waters.'

'So why do we meet here?'

'Why, my Lord of Oxford, we are here to plot rebellion and destroy York in one bloody affray.'

Oxford startled in reply.

'How? When?' he stammered.

'I will be succinct,' Maillac replied. 'You, my Lord, have an Act of Attainder against you. If captured, you would die . . .'

'I know only too well,' Oxford snapped, 'what will happen if York captures me. I will be lodged in the Tower where I will be tortured, questioned, abused and bruised, until I plead for death; but that won't come swiftly. I will then be hauled through the streets like a common felon, strapped to some hurdle or sledge. I will end my days on the execution platform at Smithfield or Tyburn, my body cut open, my heart plucked out. So, sir, don't tell me what will happen. I know that only too well.'

'And rest assured,' Maillac retorted, 'we shall do the same to York in one great bloodletting.'

'And what will be my part in this? When does it occur and where?'

'We still strike on the eve of the Feast of St George, the twenty-third of April. We will storm The Moor and control it. The archbishop will ensure that seizure of our enemies will be swift and silent. The Brothers York will be arrested and tried by martial law, as they did Somerset and others of our captains after Tewkesbury. Remember? They were seized from sanctuary and beheaded, one after another, in the market place, Edward watching from a window. Now it's our turn.'

'And my part in this?'

'You will sit in judgement. My Lord, as you have often informed York: they killed your father and you will not rest until you have killed them.'

'A promise I shall certainly keep.'

'And we will supply both the place and the occasion for it.'

'And, what else?'

'You, my Lord, will sit high in the council but, to achieve that, we ask you to provision your cog for war and flight. We would like some of your crew to join us, but it is your cog that matters. If we are successful, and God willing we are, we will ask you to spirit away Edward of York's Queen and children. You will take them to Calais, where Elizabeth, her offspring and the other ladies, can be safely lodged in Hammes Castle. Once there, no one can use them to rally the Yorkist cause.'

'And should we fail?'

'Well . . .'

Maillac stared around the desolate, lonely beach, as if listening to the surf break and the seabirds call into the night. Oxford stared up. The sky was clear, providing good sailing weather. Nevertheless, for how long could he prowl off the coast, only a short distance from his estates, his very own God-given inheritance?

'My Lord?'

'And if we fail?'

'If we fail, my Lord, we shall certainly need you. Flight by horseback would be fruitless. We would soon be ridden down by York's huntsmen. No, we would flee here, take refuge on this lonely beach, waiting to be taken out to your life-saving cog.'

'Could we fail?'

'My Lord, look at the fight at Barnet! That battle, like many such struggles, teetered on the edge of both defeat and victory. But my Lord,' Maillac stretched out his hands to the fire, welcoming its warmth, 'we shall succeed. There are others at The Moor who will join us. No less a person than Margaret, Countess of Richmond, with her henchmen.'

'I've heard the same, but I have also learned that a pretender, an Imposter, has emerged, claiming to be the countess's son, Henry Tudor.'

'One farrago of nonsense amongst many. The Imposter does not concern us. The countess certainly does. We will win her support. You, my Lord of Oxford, have the deepest respect for her.'

'As she does for me.'

'Precisely, my Lord. Your support and hers are crucial.'

'Very well, let us say we are successful.'

'The Brothers York, together with whatever henchmen accompany them, will be despatched into the dark to join the legion they have sent there.'

'And what then?'

Maillac gestured at Robin of Redesdale, inviting him to speak.

'I will gather men, there are now enough who want to settle matters with York, including veterans from your own estates, my Lord. We may well need your cog to ferry troops from the mouth of the Humber to this beach. We will certainly be with you at The Moor. We will take care of any escort. Once York has been seized and despatched, we will march on London. Others will join us from the shires, as well as from the city. There will be little resistance. Our merchants do not like turmoil; it ruins the markets and is bad for business.'

'In whose name?' Oxford interrupted. 'In whose name do we proclaim the peace?'

'Why my Lord, Henry Tudor,' Maillac replied. 'As for the mammet, he will soon disappear. Countess Margaret will take care of him. More importantly, she will despatch couriers to Duke Francis. The good duke, together with Lord Jasper and others of our coven, will arrange for young Henry to sail immediately for England. He will land safely, to be acclaimed as King and crowned at Westminster.'

'And in the meantime?'

'A regency under my Lord Archbishop, or, if she accepts it,
Margaret Countess of Richmond. She is a Beaufort, with royal
blood in her veins.'

Oxford turned and gazed back at the sea. Maillac's news had
seriously disturbed him. Here he was again, readying for battle,
as he had on that fateful Easter Sunday at Barnet, with that
dreadful mist seeping in and the Lancastrian camp being roused
to war. Life was like a game of hazard. Fickle Fortune spun her
wheel, the dice would roll, the cast be made, but how would it
all play out? If he joined Archbishop Neville what, apart from
life, could he lose, and what life was that? Sailing up and down
this bleak coast, like some corsair waiting for an opportunity
such as this. And if they were successful? Fortune would reward
him. Many invasions had proved successful. Indeed, the House
of Lancaster first won the Crown by a successful incursion against
Richard II over seventy years ago. He thought of The Moor and
those who lodged there.

'Lady Margaret,' he declared, 'is she party to this? Will she
support us?'

'I am sure she will. She constantly lives under the shadow
of the axe whilst her beloved son Henry has to shelter abroad,
fearful of betrayal or violent death at the hands of some hired
assassin. She too must baulk at the power of York. Now the
countess is cunning and astute. She keeps her own counsel.
Indeed, on a venture like this, I doubt if she even reveals her
secret thoughts to her most loyal henchmen. Don't worry. I
am sure when we strike, she'll be with us. What else, my
Lord?'

'There have been murders, so it's reported, at The Moor?
York's man killed in the maze there? Another had his throat cut.
One of the Five Wounds company also slain.'

'In truth, my Lord, I – we – do not know the truth of that,'
Maillac explained, 'except all three victims were protected by
the Crown. This may well sharpen King Edward's appetite to
visit The Moor and view matters for himself. My Lord, we live
in highly dangerous times. Sudden, violent death is an unexpected
guest at many a table. I cannot explain or answer everything.
What I must do is answer for you to my master, the Lord

Archbishop. Are you with us, yea or nay? Will you be with us
on the eve of the Feast of St George?'

Oxford crossed himself and clambered to his feet, hand
extended for Maillac to grasp.

'Yea,' the earl exclaimed. 'Except . . .'

'Except for what, my Lord?'

'You talk of sudden death. You mention the murders at The
Moor. I realize you cannot have an answer for everything, but
someone must have a hand in such a murky, murderous muddle.
I just wonder if that prince of mischief, that sly subtle Satan of
a man has emerged yet again.'

'My Lord?'

'Achitophel. A spy who served both York and Lancaster and
merrily betrayed them both if the price, whatever that might be,
was right. Achitophel prowled the camps of both York and
Lancaster. The chaos you describe could be Achitophel's work,
and would that be for our good or for our damnation and loss?'

'My Lord, I cannot answer that now. Our business, our affairs
must not be brought to nought. We are committed to this venture.
Are you?'

'Oh yes. I am. To the death, and so damn Achitophel.'

Oxford and those he met truly believed they were shrouded,
protected, by the lonely darkness of Walton Cove. They were
not. The fisherman who had first brought the news to *The Glory
of Lancaster* when it stood off the coast of Norfolk was also
there. Hiding high up on sand hills, together with his son. The
fisherman was well paid by Oxford. He was a collector of news,
rumour and gossip. He could regale the earl with all kinds of
tales, but he was also Sir Thomas Urswicke's man, answering
directly to the Recorder, or one of his henchmen. Now they were
here to view what would happen and they had. The fisherman
peered down at the beach and wondered what Sir Thomas
intended. The fisherman had supplied the Recorder with Oxford's
answer, giving the time and place for this meeting. But why?
Why just watch and let them go? He had dared to ask the same
question when he and Sir Thomas had met in that deserted priory
close to The Moor. If Oxford was to bring his cog in. If the rebel
Earl was to disembark and meet with others, then why not scoop
all the traitors up as he would fish in a net? Soldiers could watch

the beach, whilst royal cogs would appear from over the horizon to pin Oxford's cog against the coast and utterly destroy it. Sir Thomas had just laughed softly and told the fisherman to simply watch and collect whatever information he could. More specifically, if the meeting actually took place. Sir Thomas then clasped the fisherman on the shoulder as he handed across a purse of coins.

'My friend.' Sir Thomas then squeezed hard. 'I have others well placed amongst the traitors, but they have their task and must remain deeply hidden until the very end. Each to their own. Look, when you go fishing, have you ever ignored the minnow, the mackerel, so you could net a plump porpoise?'

'Of course, my Lord.'

'Well, my friend, I am hunting a veritable shoal of the plumpest porpoise, and I intend to feast on them all.'

Christopher Urswicke grasped the guide rope more tightly as he slowly threaded his way through the maze at The Moor. Days had passed, time so swift it was startling. Reginald had slipped into the city to begin his own hunt, whilst the countess prepared to leave London, ordering Urswicke to keep Mauclerc, Patmore and the Imposter, whom she now described as the 'Unholy Trinity', out of her sight. In truth, Christopher did not find this difficult because all three unwelcome guests kept very much to themselves. Urswicke ensured that they remained so, although he was growing more and more fascinated by the burgeoning friendship between Mauclerc and the Imposter, as if they truly were father and son. As Urswicke reported to the countess, they acted like blood kin, reconciled after a long absence. The countess did not care but she was delighted to learn that Mauclerc and his two accomplices would be leaving London before them and would not join their own cavalcade to The Moor. Urswicke was also relieved.

In the end, the journey into Hertfordshire had proved very pleasant; warm sunshine, the ground underfoot hard and firm, ensuring a pleasant ride. They had skirted Rickmansworth and took the path to The Moor to be warmly welcomed by the Lord Archbishop and his sister Lady Grace, together with the dark-faced former soldier Maillac, Neville's chief steward and hall

marshal. The countess, Urswicke and their small retinue were
provided with the most comfortable lodgings, the countess's
chamber in particular being furnished with every luxury. The
'Unholy Trinity', however, or so Urswicke learnt from Maillac,
had been greeted with a cold diffidence and provided with rather
bleak lodgings at the rear of the mansion, close to the servants'
quarters.

The countess also feasted well. Every meal turned out to be
a veritable banquet; lampreys, eels, venison, beef, carp and pike
were served, all picked out in delicious and savoury sauces. The
best wines of Bordeaux, Alsace and Avignon were poured, along
with sweetmeats of every kind heaped on platters. All the meals
were served in the Great Hall, magnificently furnished, with its
finest oak and elmwood furniture polished to a glittering
shine. Tapestries, paintings and drapes adorned the walls.
Catherine wheels, crammed with candles, provided more light
when the sun could no longer pierce the windows, many of which
were filled with painted glass of the most glorious hue. The Moor
truly was a lavish, episcopal palace, a place of dancing light.
The air was constantly perfumed with the mixed fragrances of
crushed herbs, incense as well as the mouth-watering smells from
the well-furnished kitchens and buttery. Thick, rich turkey mats
covered the floor and deadened sound. For the rest, The Moor
would have been the envy of any manor lord, with its carp ponds,
pheasant runs, stables, piggeries, hen coops; its rich meadows
cropped by a wide variety of livestock.

Lost in such thoughts about his new lodgings, Urswicke
grasped the guide rope more tightly, following the twisting paths
until he reached the centre of the maze, which was dominated
by a lofty stone cross of Celtic design. Catching his breath,
Urswicke sat down on one of the benches which flanked the
cross. He blessed himself and wondered again about his hosts,
Lord George and Lady Grace. Both Nevilles were truly handsome, with their thick golden hair, large blue eyes, full lips
and fair skin. Ever-pleasant, both brother and sister viewed the
world under heavy-lidded eyes, lips slighted parted, always ready
to smile. Twins, as the countess remarked, they certainly were
peas from the same pod and, as the countess had added, as
treacherous and cunning as each other.

'I wouldn't trust either of them, Christopher. They are snakes – beautiful snakes, but just as venomous as any reptile from hell. Now, Christopher, you must do what you have to. I must reflect on certain letters and memoranda I must draw up.'

'Do you wish to dictate?'

'No, no.' The countess had beckoned Christopher as close as she could. 'What I write,' she whispered, 'must be by me alone. The old phrase "the walls have ears" is certainly true here, with the added warning that they also have eyes. We will be closely watched and listened to. We must be prudent, as I keep saying; we must wait and watch.'

Christopher had left the countess in her chamber. On reflection he had ruefully conceded the countess was correct. If they had to speak on confidential matters, it would be most prudent to meet outside.

'Though not here,' Urswicke murmured to himself. He glanced around at the strange world of the maze. Wall after wall of greenery – thick, closely packed hedges reaching at least four yards high – housed a place of sinister stillness.

Maillac's steward had informed both the countess and himself about The Moor, its ownership by the Templars before all their property and goods were seized by the Crown. The story of Fitzallen was chilling enough to cast a long, deep shadow over this place. Urswicke wondered what other macabre secrets The Moor hid behind its magnificent front.

'Oh yes,' Christopher murmured to himself. 'Sudden death, brutal murder . . .' Urswicke froze at the sound of footsteps on the gravel path. He rose, half drew his dagger, then sighed in relief as the countess, wielding a pointed walking stick, turned on to the path leading to the cross. She let the guide rope drop and walked over to her henchman.

'Christopher, I did not mean to startle you. I tried,' she smiled, 'to be heard. There,' she gestured at Urswicke to sit back on the stone bench where she joined him. 'This,' she declared, 'is a true maze, created by a master, Daedalus. I have read about him, Christopher. Anyway, a place of mystery. Now, you have not yet broached the matters covered by your father's commission.'

'My Lady, I intend to do so later on. I would dearly love you to join me, even if it's just to sit and, as you say, watch and wait.'

'Of course I will, yet what do you have here, Christopher? What have you learned? What scraps of information have you collected?'

'Not much. Brasenose was one of my father's henchmen. He and his manservant Rutger visited The Moor, ostensibly to ensure that all was well before the arrival of the Brothers York. For all I know, he may have had other business, but that is nigh impossible to establish. As for his murder, he apparently entered this maze using the guide rope as we did, only to be attacked from behind, stab wounds to his back. No sign of resistance or a struggle. According to Maillac he was lying face down. As for why he entered the maze, there is a rumour that he saw someone else enter, but that is impossible to prove. How he was murdered so quietly, so effortlessly, is a complete mystery.'

'Then there are the others?'

'Yes, Simon Fladgate, one of the Five Wounds. He was slain in a yard adjoining the petty buttery. Apparently, he went across to the jakes cupboard, opened the door and found Rutger, hose down, slumped on the turd bench, his throat sliced from ear to ear. From what I can gather, Fladgate was then slain. The assassin crept up behind him. Fladgate turned and took a bolt to the head, shattering bone and brain.' Urswicke rubbed his face. 'That's all I can say about the deaths. Nothing else, nothing more. Of course, I still wonder why my father commissioned me to investigate.'

'Enough, Christopher, we have discussed this. As I have said before, your father doesn't want anyone else coming to The Moor to investigate. For his own secret purposes, your father wants to keep this tightly within his control, which only sharpens my anxiety.'

'My Lady?'

'The Moor is a lavish palace, soon to host King Edward and his coven. Nevertheless, I sense something very wrong. A malevolence, a malignancy gathering in the dark. I do not know the where, the when or the why-for – nonetheless, Christopher, I truly suspect we are in great danger.' She drew a deep breath and got to her feet, driving the pointed walking stick repeatedly into the pebble-dashed path. 'We can only pray,' she declared, 'for us both, and for our good friend Reginald.'

PART THREE

'The Manor of The Moor which the Archbishop had purchased and built right commodiously.'

Reginald Bray sat facing the garden of The Mouth of Hell, a spacious but greatly decayed tavern standing at the heart of Whitefriars. The hostelry was one of the manors, as he described it, of Lord Nightshade. The King, the mayor, the noble Recorder, and all the masters of the Guildhall might well boast how they completely ruled London. Bray knew different. In truth, Lord Nightshade and his council of demons controlled, with an iron fist, the nightmare underworld of the city, be it the rat-infested mumpers' castles of Whitefriars, or the shabby tenements which lined the Thames. Harlots, both male and female, tricksters, cunning men, naps, foists, thieves and pimps, were, whether they liked it or not, Lord Nightshade's subjects. He ruled with sheer terror. God help anyone who committed a felony without his support. Even the most ragged of whores or the poorest pickpocket fully recognized Lord Nightshade as a true Prince of Darkness. This Lord of Hell often held court in the Poison Pot, which stood nearby, but today he had chosen The Mouth of Hell, informing Bray that he would meet him there three hours after midday.

Bray had arrived early and now stood examining a gruesome wall painting, crudely but vigorously done by some itinerant artist. The garish tableau reflected the tavern's grim title, portraying hell and all its torments, a startling memento mori. According to the painting, hell was a place of torture, the tableau being dominated by two great columns of roaring fire. From these pillars hung a host of the damned, with razor-sharp spikes thrown through whatever member of their body they had sinned with during their life on earth. Fornicators, whores and pimps had their genitals pierced with daggers as they roasted in the flames. Thieves had their hands rent, liars their lips and tongues shredded; others were being punished in baths of boiling lead, pitch and brimstone. So immersed in these horrific depictions, Bray startled as he heard a sound behind him. He turned quickly. Lord Nightshade, Deadly Nightshade, stood grinning at him; on either side his bodyguard, all armoured and buckled for battle.

'My dearest, dearest Reginald,' Nightshade lisped. 'So very good to see you.' Nightshade stretched out his hand for Bray to clasp. Bray did so and the riffler chief pulled him closer. Bray stared hard at this creature from the pit. Nightshade loved to dress as a woman, as he was now, garbed in a gown of dark green sarcenet over a white chemise gathered high at the throat, so as to conceal the weals left by hangings. Nightshade had been hastily plucked from there at the insistence of this person or that. Bray knew this of old. After all, on a number of occasions he had rescued this lord of the underworld from Newgate or the execution cart and, on occasion, the gibbets at Tyburn and Smithfield. Bray had always arrived just in time for the rope to be cut before Nightshade's soul joined the choir invisible. In thanks, Nightshade had become Bray's guide in threading the dangerous streets of London's underworld.

Nightshade looked as singular as ever; his face had more paint than that of a whore, his richly carmined lips made even more hideous in a face plastered as white as snow. Nightshade held on to Bray's hand.

'Good to meet you, Master Reginald.' He lisped again. 'I hear such interesting news. I wondered when you would come to seek me.' Nightshade released his grip and thrust a small parchment scroll into Bray's hand. 'Three of my most faithful parishioners,' he whispered, 'beautiful boys, lovely lads, now lodged in Newgate over some very serious misunderstanding. I would like a pardon for each. Yes?'

'The countess,' Bray replied, 'is absent from London at the moment, but I will serve a stay of execution until she actually petitions the chancery. You know, my Lord, we will do all that we can.'

'Well, it's either that,' Nightshade laughed, 'or we are going to storm the execution cart: those boys cannot hang.'

'As I said, I will see to it.'

Deadly Nightshade nodded and waved Bray to join him in the window seat whilst his escort mounted guard on the taproom doors.

'No one will disturb us. Minehost has been given instruction.' He turned and beckoned across the rather nervous taverner standing just within the door leading into the kitchen.

'Food?' he asked.

Bray just shook his head

'Ale,' Nightshade bawled. 'And the best.'

Once the tankards were served, Nightshade gulped his eagerly then leaned against the table.

'So, my friend,' he murmured, 'Master Patmore? Former lawyer, and not such a good one. He is now the official custodian of a young man who claims to be the only beloved son of Margaret, Countess of Richmond.'

'An Imposter!'

'As some people say, Master Reginald, and of course he is. Whatever is intended, they have certainly caused chaos. They've upset the beehive and we can all see the consequences. Poor Caiaphas, hanged outside the countess's door. Young Haddon rotting in Newgate, though rumour claims he will be released, or has been. A number of the countess's good servants and retainers have decided that London is not for them and have moved out to hide in the shires or fled across the Narrow Seas. Now, we all know a great lie is being peddled, but what can we do about it? The more the countess protests, the greater the confusion. And of course, Master Bray, that would be very dangerous, yes? Our noble King has defined the way things are. God help anyone who tries to contradict him. But it is good that you have turned to me for help.' Again, Nightshade paused to drink from his tankard.

'My friend, I wait with bated breath.'

'Of course you do, Master Bray. I have learned, or discovered, that before their emergence into the open, Patmore and his mammet came out of Wales. They journeyed here and stayed hidden in London before travelling to one of the Cinque ports to secure passage back to the port of London, where they proclaimed themselves for all the world to hear.'

'How did they hide in London?'

'Well, my minions cast about and discovered Patmore and the Imposter lodged at The Golden Boy, a prosperous tavern close to the Inns of Court. Indeed, very expensive.'

'Ah yes,' Bray intervened, 'and The Golden Boy has a distinctive reputation.'

'So true, my friend. A place where young men – or not so young – can meet to have their pleasure of each other. A hostelry much suspected, though the lords of the Guildhall are most reluctant to intervene with a forced search. Heaven knows who, or what, they may find there.'

'I would agree. So, Patmore and the Imposter lodged there?'

'They did more than that, my friend. According to my spies, the noises from that chamber could be heard out along the gallery. The tryst of raucous though forbidden lust.'

'So, the Imposter is or was Patmore's catamite?'

'So it would seem. But I've also received intelligence that it is Patmore who likes forbidden fruit, not the young Imposter. He apparently absents himself when his mentor and master entertains someone else. Ah well, to continue. I have learned that Patmore took Minehost of The Golden Boy aside. He asked for the name of a cog which could spirit him away without any interference from the harbour masters.'

'And?'

'Listen, my friend.' Deadly Nightshade turned, snapping his fingers, issuing a spate of orders to one of his minions by the door. The fellow left and returned with a pot-bellied barrel of a man. From his rolling gait and rubicund, weather-chastened face, Bray suspected that he was a mariner.

'Josiah Wallington,' Nightshade intoned, gesturing the new arrival to an empty chair. 'Josiah the Jovial,' he continued, 'master of the small cog *The Rebec*, out of Queenhithe. The conveyor of all sorts of goods, be they alive or dead.'

Wallington beamed a gap-toothed smile and gratefully accepted the tankard thrust down on the table before him. He toasted Nightshade and peered at Bray.

'You're the comrade of Urswicke's son, yes?' Wallington's voice had a rich northern burr. 'I trust that he is not as merciless as his father. Sir Thomas Urswicke has a reputation much feared by us river folk.'

'My friend Christopher,' Bray retorted, 'is his own man. So, my friend, what can you tell us?' Bray pushed a coin from his purse across the table. The piece of silver disappeared in the twinkling of an eye.

'Tell him,' Nightshade grated.

'I was approached at Queenhithe by Patmore. He gave me his name and proof of who he was. I always demand that. He'd come to The Salamander tavern, seeking me out. He said I had a reputation for spiriting people out of London to some port across the Narrow Seas. I told him that he was correct and asked what he wanted. He replied: swift passage to Dordrecht, sometime between St George's Day and the end of the month.'

'Twenty-third April,' Bray declared. 'That's St George's feast day, yes?'

Wallington nodded.

'Of course,' the seaman declared, 'I cannot give a precise hour or a specific day. However, I advised Patmore that if he lodged at The Salamander, he could wait for me there. He paid some coins as his bond and left.'

'And he wanted passage for two people? Did he mention his companion?'

'Oh no, definitely not. He talked of no one else but himself. He was insistent on that and so was I. *The Rebec* is a small cog. I need to ensure that only so many are aboard with what baggage they carry.' He waved a hand. 'You must know how it is.'

'Of course, of course,' Bray murmured. 'So Master Patmore intended to flee England some time towards the end of April.'

'So it would seem.'

But why? Bray wondered to himself. Why the haste? What was so crucial about those dates? Just as importantly, Patmore had apparently decided that the Imposter would not be travelling with him. Why not?

'My friend,' Nightshade stretched across to pat Bray on the arm, 'you are finished here, yes?'

'For the present,' Bray answered absentmindedly. 'Yes, yes, so much to think about.'

'And I have got more grain for the mill,' Nightshade declared. He gestured at Wallington. 'Thank you, comrade, we no longer need you. Keep me informed of developments but go in my peace, as well as that of the good Lord.'

Once Wallington had gone, Nightshade leaned closer in a powerful scent of ale and cheap perfume.

'Master Bray, you are being followed.'

'Impossible,' Bray declared. 'I can thread the streets as cleverly as you can. I know when I am being followed and I have glimpsed nothing.'

'Oh, they keep you under close watch, that's all. That's why my friends and my good self will leave the tavern cloaked and cowled. Now,' Nightshade continued, 'do not be too concerned, we know that they are not footpads. None of my villains would dare do that without my permission, and that also goes for the dagger boys and their ilk. So, the only conclusion that I can draw is they . . .'

'They are Guildhall spies?'

'Correct, my friend, despatched by our noble Recorder, Sir Thomas. They will organise a close watch over you, one man replacing another so that you cannot mark an individual pursuing you. They are constantly changing. An old trick, sometimes I use it myself. But to move on. Tell me, Master Bray, where is your accomplice Urswicke? I've heard rumours . . .?'

'You mean you have gathered information from your legion of snoops and pryers . . .'

Nightshade tittered behind his hand.

'Sharp, Master Bray. Oh yes, we have heard that the countess, God bless her, is for The Moor, and that the snake in the grass, Lord George Neville, Archbishop of York – that fox in human flesh – will be her host. We have also heard tales about gruesome murders, including that of Brasenose, Sir Thomas's henchman. I knew that bully boy well, as I did his shadow, Rutger. The gossips talk of killings in a maze as well as outside a shit shed. There's also a story about a knight, one of the Five Wounds battle group, having been murdered. So, Master Bray, I can tell you a tale which, in the circumstances, might intrigue you, your good friend Christopher and your mistress.'

Bray turned and called across to Minehost to bring more tankards. Once he had, Bray toasted Nightshade with his.

'Tell me,' he declared. 'Tell me your tale.'

'I have your word that should at least three of my parishioners seized by The Recorder's bully boys . . .'

'As I have said, the countess will do what she can. But come, Lord Nightshade, the hour passes, the candle burns and I am becoming tired.'

'Ah yes, but the information I will bring you might well be worth a barrel of candles and freshen your heart. So, stay here, drink, think, sleep. I will be back by the vespers bell.'

Lord Nightshade clambered to his feet, pulling his cloak tighter, hiding both head and face in a deep cowl: his escort, similarly attired, followed their master out of the tavern. Bray slouched in his chair and reflected on what he had learnt. Nightshade's revelations about the emergence of Patmore and the Imposter were as expected. What had provoked deep surprise was the news that Patmore was already preparing to leave so abruptly, so swiftly, that he'd already decided he would be travelling by himself with no care for the Imposter. So, what did Patmore intend? Why did he bring the Imposter to London and proclaim who he was supposed to be? Chaos and confusion had been plotted and carried out, but what then? Bray drained his tankard, gathered his cloak and warbelt on to his lap and then, one hand on the hilt of his dagger, slipped into sleep. He was shaken awake by a grinning Nightshade, who sat opposite, forcing the man he had brought with him into a chair on his right. Nightshade made himself truly comfortable, ordering blackjacks and a platter of croutons grilled in a sharp, peppery sauce.

'This,' the lord of the underworld declared, gesturing at his guest, 'is Bardolph. Bardolph the Beanpole. Have you ever seen such a thin man?'

Half awake, Bray stared at Bardolph, who richly deserved his title. Slender as a wand, garbed in dark blue, he had the narrowest face, bruised and wounded, with a patch over his right eye. Nightshade made the introductions and invited his two guests, as he called Bray and Bardolph, to eat and drink, whilst Minehost ushered two shabbily dressed tinkers and their caged pet weasels out of the taproom. Once they'd gone, Nightshade, clearing his teeth with a finger, urged Bardolph to tell Bray who he was and what he knew.

'I am a camp follower,' he began in a thin, reedy voice. 'I follow the armies.'

'You mean you're a scavenger? A crow in human form?'

'Gentle Master Reginald,' Nightshade murmured.

'Yes, I am a scavenger. I harvest the dead. I and my comrades follow the armies and, as the fighting fades, we search amongst the slain for anything valuable.'

'And bring it to me,' Nightshade interjected

'We were at Barnet,' the Beanpole continued. 'The fighting was ferocious; a mailed mass of men clashing backwards and forwards through a thick, swirling mist. My comrades and I reached a copse which housed a horse line. Magnificent destriers all saddled and harnessed.' Bardolph sipped from his blackjack. 'The scavengers were already busy. The squires who tended the horses were no longer bothered about anything, except fleeing the battlefield as swiftly as possible. They did not bother us or try to stop us. By chance I stumbled to the edge of the tree line. I crouched and stared out at a lord, I could tell this from his armour and battle harness. He had taken off his helmet and, sword in one hand, dagger in the other, was staring in the direction of the fighting. Now and again, he'd turn as if searching for someone. The mist shifted and I could see the knight had his standard half-driven into the ground beside him. It displayed the Ragged Staff. I guessed it was Warwick. Now the battle was lost, Warwick seemed to regain his wits. He turned, staggering towards the horse lines. Then I saw a group of Yorkists. Despite all the dirt, I could make out their surcoats emblazoned with Yorkist suns. It was like watching hunting dogs bringing down a wounded deer. The Yorkists caught up with Warwick. He slipped, crashed to the ground, then they were on him. Dagger blades rose and fell, the bloody threshing stopped and the Yorkists began to strip the corpse.

'I decided to wait. Time passed. Sounds behind forced me to shelter behind thick gorse. I peered through a gap. I saw five men hastily mounting their horses. One of them called out, "He's gone and so must we." The men turned with their horses and galloped off. The Yorkists were still revelling in their finds, so I remained hidden deep in the gorse like a beaten dog. Another man appeared, dark faced, his shoulder emblazoned with the

Neville coat of arms, a white cross against a red background; it was clear enough. Anyway, this rider waited for a while then he also left.' Bardolph paused. 'Once it was safe, I did approach Warwick's corpse. It was all bloodied and wounded. Knife thrust after knife thrust.' Bardolph shrugged. 'I found a broken bracelet; I rejoined my companions and we returned to London to report all to Lord Nightshade.'

'And what did you make of all this?'

Nightshade pulled a face. 'Intriguing, Master Bray. I have learned all about the battles of Tewkesbury and Barnet, but Bardolph's tale is truly intriguing. I keep such stories here.' Nightshade tapped the side of his head. 'God knows, but one day I might need such information.'

'I'll ask you again, what do you make of it?'

'Come, my friend. Bardolph, stay here.' Nightshade rose, beckoning at Bray to follow him across to view a painting on the far wall. A bizarre, colourful fresco depicting snakes with two heads, their eyes shining like lamps. 'I know the artist,' Nightshade murmured. 'He claims to have travelled through all of Asia. He maintains he has seen giant ants as big as dogs, each with six feet and a body like a lobster. They have long, sharp fangs, black in colour. He also met forest women with hair down to their ankles; cow tails grow from the base of their spine; their bodies are rough-skinned as any camel's.'

'And, with all due respect, what does this have to do with me or what I seek?'

'Because the artist, Fitzwolf, as he calls himself, has survived many a sheriff's hunt and he knows this city like the back of his hand. We are finished here, I will leave, you will leave. You must go along the Street of Sighs, which leads out of Whitefriars on to the Place of the Tombs. Fitzwolf will be there, waiting for you, garbed in another of his guises, "The Teller of Tales". He's proclaiming how he is a pilgrim who has travelled to the far side of the moon. God knows, the man is as mad and frenetic as a box of frogs. Anyway, he and all of his company will be there.' Nightshade plucked at Bray's sleeve. 'Fitzwolf will see you safely back to the countess's mansion. I didn't want Bardolph to know about this because, in this vale of tears, you can only trust a very few.'

'Which includes you?'

'For the moment.' Nightshade laughed. 'Reginald, I am speaking the truth. What's the use of you coming here and learning all this if you're seized, even silenced, within a few heartbeats of leaving this tavern? No. You arrived safely and I will ensure you will leave safely with the information I have given you. Now, what do you think of Bardolph's tale?'

Bray opened his purse and took out two freshly minted silver coins and pressed them into Nightshade's mittened hand. The riffler chief inspected these closely and whistled his approval.

'Freshly minted,' he declared. 'Oh, Reginald, you are a friend.'

'I know what I think about Bardolph's tale but what do you make of it?'

'Simple and logical, Master Reginald. Warwick was deliberately left vulnerable: his battle group, his personal bodyguard, deserted him in his hour of need. Warwick was cut down. He was slain, his corpse abused. From what I gather, the Company of the Five Wounds were not even scratched. Oh, they had a story,' Nightshade waved a hand, 'the mist, the shifting battle lines; yet, I repeat, not one of them was wounded. In my view they appear to have hung back.'

'Why?'

'To leave their master vulnerable.' Nightshade took a deep breath. 'Hence that famous phrase from Augustine who borrowed it from Juvenal: "*Quis custodiet ipsos custodes* – who shall guard the guards?" If you wish to carry out swift and sudden assassination, you must first ensure your victim's bodyguard is nowhere in sight. Believe me, if I woke up to discover my lovely lads had disappeared, I would be desperate for my warbelt, my purse, and the nearest open window.'

'So,' Bray declared, 'this begs one more question. Did that bodyguard do it on their own whim?'

'Or did someone suborn them?' Nightshade whispered.

'If it was the latter,' Bray declared, 'the list of suspected traitors is as long as long can be.'

'Possible!'

'But you believe different. Who would arrange Warwick's assassination?'

'Well,' Nightshade whispered, 'it has to begin with Warwick's brother, His Grace the Archbishop from Hell.'

'George Neville? But . . .'

'Gaze into the visions of the night, Master Reginald. Stare into the past! George Neville is as treacherous as any Judas. He was supposed to defend London and the old King Henry. In fact, he couldn't sell him swift enough to Edward. He won the King's favour and, once settled, he secured pardons for the Company of the Five Wounds, saying that he would stand guarantor for them. He has even taken them into his household. But you must know all this. Now,' Nightshade stared around, 'I have said enough. I must be gone and, once I have, remember the Street of Sighs and the Place of the Tombs. You won't forget them, will you?'

'Of course not.'

'Oh, by the way, Bardolph's description of the other horseman in that fate-filled copse.' Nightshade made a face. 'I would wager those two silver coins you gave me that the rider was no less a person than Henry Maillac, Archbishop George's principal steward, a fervent adherent of the Earl of Warwick. Heaven only knows what he was doing on the battlefield. Anyway, farewell my friend.'

Nightshade and Bardolph left.

Bray visited the jakes closet and made his own way out into the street. Daylight was fading, the darkness gathering. The narrow runnels and corpse paths of Whitefriars were thin streaks of darkness with the occasional candle or lantern gleaming through the gaps of battered shutters. Bray made his way carefully, keeping to the side, as far as possible from the long mound of dirt, mud, offal and human waste. The reek was so horrible, Bray had to cover both nose and mouth with the muffler of his cloak. Rats and mice swarmed, screeching and scratching. Now and again a piercing scream echoed as one of the legions of feral cats and dogs made their own killing amongst the swarming horde of vermin. Voices rang out, eerie hollow sounds. Shutters clanged closed. Doors slammed. Beggars, hideous in aspect, crawled out of their enclosures, clacking dish in one hand, dagger in the other, only to hastily retreat when Bray drew his own blade.

The rotting houses rose like a wall on either side to lean closer, like conspirators eager to block out the strip of clear night sky. Bray turned a corner and crossed a narrow, cobbled square. The houses on either side were brothels and the ladies of the night, garish in their cheap clothing, called plaintively out to him. He crossed the square and went down the Street of Sighs to the Place of the Tombs, which marked Whitefriars from the rest of the city. Here the legion of nighthawks, dark-dwellers, sewer-squires, bully-boys and rifflers gathered to do business. They ignored the warning signs which soared above them: three massive, four-branched gallows, each with its own gruesome burden; the corpses of felons executed and left to hang until they rotted.

All the canting crew of Whitefriars thronged here. Itinerant cooks had set up stalls to grill the food they'd collected or stolen from city shops; the different meats were basted with the cheapest oil and the stench made Bray's stomach churn. Torches and candles were lit to send the shadows dancing; the taverns and alehouses bustled with business. Bray knew that sooner or later every villain in London would visit this haunt of wrong-doing. He needed to be through it as swiftly as possible. He pushed his way forward, then abruptly turned. Nightshade was correct. Three cowled, cloaked figures were standing close behind him. Bray glimpsed their polished cudgels. 'City bailiffs.' He breathed.

'Come sir, you!'

Bray turned back. A Teller of Tales now stood on one of the ancient tombs, surrounded by what he called his 'minions of the moon'. A gaggle of the most fantastically garbed individuals: some were dressed in horsehair, cow hide and deerskin, their faces painted a bright red, with black circles around their eyes.

'Come.' The Teller of Tales pointed at Bray, who now allowed himself to be gently seized by the minions and pushed closer to their master, who promptly climbed down from the tomb. He plucked at Bray's cloak.

'Come with us, my friend,' he declared in a carrying voice. 'And I shall tell you about the Portunes, who warm themselves at our fires. They eat little frogs. Many do not see these creatures, for they are only as big as a half-thumb. They are of aged appearance and wear tiny rags sewn together. They slip through the shadows of the night and keep us humans under close scrutiny.'

The Teller of Tales pushed his swarthy, manic face closer. 'As we shall you, Master Bray,' he whispered hoarsely. 'So, let us escort you, we pilgrims from the dark side of the moon!'

Bray just grinned, shrugged, and allowed himself to be hurriedly escorted out of the Place of Tombs and down through the city streets. Surrounded by this gang of moon-touched charlatans, Bray was safely escorted along the river path to the countess's mansion. Once there, the Teller of Tales grasped Bray's hand and pulled him closer.

'Get out of the city for a while,' he warned. 'Do not tarry. There's only so much protection we can offer.'

'And what you have already offered, I am grateful for. Tell your master, the Lord Nightshade, that I'll be gone before dawn to lodge in the most comfortable tavern in Rickmansworth.'

Countess Margaret and Christopher had barely left the maze when the alarm was raised by the mournful call of a hunting horn and the discordant clanging of the chapel bell. They hurried across a small garden and in through a side door leading to the Great Hall. Servants flocked about all in a panic. Christopher stopped one and the servitor, a spit-boy from the kitchen, gasped out how a horrid murder had occurred. Urswicke asked where? Mumbling in fear, the boy pointed down in the direction of the servants' quarters at the rear of the house. Christopher eventually learned from the servant's gibbering that one of Warwick's men had been murdered, a member of the Five Wounds.

'Let us see for ourselves,' the countess declared. 'Christopher . . .'

Urswicke needed no further urging. He ordered the servant to lead them. They went down through hallways and along galleries, places of comfort and light with their long windows and polished woodwork. The pink plaster above the precious wainscoting was decorated with crucifixes, diptychs, as well as the emblems and arms of both Warwick and Neville. They reached the entrance to the servants' quarters, now thronged with the anxious and curious. Urswicke forced himself through and led the countess up the steep stairs. Members of the Five Wounds gathered at an open doorway. Patmore, the Imposter and the cruel-faced

Mauclerc were also there. Maillac came out of the room. Urswicke had urgent whispered words with him, but the steward just shook his head, all fearful, pointing back to the chamber.

'Disgusting,' Maillac whispered. 'In heaven's name, why?'

Urswicke, grasping the countess by the arm, pushed past him into the chamber. The room reeked of fetid smells which even the open windows, their shutters pulled back, could not dispel. A narrow chamber with paltry, shabby furniture and little comfort. The chancery table had been turned on its side and a man, naked as he was born, had been set up against this, his arms extended, and kept so, by the razor-sharp spikes hammered through each wrist. The man's head hung down. Nevertheless, Urswicke could still glimpse the leather gag pushed into the dead man's mouth and tied securely by tight lacing to the back of the victim's head.

'In sweet heaven's name,' the countess whispered. Urswicke looked around, noticing the items of clothing, saddlebags and a warbelt, its weapons still sheathed. The narrow cot bed looked dishevelled. On a small table beside it stood a pewter jug and goblet. Urswicke went across and sniffed them both, yet he could detect nothing but the rich scent of Bordeaux. He looked back at the blood-drenched corpse; the gruesome mess was already beginning to thicken. Urswicke crouched down. The gag was a very tight roll of leather. Urswicke had seen similar used on felons who refused to keep quiet during their trials. The gag, thrust deep into the dead man's mouth and tied securely behind the head, would certainly prevent the victim from crying out. Eventually, he must have sunk into that eternal sleep as he bled to death. Urswicke shifted to study the spike in the left wrist of the corpse. Urswicke knew enough about physic to deduct that a deep wound through that part of the wrist would lead to a sudden, hideous loss of blood, a veritable torrent.

'What is this?'

Urswicke rose and turned. Archbishop George and his sister, the Lady Grace, stood in the doorway. Both were garbed in gorgeous, sleeveless cotehardies of blood-red with golden stitching. The archbishop seemed assured, certainly not troubled, by the gruesome mess, though his sister looked as though she was on the verge of fainting. Lady Grace leaned against the wall just inside the door, lifting a pomander to her pretty face before offering it to her twin brother, who sniffed it appreciatively before flicking his fingers at Urswicke.

'I know what you are doing,' he called out. 'You are already investigating this grisly murder, but by whose authority?'

'A very good question, my Lord Archbishop. My authority comes from the King, through my father, Sir Thomas Urswicke, Recorder of London. Yes, I should investigate, and the sooner the better. I suggest we remove the corpse. What is the victim's name?'

'John Forester.' Maillac, who had come in behind the Neville twins, interjected. 'John Forester.' He repeated. 'Late member of the Company of the Five Wounds.'

'The corpse will be removed,' the archbishop declared, staring from under heavy-lidded eyes at Urswicke, whilst his twin sister, pomander close to her nose, arrogantly inspected Urswicke from head to toe.

'My Lady, we are well met.'

'Master Urswicke,' she laughed, 'I think not.' The smile disappeared from her face as she gestured at the corpse. 'Not well met, Master Urswicke.'

'In which case, my Lady, we should meet more formally. My Lord,' he stepped closer to the archbishop, 'I carry the King's commission. I must see you and others I shall name now in the hall below. A court needs to be convened. I shall tell you what I need and then . . .' Urswicke turned back to the Lady Grace, 'then we shall all be well met.'

Two hours later, with the daylight fading, Urswicke sat beside a long trestle table on the dais at the end of the Great Hall. The table was positioned just beneath one of the Catherine wheels, lowered so that Urswicke could clearly see everything on the table before him. He had laid out his commission and warrants, which had been closely inspected by the archbishop and his sister, who now sat either side of Urswicke. Christopher had also insisted that a row of slender beeswax candles be lit and placed in their spigots along the table, together with a Book of the Gospels, his own sword and a crucifix on its stand. The countess sat in a throne chair to Urswicke's right. Others, members of the Five Wounds, together with Maillac and

Mauclerc, sat on a high-backed bench facing what was now a place of judgement similar to King's Bench at Westminster. Urswicke used the pommel of his sword, banging the table for silence. He ignored how the archbishop and the Lady Grace stiffened at this, but Urswicke was now determined to hasten matters along. He swiftly read out his commission and then pointed at the members of the Company of The Five Wounds.

'Two of your coven,' he began, 'have been murdered, yes?'

He was answered with a mumble of agreement.

'Why?' Urswicke demanded. 'Do you know of any reason or cause, some motive for why two of your comrades should die here?' He paused. 'Not because of Barnet, surely?'

'I can't think of one,' Matthew Poppleton replied hoarsely, 'and, if you agree, sir, I will answer for all my companions, unless they themselves have something to offer?'

'As long as it's the truth,' Urswicke retorted. 'I will now go back to my question. Why have two of your shield comrades been slaughtered?'

'Simply put, sir, we do not know. Fladgate died in a muddy yard at the dead of night. For God's sake, Master Urswicke, it could have been anyone – either within or without.'

'And Forester?' Urswicke asked. 'Slain in macabre circumstances. Did you see him earlier in the day?'

'Yes, he came out with us to the stables.'

'I can vouch for that,' Maillac declared. 'I saw them there.'

'And nothing untoward was noticed? Did Forester say or do anything which caught your attention?'

'He seemed happy enough,' Poppleton replied, 'didn't he?'

Again, a mumble of agreement answered his question.

'We saw nothing. We heard nothing amiss, but the same is true of poor Fladgate's murder. Ah,' Poppleton beat his hand against his knee, 'there is one thing I've forgotten.' Poppleton opened his purse and pulled out a small piece of parchment. He pushed this across the table for Urswicke to study. Pulling a candle closer, Urswicke read aloud what was scrawled there.

'*Company of the Five Wounds,*

'*Ride not so bold,*

'*For your treachery and treason,*

'*Will be told.*

'Where did you find this?' Urswicke glanced up. 'It's a clear threat.'

'It was pinned to the chapel door.'

'You should have mentioned this earlier. Examine those doggerel lines. This is an accusation that you, Poppleton, and the others committed treason and treachery against your master, which will be proclaimed for the world to hear and understand.'

'Master Urswicke,' Poppleton replied, 'we are warriors. We have hacked and cut our way across many a battlefield. We are not gentle Franciscans, pious parsons. We have enemies who served with York. We also have others, who should know better, who believe we should have stood and died with our master at Barnet. For heaven's sake we tried, stumbling around that battlefield: that note could be a threat or it might just be someone mouthing their nastiness.'

'No, I think it's more than that, Master Poppleton. I strongly suspect that the person who scrawled this and pinned it to the chapel door probably murdered your comrades. But let's move on.' Urswicke stared down at the manuscript before him, deliberately allowing the silence to deepen. He lifted his head and pointed at Poppleton. 'You have sworn on the Book of the Gospels to tell the truth.'

'And I have, and I shall.'

'Yes, yes, I hope so. Anyway, the company, this battle group of the Five Wounds; tell me more about it.'

'Our history is well known.'

'Tell me about it.'

'We were the household knights of Richard Neville, late Earl of Warwick. He first formed our company when he broke with the power of York to form an alliance with Queen Margaret, Somerset and his ilk.'

'My kinsman,' the countess interjected.

'God rest him, my Lady, but he is dead and gone. We served our master well. We knew that whenever he engaged with the enemy, they would have their own company or cohort dedicated to seeking out and killing my Lord of Warwick and his brother the marquess. We were Warwick's response to that.'

'As I have said, not much of a response,' Urswicke replied. 'At Barnet, Warwick was left deserted and desolate, highly vulnerable to his enemies.' Urswicke paused. He realized he had sorely provoked Poppleton and the rest, yet he truly believed that the murderous mysteries which now enmeshed this house had their roots in the Battle of Barnet. After all, the leader of the Neville family had been slain there, yet his so-called bodyguard had escaped without wound or injury of any sort. He took a deep breath. 'I need,' he measured his words slowly, 'to create a reality to explain these murders. My first step in doing that is to understand the Company of the Five Wounds. So, gentlemen,' Urswicke gestured at Poppleton, 'you act as their leader, you want to be their speaker: so how were you formed? You swore an oath of loyalty to Warwick as well as sealed indentures with him?'

'Yes.'

'For how long?'

'Three years ago, on the Feast of the Five Wounds.'

'Hence your name?'

'Yes, in a chapel bearing the same title at Warwick Castle.'

'And you shared your master's fortunes both good and bad?'

'Yes. Except at the very end.'

'So, it would seem. I would like to know what actually happened at Barnet.'

Poppleton moved uneasily in his chair. He stared at his two companions. They simply shook their heads. Poppleton turned back to his interrogator.

'Master Urswicke, you must know about that mist-bound Easter Sunday morning?'

'Oh yes but, despite all the words, I have not listened to you describe your part in that battle. You did take part?'

'Of course we did,' Poppleton heatedly replied. 'But that mist shrouded everything. Warwick had agreed with his brother that both of them, together with their captains, should fight on foot in order to reassure the common soldiers. And so, they did. The conflict swiftly swung backwards and forwards. Battle groups and phalanxes became confused. Commanders were cut off from their retainers. Because of the poor dawn light and that devilish mist, it was nigh impossible to distinguish one banner from another, or even to make out the different markings.'

'The chaos caused by Oxford being taken for that of Edward

of York is proof enough,' Colworth burst out, beating his fist against the table. 'By the feet of the Virgin, how can we be held accountable when the generals on both sides were confused?'

'We were swept away.' Poppleton turned slightly, gesturing at the angry Colworth to remain calm. 'I admit,' he continued, 'we were not in the thick of the fight, but why should we be?' Poppleton put his hand on his chest and bowed at the archbishop and his sister, who'd sat like statues throughout Urswicke's questioning. 'With all due respect, Your Grace, my Lady, but the Earl of Warwick made decisions that morning which cost him and others dearly. Indeed, I would argue that the battle was lost before it ever began.'

'True, true.' Archbishop George stirred in his chair as both he and his sister crossed themselves.

'Warwick, my brother,' the archbishop continued, 'was his own man. He could not be told. Sweet reason and pure logic failed with him. If he set his heart on doing something, then he'd do it. At Barnet he decided to fight in a certain way at a chosen place and, to a greater extent, he paid the price for his own foolishness.'

'And impetuosity.' Lady Grace's voice trembled with emotion. 'My brother,' she sighed, 'the great Warwick.' She flailed a hand at Poppleton and his two comrades. 'I do not hold you responsible. Fickle Fortune made her throw. My brothers, both of them, should be sitting in glory at Westminster. Instead, their corpses, bruised and wounded, were carted into St Paul's in an arrow chest: hunks of slaughtered meat no different from offal on a butcher's stall.'

'They are now at peace,' the archbishop soothed. 'They lie with our forebears at Bisham Priory.'

'And you?' Urswicke demanded, gesturing at Poppleton. 'Are you at peace now?'

'We live with our consciences,' Poppleton retorted. 'As everybody in this room must.'

'And what happened after the battle?'

'We hid,' Poppleton snapped. 'And you know the reason why. Oh, there are many, and their name is legion, who stand wagging their fingers at us, accusing us of this, that and the other. People who have never seen a battlefield, who've never wielded a sword, who've never seen a pile of corpses stacked high. I'll tell you what, Urswicke, York thought differently. They described us as their enemy. All our names were included in an Act of Attainder. We were proclaimed as traitors, rebels against the King. We were outlaws, *utlegatum*, wolfsheads who could be killed on sight. Now why should York think that? Because they'd recognise us for what we really were: loyal, fervent Lancastrians. True, we sued for pardon later on, but what else could we do? Where could we go? What did the future hold?'

'What Poppleton says is true,' Archbishop George declared in a ringing voice. 'I can vouch for what he said. In those hate-filled days following Barnet, Poppleton and the rest could have been cut down and no one would have objected.'

'My question still stands. What did you do after the battle?'

'We hid out in Epping Forest and cast around for someone to help us.'

'I was their help.' Archbishop George drew himself up in his chair. 'At my insistence, my pleading, the Act of Attainder was nullified and pardons were issued. I was to stand as their guarantor, which I did. They entered my household, and I truly welcomed them here. I did this to reward them for their years of service.'

'Yet you have not found peace,' Urswicke observed. 'Not here at The Moor. Only murder and mayhem. My father, Sir Thomas Urswicke—'

'I know who your father is.' The archbishop's voice sounded more like a hiss. 'He was instrumental in issuing the pardons I have mentioned.'

'Now the murder of two of the Company of the Five Wounds is a grave matter,' Urswicke continued, ignoring the archbishop's outburst, 'but my father must be, in fact he is, deeply concerned at the brutal murder of two of his henchmen, Brasenose and Rutger. So let us turn to these.' Urswicke stood up to ease the cramp in his legs. He walked backwards and forwards then returned to his chair. 'Brasenose,' he demanded. 'Why was he here?'

'Ask your father,' Lady Grace replied.

'Not now, not now,' her brother replied quickly. 'To answer your question, Master Urswicke, Brasenose kept close counsel with himself. He was a man who waited and watched. However, to be blunt, he probably came to The Moor to ensure all was well. You must know that King Edward and his entourage will journey here on the eve of the Feast of St George for the most splendid celebrations?'

'Did he talk to you about that?' Urswicke turned to point at the dark-faced Maillac who had sat aloof throughout the proceedings. 'Come on man,' Urswicke urged. 'Brasenose must have conversed with you.'

'He spoke but in actual fact said very little. He was intrigued by The Moor, the maze and all the legends and histories about the manor.'

'So, it was strange that he was murdered in the maze.'

'Yes, he followed the guide rope. He'd almost reached the centre where the Creeping Cross stands.'

'Excuse my interruption.' The countess raised her hand. 'Maillac, did you show Brasenose around The Moor and gardens?'

'No, no,' he replied. 'Brasenose and Rutger wandered at will.' The steward shrugged. 'He bore the royal commission, so I let them be.'

'And the day he was murdered?' Urswicke asked.

'Apparently,' Maillac replied, 'he and Rutger had a conversation shortly before Brasenose entered the maze. Brasenose claimed that he had seen a figure, maybe an apparition, entering the maze. He was intrigued and decided to follow. The rest is well known. Rutger became concerned and went searching. Brasenose was found lying face down with wounds to his back.'

'And this fighting man, this mailed clerk, who'd hacked and cut so strenuously at Barnet and elsewhere appears to have offered no resistance, no sign of a struggle?'

'None whatsoever,' Poppleton declared. 'I accompanied Rutger back to collect the corpse. I know what I saw.'

'As did I,' Maillac murmured. 'Master Urswicke, I supervised the arrangements for Brasenose and Rutger to be kept in the manor death house. I await your father's instructions whether he wants them to be buried here in God's Acre or in the cemetery of some London church. He definitely wants both disposed of quietly and quickly.'

'In which case I need to view all four corpses. So, we come to the other three murders. Rutger was found with his throat slashed, squatting in a jakes closet. Fladgate lay sprawled nearby.'

'That's true,' the archbishop interjected, leaning forward and tapping his own brow. 'A bolt here, death must have been instant.'

'Tell me,' Urswicke pointed at Poppleton, 'you had dealings with Brasenose – you and your comrades?'

'We had short, sharp words about how long we were to stay at The Moor. We need licences and passes to travel safely wherever we wish.'

'And?'

'Brasenose refused to be drawn – said it was a matter for Sir Thomas. We asked him to intervene for us – he replied he'd think about it.'

'So your encounter with him was not amicable?'

'Of course not! A year or so ago we were mortal enemies.'

'And now?'

'I did not, we did not, like Brasenose, but we had no hand in his murder.'

Urswicke glanced quickly at the countess. She sat, one hand on the arm of the chair, the other held her ave beads, wrapped like a string of jewels around her fingers. She turned, caught his gaze and shook her head perceptively. Urswicke realized the countess was signalling that he would make little, if any, progress here.

'Very well.' Urswicke drew a deep breath. 'Is there anything at all which would account for – or explain – this sudden rash of murders in this beautiful palace? Why these victims? Why now?' His questions were met with a fraught silence and Urswicke caught it. A feeling that these brutal killings masked deeper, more lasting hatreds. But what were these?

'I ask you again,' he repeated.

'I cannot speak for all who are here,' Maillac retorted, 'but all I can report is a remark made by Rutger in the days following Brasenose's murder. I found Rutger standing over his master's corpse in our death house. I thought he was praying, but he heard my footsteps and abruptly turned and, without any questioning, said that, in the end what was most important, never to be forgotten . . .' Maillac paused, eyes closed, lips moving sound-lessly. 'Yes, that's it: "that what we did in life was more important than who we were". And, Master Urswicke, I don't know what he meant.'

'Well, Rutger has followed his master into the dark,' Urswicke declared. 'One other matter. Have any of you had dealings with Master Patmore, or the young man who accompanies him?' The question was greeted with shakes of the head and murmured denials.

'We have nothing to do with Clarence's henchman Mauclerc, or the precious pair he guards.' The archbishop's voice was clipped. 'Whilst my Lady Countess here was invited to partici-pate in our festivities around the Feast of St George; she is a special guest, she is most welcome, which is more than I can say for them. God knows what mischief is being plotted.' The archbishop let his voice trail off as his sister coughed loudly.

'Oh, by the way,' Urswicke demanded, eager to press matters on, 'Brasenose and Rutger, where are their possessions?'

'In the store of our death house.'

'Any papers, commissions, warrants?'

'Nothing more,' Maillac replied, 'than a writ from your father, indicating that both Brasenose and Rutger were his henchmen and to give them every support and assistance here.'

'For what?'

'I asked the same.' The archbishop laughed sharply. 'Brasenose dismissed my question with the enigmatic response that what-ever was coming. I asked him what he meant by that? I didn't get an answer.' The archbishop pulled a face. 'Brasenose arrived here, he then walked and waited . . . Master Urswicke, the hour draws on, I am hungry, tired.'

'Aren't we all?' Urswicke forced a smile as he pointed at the Company of the Five Wounds. 'Why did you take that particular name?'

'It was our master's idea. He had his personal chapel in Warwick, which was dedicated to the Five Wounds of Christ. We took our oath of fealty there on the chapel's feast day and we assumed that title. We became the earl's battle group. We were his liegemen,' Poppleton continued, his voice growing

strident. 'We swore loyalty in both body and soul, in this life
and the one to come.'

'Of course you did,' Urswicke soothed, his voice just above
a whisper. 'And, talking of the life to come, two of your companions are already there, whatever state of grace they are in. Fladgate
died swiftly, but now, before we close, let us turn to Forester's
murder. Did he say or do anything before he was killed which
might explain that foul act?'

'He was a keen soldier,' Colworth answered.

'A born shield man,' Chadwick declared.

'As you all are,' Urswicke replied. 'And that's part of the
mystery. Look, I can understand Fladgate's death, the assassin
striking swiftly out of the dark, giving no sound or sight to his
victim. But Forester's murder surely is another matter? You
viewed his corpse; you've seen his chamber. Nevertheless, I
detected no sign of resistance, defence or alarm; nothing but
that poor man's corpse nailed by his wrists to a table. Why did
the assassin kill him in such a way? How did he achieve that?
Let me repeat my question: do any of you here know anything
which might explain Forester's brutal murder?' He glanced
around. 'No, that's what I thought.' Urswicke sifted amongst the
pieces of manuscript on the table. He then rose, walking the full
length of the dais. 'Forester,' he declared, 'was found murdered,
naked as the day he was born, nailed to that table. Can anyone
explain why he was naked?'

'Bathing,' Poppleton retorted. 'Forester was always one for
cleanliness. He must have been preparing to go down to the bath
house.'

'Possible,' Urswicke conceded. 'Or waiting for someone.'

'Who?'

'Master Poppleton, if I could answer that,' Urswicke shrugged,
'then the mystery would be solved. But we all live our own
hidden lives. Was Forester involved in some secret relationship,
be it with a servant girl or anyone else?'

'Not that I know of,' Poppleton declared. 'And I think that I
speak for my companions.'

'Then let us try and imagine what happened in that room,'
Urswicke continued. 'Forester had stripped. He could be a man
getting ready for a bath, eager to clean the dirt and dust from

his body, or he could have been sleeping, or he could have been waiting for someone to come, the ardent lover. If he was naked and there was a knock on the door, he'd suddenly cover himself up. Now Forester's assassin must have knocked on that door. Most people lock or bolt themselves in when stripping themselves. Oh, there can be exceptions but, in the main, I am sure Forester would have done what all of us would have done, wrapped a sheet around himself. He would most certainly have asked who it was? Forester then opened the door, so he must have not only known his visitor but regarded him or her as a friend, a comrade: such a title applies to virtually everyone in this room.'

'Including ourselves?' the archbishop interjected.

'Of course, my Lord, this is your house. You can go where you wish, whilst you Mauclerc,' he gestured at his enemy who'd sat, eyes half-closed, a silent witness throughout the entire proceedings, 'as our archbishop said, you are the henchman of Lord Clarence. You wield great authority. Forester would have opened the door to you. Indeed, I cannot think of a reason why he would refuse entry to anyone here at The Moor. Forester would not have expected an assassin in the full light of day. The other three murders were committed under the cover of deep darkness. Anyway, he opens the door, his killer stands smiling there. He has brought with him a carafe of wine and two goblets, or perhaps he was prepared to use the goblets in the chamber: anyway, into one of these the killer sprinkles a sleeping potion. Forester falls into a deep sleep. The assassin turns the table over, moves Forester to rest against it, securely gags his mouth and then carries out that hideous slaying. I appreciate this is conjecture . . .'

'It's logical,' the archbishop agreed.

'Yes, yes it certainly is,' Poppleton declared. 'You are right, Master Urswicke, Forester would have opened the door to anyone here, and he did like a goblet of wine, but why kill him in such a gruesome fashion?'

'That, I still have to establish. Now, to assist me, I must view all four corpses.'

PART FOUR

'And the Archbishop believed he stood in great favour with the King.'

'Death in all its guises is horrific: murder even more so.' Urswicke recalled the lines from a treatise he had recently read. He pushed the pomander, soaked in pine juice and other herbs, against his nose and mouth as he stared down at the four battered corpses laid out on narrow tables next to each other in the manor death house. Urswicke crouched closer to inspect Rutger's slashed throat.

'Swift as death's own scythe,' Urswicke whispered. 'You were sitting in that jakes closet, hose about your ankles, your belly bubbling with ale. You'd be half asleep. The door to the closet opens. You fall back, head tilted in surprise, offering your throat like a pig in the slaughter house. And you . . .' Urswicke turned to Fladgate, his head and face brutally shattered by a powerful bolt. 'Delivered at such close quarters, death would swoop like a hawk in that dark, muddy courtyard. You'd turn, the bolt was loosed, then you were gone. As for you . . .' Urswicke went to stand over Brasenose, trying to ignore the badly disfigured face, made even more gruesome by death. He gently turned the naked corpse over and studied the wounds to the victim's back. 'Time and time again,' Urswicke declared, 'the assassin plunged his dagger, except here.' Urswicke peered at the horrid gash just by the nape of the neck. Nothing more than a jagged wound, the skin and flesh rupturing before turning hard. Urswicke had seen such wounds before and suspected what had happened. He then moved to Forester's naked cadaver, with those hideous piercings to the wrist. Why, Urswicke wondered, had the man been slaughtered in such a barbaric fashion? Forester, gagged and hapless, had been nailed to that table, unable to move, just left to bleed to death. So, as with the other murders, how was it done? Why? By whom? Why now? All these gruesome slayings, erupting one after another like the buboes of some malignant pestilence. 'And why were you naked?' Urswicke murmured. Once again he carefully scrutinised Forester's corpse, the flaccid genitals, the distended belly, the muscular arms and legs. How, Urswicke wondered, had this mailed clerk, this survivor of many battles, been trapped so easily? Had he been drugged with some potion? Urswicke and Maillac had taken the wine into the courtyard, where a cage of rats was kept to detect tainted food and drinks. The rodents had been given the wine with no ill-effects whatsoever.

Sickened by the grisly sight and the reek of corruption, Urswicke walked across to the open window and breathed in the bright morning air. He had brought his investigation to an abrupt end the previous evening. The countess, tight-lipped and anxious, had bade him goodnight and left. Urswicke was certain his mistress was deeply troubled, but for the moment he could do little to help. He had then retired himself and risen early for the dawn mass in the palace chapel.

'Master Urswicke, are we finished?' Maillac called from where he stood just inside the doorway, clutching a pomander.

'I am finished here. However, I need to see the dead men's clothing. Could you lay them out in the yard so I can examine them in the daylight?'

Maillac nodded and hurried out. A short while later, Urswicke joined him in the yard, where the steward had laid out along a fence the clothing of each of the victims. Urswicke searched them all, paying particular attention to Brasenose's clothing and boots, hoping to find that secret pocket, but he couldn't. He then inspected Brasenose's doublet. He could make out the blood-encrusted slits where the assassin had struck with a dagger and, finally, that ragged rent just beneath the nape of the neck.

'At least on that I am correct,' Urswicke exclaimed to himself. 'But where is that secret hidden pocket? I am sure he had one!' Urswicke finished his searches, thanked Maillac and walked slowly back to the house. Lost in thought, he heard a horse whinny, a high, piercing call which cut the air. Urswicke stopped and shook his head.

'Of course, of course.' He smiled to himself. 'Brasenose's saddle!' Urswicke knew his father of old: his henchmen invariably carried secret papers of one kind or another and what better place than a battered saddle which would hardly warrant a second glance? Urswicke made his way to the stables and asked the chief groom to bring Brasenose's harness to him. Once he had done so, Urswicke crouched down, and eventually he found the secret pouch on the inside of the saddle, just beneath the horn. Urswicke made sure there were no other such pockets before drawing out two scrolls, tightly rolled and tied fast with chancery cord. He had barely slipped the scrolls into his own pouch when Maillac came hurrying into the stables, all breathless.

'Master Urswicke,' he gasped, 'you have a visitor . . .'

Urswicke found Bray waiting for him in the porter's lodge. He assured Maillac he would stand guarantor for him and, putting a finger to his lips, took his comrade up to their mistress's chamber. The countess was at her prie-dieu reciting her psalter. She rose as they came in, extending her hand for both of them to kiss, before gesturing at chairs around the chancery table. Countess Margaret looked decidedly better. She was garbed in a dark blue gown with a broad lace collar, which matched the icy white wimple fastened over her hair. Once seated, she also raised a finger to her lips; a warning to be prudent, before getting to her feet and crossing to a glass-filled door window. She pushed this wide open, then turned and smiled at them mischievously.

'So good to see you, Reginald and Christopher. I was just reciting a psalm, "The Lord is my help; there is nothing I shall want". There is a line: "He gives me green pasture to lie in", and that prompts me. Look, it's a beautiful morning, I have little to say, so let us walk. Let us stroll under the sun, catch the breeze and marvel at our good fortune.'

Both henchmen agreed and, with the countess now in a cloak matching her gown, they left the chamber. They went downstairs and out across the palace gardens into a broad, richly grassed meadow dotted with thick copses. The countess led them across to a line of hedgerow with a number of strong wooden seats placed to capture the full glory of the sun. Once comfortable, with her henchmen seated either side, the countess pulled back her cowl.

'I thought this would be the safest place,' she murmured. 'No one can approach us without being seen. We will sit here, talk and wait for Callista.'

'Who?'

'In a while, Christopher, when the Angelus bell sounds. Now, Reginald, what have you found? Who have you talked to besides Wolkind, who should now be lodged at The Blossoms of Heaven, the finest tavern in Rickmansworth?'

'Madam he is, and very comfortably so, awaiting your orders. He says it's an easy task but he is ready to leave at the drop of a feather. He has two good horses, sturdy-footed garrons. But mistress, what is he waiting for?'

The countess grasped Bray's wrist, nipped the skin gently and let go.

'In a while, Reginald, in a while. And what have you learned?'

Bray, leaning forward slightly, quickly described his meeting with Nightshade. The countess and Urswicke listened carefully, now and again interrupting with a question. Once he had finished, Bray sat back.

'Very good,' the countess declared. 'But let's leave that for the moment. Let us see if the pieces fit with what you have learned, Christopher.'

Urswicke tersely described what had happened at The Moor since their arrival; now and again the countess added the occasional detail. Christopher then explained what he'd discovered that morning, pulling out the two scrolls. He cut the twine and handed them to the countess, who unrolled both, studying each carefully before handing one to Bray and the other back to Urswicke. Both henchmen studied the scrawled plan etched on each of the scrolls before returning them to the countess.

'One is certainly a plan of The Moor,' Bray declared, 'and the other is a map of a priory or small monastery. As for why Brasenose was carrying them . . .' He pulled a face.

The countess was about to reply but paused as the Angelus bell began a merry pealing, which carried clear and strong through the fresh spring air. The countess rose, pointing across the meadow.

'And here she comes,' she exclaimed. 'My little grey mouse.' The countess sat down as a hooded figure came tripping across the grass. The new arrival reached the countess, pulled back her hood, sketched a curtsy and sat down on the ground before the countess, pulling her grey gown close. Urswicke stared hard at her and smiled. Callista, as the countess introduced her, truly was a little grey mouse of a girl, with her narrow face, darting eyes, and snub nose above lips which seemed parted in constant surprise.

'Callista is my little grey mouse,' the countess declared. 'Here are my henchmen, Masters Bray and Urswicke.'

Callista darted a smile at each before returning to stare fixedly at the countess.

'Callista, my little mouse,' the countess repeated. 'She scurries about and people hardly give her a second glance. They dismiss her out of hand. But I don't, do I, Callista?'

The young woman nodded in agreement.

'Callista sees all kinds of things,' the countess continued. 'Who goes, who comes, who talks to whom, where and when. So, tell me, little mouse, what do you know, what have you seen?'

'My Lady.' Callista's voice was surprisingly harsh and clipped. 'First, the Lord Archbishop and the Lady Grace are deeply involved in preparing the festivities planned for the Feast of St George. Carts crammed with provender and purveyance to restock the kitchens and buttery—'

'Yes, yes,' the countess interjected. 'But tell us about the others, the Company of the Five Wounds. I mean from the beginning.' The countess turned to her henchmen. 'I very rarely have the opportunity to talk to Callista. So,' she turned back to the maid, 'the Five Wounds?'

'They arrived here as warriors, veteran soldiers, once the bodyguard of the great Earl of Warwick but, in truth, that was not so.'

Christopher watched intently. The countess had chosen well. Callista, for all her mouselike ways, was a cunning, astute observer of others. Christopher silently scolded himself. He had committed, once again, that great mistake, which he always ruefully regretted. Never underestimate anybody, and never judge by appearances.

'Yes, the Five Wounds arrived here,' Callista continued, 'acting like valiant paladins. In fact, they were treated more like prisoners, chaffing at the restraints placed on them. The months passed and they became five layabouts around this palace. Lord and Lady Neville had very little time for them, even though the good archbishop had stood guarantor for all five. I think he did that to honour the memory of his fallen brother. I once overheard a conversation in which the Lady Grace said that, in their day, the Company of the Five Wounds were truly valiant and brave. All that changed at Barnet. Mistress, you know how it goes. Warwick was cut down, they escaped, and life moved on.'

'Did you notice anything untoward about the Five Wounds?' Urswicke asked.

'No sir, as I said, they were given chambers, they dined at the common board. At each quarter of the year, they would receive coins, fresh clothing, and so on.'

'And what was intended for them?' Bray demanded.

'From the little I know, time would pass and the archbishop would be permitted to allow them to leave. I suspect they are looking forward to that. Anyway,' Callista shrugged, 'nothing really happened, not until the messenger came, the man with the battered face.'

'Brasenose?' Urswicke replied.

'Yes, that's it. Sometimes he would meet with them, I mean the Five Wounds.'

'Where?'

'My Lady, wherever they could. Free of any eavesdropper. In fact, they came here on more than one occasion. I attended their last meeting just before Brasenose was killed in the maze.'

'What do you mean "attended"?'

Callista grinned in a display of fine white sharp teeth.

'Well, they didn't know, but I found out that they'd planned to come here. One of them asked the buttery for a wineskin. The kitchener asked them why, where they were taking it? He said to the meadow. I overheard this so I came before them.' She pointed at the trees close by. 'I sheltered in that copse. I hid there. The meeting, as usual, was very brief. I could not hear what was actually said. Some words, and they were bitter. Accusations of being kept prisoner, of promises not being honoured. I also heard a name repeated three or four times.'

'What was it, child?'

'It's hard, my Lady, a long word, a long word,' she repeated, closing her eyes, 'ack, ack . . .'

'Achitophel?' the countess demanded.

'Mistress, that's it, Achitophel. Who is it, mistress?'

'In origin, it's from the Old Testament. The name of a great spy, a traitor, who betrayed King David and came to a gruesome end. I've heard that name in other chatter. Callista, can you tell us more?'

The young woman just shook her head.

'Very well.' Urswicke glanced to his left at the copse of trees. What Callista said was possible. 'Very well,' he repeated, 'you watch, you observe. Do you ever suspect who could be responsible for the killings which have occurred here?' He smiled at the young woman. 'Callista, as my mistress says, you scurry about this splendid mansion like a little mouse. You must have seen something suspicious?'

'No, not really,' she retorted. 'True, the servants chatter amongst themselves and they have reached one conclusion, one that I agree with. It can't be the Lord Archbishop or his sister, the Lady Grace.'

'Why not?'

'It's well known,' Callista blinked, 'or it is here. Both brother and sister cannot stand the sight of blood.'

'Yes, yes, now you mention it,' the countess replied. 'I have heard similar rumours.'

'But they came into the chamber where Forester was killed. A truly grisly sight,' Urswicke intervened.

'Ah yes, sir, but they didn't draw close, did they? As long as there's a distance. The servants,' Callista hurried on, 'say that's why Lord George became a priest. He swoons if he touches blood and the Lady Grace likewise. Both of them vomit and fall into a faint. Neither of them ever visits the kitchen, parlour or buttery when fowl or beast is being sliced and cut. Indeed, woe betide any cook who serves meat with a trace of blood.'

'Of course,' the countess declared. 'Lord George has never, despite his family name and the warriors of his house, been involved in any physical confrontation. Little wonder after Barnet that he handed both London and the old King over to York on a platter.'

'And the rest?' Urswicke demanded.

'Well, sir, we know that Maillac was devoted to Warwick. He constantly mutters that his former master was betrayed. He has little – if anything – to do with the Company of the Five Wounds. And of course, there's the new arrivals.' Callista blinked furiously. 'What's his name? He looks after the boy and the strange silent man who accompanies them everywhere Pat . . .'

'Patmore,' Bray declared.

'Yes Patmore. He, the boy, and the tall, pock-faced creature who disports Clarence's insignia.'

'Mauclerc?' Urswicke declared. 'But all three arrived—'

'Before us,' the countess interjected. 'Remember, I insisted they travel ahead. They arrived here very late on the day Fladgate and Rutger were murdered. We joined them reluctantly the day afterwards.'

Urswicke closed his eyes, recalling the preparations to journey to The Moor. He mentally sifted through the happenings of recent mornings and afternoons. He then stretched out and touched the countess on the back of her hand.

'As ever,' he smiled, 'you are correct. Now, Mauclerc is Clarence's creature and . . .' Urswicke felt his boot gently tapped by that of his mistress. He fell silent, staring across the meadow, now a glorious shifting sea of green under the strengthening sun. He glanced quickly at Callista. His mistress was correct. Callista was a little mouse but, did she work for others?

'Callista,' the countess declared, 'continue.'

'Well, there's Mauclerc, as you call him. But he seems only interested in that strange, pale-faced boy, fussing over him like a favourite child. But more than that I cannot say.'

'Very well.' The Countess delved into her purse and plucked out a silver coin which she placed into Callista's outstretched hand. 'That, my dear, is your reward for the time being. Now, I am sure that if you watch, others may well watch you. So, if they ask, tell them the truth, that I am so pleased with your assistance, I have invited you into my household, which I now do. Believe me, Callista, when we leave here, and God willing we shall, you will accompany us.'

All excited, Callista clambered to her feet. She was about to leave then turned and came back.

'One thing I did hear,' she declared, 'when I was hiding in that copse . . . One of the company – Chadwick, I believe, as I've got to know their faces and names – well, he protested stridently that he was innocent of any wrongdoing, either now or in the past. I remember this because Chadwick appears to be constantly agitated. I know he has visited, on more than one occasion, Father Benedict, the old chaplain here. Anyway,' she pocketed the coin and flounced out in her grey serge gown, 'I'd best be gone.'

The countess and her henchmen watched Callista hurry back across the meadow.

'Now that's something I shall remember,' Urswicke murmured. 'The power of servants, eh?'

'True,' Bray agreed. 'So many of us act and talk as if such minions are nothing, almost invisible.'

'So,' the countess drew a scented cloth from the voluminous sleeve of her gown and gently patted her face, pausing to move a ring from one finger to another. 'So,' she repeated, 'let us make a summation about what we know has happened. Christopher, we will be guided by you. Reginald, add what you think.'

'First,' Urswicke declared, 'we have Patmore and the Imposter. We now know they arrived in London through a devious route. They no more came out of Brittany than my father did. All they said about Brittany was a farrago of nonsense which, I am sure, Duke Francis will confirm. Patmore has acquired a close look-a-like to your son, Henry. We do not know the truth of the boy; we can only speculate. His emergence on to the stage truly is a mummer's masque but, nevertheless, a deadly one. He and Patmore have caused chaos and consternation, seriously inter-fering with our web of informants, messengers and other supporters. Poor Caiaphas's execution is an eloquent testimony to this. Secondly, my father, Sir Thomas, undoubtedly has a hand in all this deadly nonsense. But why – and what he ultimately intends – remains a mystery. He has insisted that we journey to The Moor to participate in the festivities of St George, whose feast day is fast approaching. We also know that the Brothers York will journey here as the archbishop's special guests. Thirdly we know, thanks to you, Reginald, that the situation might abruptly change. Indeed, so much so that the elusive Patmore has already, and still is, probably, preparing to flee the kingdom. Is that why Mauclerc has been commissioned to look after both Patmore and his mammet? In truth, that is all Mauclerc seems bothered with. Most surprisingly, he has formed a very close relationship with the Imposter. So, what does all this portend? As yet we do not know. Fourthly, there are the murders here in this splendid palace. Our hosts are the Nevilles, who ironically have a strong aversion to bloodshed . . .'

'But not to spilling it,' the countess interjected. 'George and Grace Neville take to intrigue and betrayal as a pigeon does to flying.'

'Nevertheless, we can detect no malice towards us on their part, indeed the opposite. However, that makes no difference to what is happening here. A world of murderous mayhem which, I truly believe, has its roots deeply embedded in the recent wars and the battle at Barnet in particular.'

'As I have said, my late husband was at Barnet. He talked about the confusion and chaos, phalanxes and battle groups becoming lost in the mist. He also talked of treachery, and mentioned a sinister presence called Achitophel. Callista heard the same name being mentioned here when Brasenose met with the Company of the Five Wounds.'

'Achitophel!' Urswicke exclaimed. 'What is his part in all this?'

'I don't know, Christopher, just a name; one sinister presence amongst others during that hurling time of vicious violence and the basest betrayal. However, as people would have it, that is now the past, though we strongly suspect it is also part of our present troubles.'

'I still cannot understand,' Bray declared, loosening his cloak, 'why we are here. Oh, I am sure that the truth will eventually emerge but,' Bray gestured towards the house, 'in a place like this, the truth will be grudgingly slow.'

'Yes, it will,' the countess agreed. 'The truth might also be very surprising, which is why Sir Thomas asked you, Christopher, to investigate. He doesn't want some clumsy justice tramping around here and setting up court, whilst he knows how skilled you are. So, Christopher, continue.'

'As I have said, fourthly we have the array of murders here

at The Moor. Brasenose and Rutger arrive here, for God knows what reason. Brasenose carried a map of The Moor, an aid surely for his wanderings around the archbishop's palace? He also possessed a crudely etched map of some church or priory. The reason for that also remains hidden. Anyway, Brasenose wanders here. We know he talked with the Company of the Five Wounds, but he is more intrigued by the maze. Brasenose believes he saw someone entering it; he follows and is murdered.'

'How?' Bray demanded. 'How is a mailed clerk killed so silently and so swiftly?'

'Reginald, quite simple. I scrutinised Brasenose's corpse. There are stab wounds to his back, four in all, and a fifth here just beneath the nape of the neck.'

'Five wounds in all. The same as the insignia of the company, Warwick's bodyguard,' the countess declared. 'Surely a reference to those men and their failure to protect their lord?'

'But Brasenose had nothing to do with the Company of the Five Wounds. He was a Yorkist swept up in the conflict, along with thousands of others.'

'I agree, Reginald,' the countess replied. 'I do not understand why Brasenose was murdered. Was it simply because he was the henchman of a powerful Yorkist Lord?'

'How he was killed,' Urswicke declared, 'is now obvious, though the assassin wished to confuse anyone who investigated. The killer either followed Brasenose into the maze or lay in waiting. Whatever. The assassin crept up behind his victim and loosed a killing bolt. Brasenose collapsed. The assassin then knifed the corpse, plucking out the barbed bolt, rupturing both flesh and clothing. That's all I can establish. The other murders are easier to analyse. Rutger was trapped in that jakes closet, probably drunk, his hose pulled around his ankles. The closet door opens, Rutger glances up, exposing his throat for that deadly gash. Fladgate was also an easy victim. He was killed in the same yard, probably going across to the closet to investigate, drawn by the light of the small lantern or the door creaking open and shut. He then heard a sound behind him. He turns and his assassin looses the bolt.'

'And Forester?'

'Reginald, his murder truly perplexes me. Why go to all the trouble of pinning a man to a table by piercing his wrists with those spikes? Anyway, the poor man was gagged and the heavy blood flow would soon weaken him. He was trapped in death, but, as I have said, why like that?'

'And why naked?'

'My Lady, I agree. There's little reason for why Forester should strip. Was he going to bathe?'

'Or meet someone for a love tryst?' The countess shrugged. 'That would explain him being naked, as well as why there was little or no sign of resistance. I do believe, Christopher, that Forester was having some romantic affair, be it with some household maid . . .'

'Or even one of his companions,' Bray offered. 'It's not unheard of for fighting men who form a company to be physical with each other, even in matters of love.'

'True,' Urswicke replied. 'If it was such an occasion, perhaps that's when Forester drank some tainted wine laced with a powerful potion. Yet there's no evidence for that. Fifthly,' Urswicke continued, 'we have just received evidence that Brasenose may have had a confrontation with members of the Five Wounds, Chadwick in particular. However, that takes us back to the same question. Why was Brasenose really here, and what is the significance of those maps?' Urswicke paused and spread his hands. 'My Lady, that's all I can say.'

She turned to Bray. 'And what conclusions have you drawn, Reginald?'

'To be blunt, my Lady, not much; indeed, nothing at all. The questions Christopher poses are difficult to answer.'

The countess moved her ave beads from her lap. She then held them up, staring at the crucifix of thick silver, letting it dangle before her eyes.

'Oh, sweet Lord,' she breathed, 'oh God be thanked.'

'My Lady?'

'Christopher, we all know about the devotion to the Five Wounds of Christ; a wound to each of his hands or wrists, and the same for his feet or ankles, the final one being to his side, opened up by the Roman soldier's lance, just before Our Saviour's body was taken down from the cross. Spiritual writers pay devotion to these, as well as the wounds to Our Saviour's head caused by the crown of thorns.'

'I see,' Urswicke murmured. 'You're saying that the slaying of each of the Company of the Five Wounds are parodies of what happened to Our Saviour. Fladgate killed by a wound to the head. Forester slain by a cut to his wrists or hands.'

'Yet Brasenose and Rutger,' Bray declared, 'do not fit the pattern you propose. They are a mystery in themselves. Why were they here? Why did Brasenose really go into that maze, and what did Rutger mean by "what we did in life was more important than who we were"?' Bray wiped the sweat from his neck.

'I agree, Reginald,' Urswicke replied, 'and perhaps that's one conclusion we can draw: that the murders are not connected. The slaying of Brasenose and Rutger should be scrutinised for what they are, the deaths of two rather powerful Yorkist henchmen, which have nothing to do with the murder of the two members of the company.' Urswicke drew a deep breath, staring across at Bray, who'd risen chewing the corner of his lip. He held Urswicke's gaze.

'So, what do you propose, Christopher?' he demanded. 'Is there a key to unlock this Pandora's box?' He smiled sourly. 'Some guide through this maze of murder?'

'What I do believe,' Urswicke replied slowly, 'is that something is being planned and plotted here at The Moor. Ostensibly a lavish celebration for the Feast of St George, to be patronised by King and court. It's logical enough. St George is this kingdom's patron saint, greatly honoured by the Knights of the Garter and all the other Lords of the Soil. A time of festival and pageant. Banners unfurled, standards flapping in the breeze. The King and his court clothed in glittering garb, ready to feast at the most splendid banquet. But it's all a sham. Something else, and it's certainly not pleasant, is gathering in the dark. A deep malevolence which, monster-like, creeps towards us, hiding beneath all the finery and opulence of this place.'

'I agree,' the countess murmured. 'We do not know the truth of that strange creature, Patmore. Both he and the Imposter are patronised and favoured by the powers that be yet, Patmore is apparently secretly planning to flee the kingdom, like some convicted felon put to the horn.'

'Then there's the Company of the Five Wounds. I believe they are being punished, eh Christopher?'

'Yes, but why now?'

'Why now, indeed?' The countess crossed herself. 'Why Patmore? Why now? Why are we really here?' She shook her head. 'In the meantime, I have pressing business with my Lord Stanley. He urgently wants to meet to discuss our planned nuptials. Oh yes,' she smiled at the surprised looks of her henchmen, 'Lord Stanley grows more passionate by the day. Just before we left London, he sent me a letter full of warm regard. I meant to tell you sooner, but these present happenings have thrown everything into confusion. Anyway come, let us return to the manor, and feast on the rich food its kitchen will soon provide.'

Matthew Poppleton, Mark Chadwick and Luke Colworth had openly confessed to each other that they were now in mortal fear of their lives. Their grey-haired, rugged-faced leader Poppleton had grudgingly admitted that the danger was now sharper than any they'd faced in battle, be it on land or sea. Poppleton and Chadwick had met, as planned, outside Angel Tower, a narrow, but formidable, lofty donjon built into the corner of the rear wall of The Moor. A guard place to provide clear view of the country-side which stretched beyond the walls of the manor house.

Poppleton had insisted that all three should gather on top of the tower; the only place, he argued, where they could be assured that they would not be spied on. Poppleton had also insisted he and Chadwick needed to meet first, as they were captain and principal henchman of their company. They would talk and then be joined by Colworth. Such an arrangement would also be to their benefit. Poppleton and Chadwick would enter the tower. Colworth, coming late, could then scour the environs of the Angel Tower to ensure that no spy, eavesdropper, or any other danger lurked close by. Poppleton had been most insistent on this, giving Colworth sharp instructions on what to look out for. If he did detect any danger, they would arrange another meeting. If he didn't, then they were safe.

Both Poppleton and Chadwick had arrived, warbelts strapped on with sword and dagger in their sheaths. They were cloaked and cowled against any cold breeze, though both men expected the afternoon to be sun-filled and warm. Poppleton ushered Chadwick into the barren stairwell, where the dust motes danced in the sunlight, piercing the lancet windows. Poppleton slammed shut the door to the jakes cupboard just inside the entrance before bolting the tower door behind them. He then held up the leather satchel which clinked as it swayed.

'I brought a wineskin and three pewter goblets. Colworth will join us when the bell rings to mark the three o'clock prayer. Now,' he drew a deep breath, 'let us climb.' Poppleton pointed at the stout poles heaped in a corner close to the jakes cupboard. 'Do you need a walking cane?'

Chadwick grinned and shook his head. 'Not yet,' he mocked back. 'I am still as nimble as you are, Matthew.'

'Then, to quote the psalmist, "let us go up to our place of rest".'

'Will we hear Colworth when he arrives?'

'Of course, I have told him to pound on the door and shout. Don't worry, we will hear him. So, up we go.'

Chadwick followed his captain up the tower steps; he quickly realized why the walking canes had been supplied. The staircase was narrow and winding, its many steps steep and sharp. The air was musty, whilst the darkness cloaked them, except for the occasional ray of sunlight piercing the lancet windows. Gasping and groaning, they at last reached the top. Poppleton pushed back the trapdoor and they clambered through, cursing the sharp pebbles strewn across the floor of the tower so as to provide a better foot-grip. They paused for a while, catching their breath, turning their faces so the breeze could cool their sweat. For a while, both men just crouched, recovering from the climb, before rising to lean against the crenellations and stare out across the rich, verdant countryside beyond the walls. A sea of green encompassing bushes, copses, spinneys, and broad sweet meadowland either side of a trackway, nothing more than a dark ribbon twisting through the countryside into the distance.

Chadwick leaned against the moss-covered stone wall and stared longingly across the countryside sleeping quietly under a warm sun.

'If I were a bird, I would fly,' he murmured. Shading his eyes, Chadwick pointed to the far left at a dark stone tower rising just above a sprawling, deeply dense copse of trees. 'Is that part of the manor?' he asked.

'I don't really know,' Poppleton replied. 'I have heard rumours, stories that the woods which circle The Moor contain villages of the dead.'

'What do you mean?'

'Villages of the dead. I found the same in the north. Entire villages, hamlets, monasteries and so on, which were devastated by the great pestilence. The peasants died in their thousands; the survivors buried or burnt the corpses then fled. They left their houses and churches, which became nothing more than monuments to the dead; haunted, eerie dwellings, avoided by many.' He nudged his companion carefully. 'Certainly not to be visited in the dead of night.'

'But refuges we could flee to! Places where we could shelter if we wanted?'

'They would certainly serve as a hideaway. I agree, Mark, it would be good,' Poppleton scratched his iron-grey hair, 'to be rid of The Moor. We should leave.' Poppleton again nudged his comrade. 'Where would you go?'

'As far from here as possible,' Chadwick replied.

'Anyway, in the meantime,' Poppleton pointed to the narrow bench built into the side wall of the tower, 'let us celebrate our freedom and plan for the future.'

They made themselves comfortable, taking off sword belts and looping them over the pegs driven into the grey stone above the trapdoor.

'Matthew,' Chadwick took a slurp from the wineskin before offering it to Poppleton, 'we must face the facts. We are trapped here, and we've been condemned to die. Who killed our two comrades? Why and why now? God save us, but it's months since Barnet, so,' he continued in a rush, 'are we being punished because we survived that battle and our master did not? Are we being blamed for his death? Heaven knows that battlefield was as confusing and as twisted as the maze this place houses.' He picked up the wineskin and gulped another mouthful. 'Matthew, you know what we did,' he continued. 'We staggered around that battlefield; the mist was so thick we couldn't see our hands in front of our faces.' Chadwick fell silent as

Poppleton patted him gently on the arm. 'No, no, Matthew, I won't hold my peace. Here we are, at the top of this tower where no one can hear what we say. Let us speak the truth. I mean, do you think our master was betrayed, but by someone else? I have racked my memory and I cannot recall anything, except that, on more than one occasion, Warwick talked of a wraith. That's how he described it; a true stirrer of troubles. Our Lord called him Achitophel. Surely, Matthew, you heard our master speak the same?'

'I certainly did. Achitophel is a name of a great traitor; his story is in the Old Testament. Now, my Lord of Warwick claimed our Achitophel was a wraith, a traitor, an informant who moved like a ghost between York and Lancaster, selling information, offering, where and when he could, to disrupt and to carry out malicious mischief. Think, Mark, of all the intrigue and treachery during the weeks before Barnet! This person refusing to fight, another claiming he would not be able to move in time; people slipping away into the dark, castles being locked against us, rumours of this, rumours of that. Warwick was certain Achitophel had a hand in all of that.'

'If he was at Barnet,' Chadwick declared, 'did Achitophel, whoever he is, survive the fighting?'

'And, more importantly,' Poppleton declared, 'is he here at The Moor? Now that's possible but for what reason, eh?'

'To murder us.'

'But why?'

'Because the world believes,' Chadwick declared heatedly, 'we deserted our lord and master. Has Achitophel offered someone, anyone, our heads on a platter?'

'True,' Poppleton conceded, snatching the wineskin from Chadwick to take a gulp.

'If that's the case,' Chadwick replied, 'we should be gone from here as swiftly as possible. Matthew, we could flee. We could hide, take service with another lord, either here or across the Narrow Seas. I am sure Colworth would join us.' He paused at a ringing of a bell deep in the manor.

'And that will be soon enough,' Poppleton murmured. 'I am just thinking, if Achitophel is flesh and blood, who could it be? Maillac was Warwick's principal steward, he was also the earl's herald. He took messages backwards and forwards, not only to fellow Lancastrians such as Exeter and Somerset, but also holding the cross and the olive branch to Yorkist leaders. Maillac was well placed to trade information and slip, like a wraith, from camp to camp. Imagine, Mark,' Poppleton peered up at the sky, 'that you are a Yorkist commander. You are asked to meet somebody in some lonely place, be it a stinking alleyway or some barren copse. All you hear is a voice offering to do something you desperately want or really need. You make a bargain and reach an agreement.'

'But surely I'd like to know who it is?'

'No, you wouldn't. The proof of the pudding is in the eating. Someone's offered you help; you don't give any money, you simply agree and you wait. If your mysterious visitor returns with proof, and you yourself will be able to judge if he has been successful or not, silver or gold is handed over, Achitophel is a little richer and he looks around for fresh business.'

'So, Maillac should be suspected.'

'Possible,' Poppleton murmured. 'But, there again my friend, we have the Nevilles, brother and sister, two treacherous peas from the same treacherous pod: a family that changes its colours as fast as fading daylight. Believe me, Mark, they've sold their allies with sweet and merry abandonment.' Poppleton paused as he stared at his friend's agitated face. 'Mark, Mark,' he comforted, 'have you found no peace, even at the shriving pew and all the spiritual ministrations of Father Benedict?'

'Oh, he has heard my confession, my protestation of innocence over Warwick's death.' Chadwick rubbed his face. 'To be brief, he has advised me to flee from anyone or anything to do with what happened at Barnet.'

'And will you?'

'I think so.'

'Don't flee,' Poppleton warned. 'Be open and honest. Just say you are leaving. Act honourably. You are innocent of any crime. You have been restored to the Crown's favour. No man can bring a claim against you.'

'How does he do it?' Chadwick snapped.

'Sorry, my friend, who does what?'

'Achitophel? How does he choose . . .!

'I have told you. However . . .' Poppleton broke off at a pounding on the door below.

'Colworth!' Chadwick exclaimed. He made to get up but Poppleton grabbed him by the arm.

'Rest here, my friend. Relax. Take another mouthful of wine.' Poppleton got to his feet. He took his warbelt off the peg then grinned sheepishly. 'I meet friend, not foe.'

He fastened the warbelt back on its peg, opened the trapdoor and began to gingerly make his way down, shouting at Colworth that he'd be there soon enough. Chadwick took another slurp of wine and leaned back against the hard grey stone. He felt sleepy but was jolted awake by the most hideous scream. Poppleton was shouting and the sound of fighting echoed up the steep spiral staircase. More shouting, cries and blows rang out. Chadwick sprang to his feet and cursed as he tried to loosen his warbelt, which was tangled with that of Poppleton. At last it was free and, holding it tightly, Chadwick made his way down through the trapdoor.

Grasping the guide rope, he began his descent but, despite the sound of raucous violence surging up the hollow tower, Chadwick made his way slowly. A fall down these steps could certainly prove fatal. He went down gingerly as the sounds of violence faded. At last, he reached the bottom. He knocked aside the shabby door to the jakes closet then opened the tower door and stared in horror at Colworth sprawled on the ground with a hideous wound to his left side. Others, alerted to the noise, were running across the garden. Poppleton appeared with one of the walking poles. He threw this away, kneeling down by the stricken man, searching for the blood beat in the neck. He glanced up at Chadwick and shook his head.

Christopher Urswicke leaned back in the high-backed chair at one end of the great oaken, oval table which dominated Archbishop Neville's council chamber. To his right sat the countess, Bray, and a stern-faced Maillac. To his left, the archbishop, the Lady Grace, Poppleton and Chadwick. The council chamber stood close to the great kitchen, which flavoured the air with an array of mouth-watering smells as the cooks and scullions grilled and roasted venison, pheasant and other succulent meats.

Urswicke remained silent as a group of liveried retainers brought in jugs of the coolest Alsace, along with goblets and silver dishes of sweetmeats.

Whilst the refreshments were served, Urswicke turned, as if distracted by the tapestries hanging on the cream-plastered walls. These created a tangle of exquisite colour, threads of every hue woven together to celebrate some triumph in the history of the Neville family. In truth, Christopher was reflecting on recent events. He and the countess had hardly reached their chambers when the alarm was raised. They went downstairs where Bray, who was about to leave, was waiting. Urswicke asked his comrade to stay with the countess and joined the others hurrying across the garden, where Colworth's corpse lay spread-eagled, soaked in still seeping blood. Poppleton and Chadwick, visibly shaken, explained what had happened. Both men were confused, still shocked by their comrade's death, so Urswicke decided to invoke his commission and hold an inquisition so as to establish exactly what had really happened. He heard a cough, turned and smiled at Archbishop George, who leaned forward, bejewelled fingers tapping the table-top.

'Master Urswicke,' he pleaded, 'with all due respect, the hour passes, the daylight fades and the candle burns.'

Lady Grace also leaned across the table, her beautiful ivory face, full mouth and lustrous eyes reminding Urswicke of a painting he'd seen of a seraph. According to the countess, Lady Grace's looks were a perfect mask concealing a mind which teemed like a box of worms or, in her case, the countess had darkly added, a nest of vipers. Lady Grace certainly knew all the tricks of dalliance. She just stared at Urswicke, lips half opened, watching him carefully. She then relaxed and smiled dazzlingly.

'Master Christopher,' she declared, 'in a few days we celebrate the Feast of St George, not to mention the arrival of our King. We have so much to do. So why all this?' Beside him, the countess coughed sharply, a warning to move matters on. He did so, tapping the table as he stared around.

'The servants have gone, yes, Master Maillac? Are doors and windows closed?'

'They certainly are. We are now alone.'

'But we are not alone, are we? A killer lurks in our midst.'
Urswicke touched the manuscripts unrolled on the table before
him. 'These,' he explained, 'contain my commission, my licence,
my authority to carry out an inquisition. I could read them out
once again but you, my Lord,' he bowed in the direction of the
Nevilles, 'are correct. Time passes swiftly. So let us ignore
the formalities and move to the meat of the matter.'

A chorus of agreement confirmed this and Urswicke pointed
at Poppleton.

'So, what happened in the stairwell of Angel Tower?'

'Mark and I . . .'

Poppleton clapped his hand on Chadwick's shoulder. 'Climbed
that tower for rest and respite, as well as to discuss our future.
The murder of two of our companions deeply disturbed us. We
wanted to confer alone. Both of us are, or were, the leading
henchmen of the Company of the Five Wounds. We thought it
best for us to gather in a place we considered safe. a pleasant
enough meeting, yes?' He nudged his companion, who nodded.

'Then you tell him,' Poppleton urged.

'Oh, we chatted away, sharing a little wine, enjoying the sun,
the warmth, the cool breezes. We were waiting for Colworth to
join us. Eventually he did, banging on the tower door and
shouting. I volunteered to go down but Matthew said he would.'

'And I collected my warbelt,' Poppleton declared.

'Yes, yes you did. You went to strap it on but then thought it
wasn't necessary, so you left it there.'

'I went down the steps,' Poppleton took up the story, 'and
reached the stairwell just as Colworth emitted a most chilling
scream. I threw open the door. Colworth was on his knees
clutching a deep wound to his side. The blood spurting through
his fingers. Close by, armed with sword and dagger, a cloaked,
hooded figure. I had no weapon, whilst Colworth's warbelt was
out of reach. I dared not stretch down to unbuckle the belt or
draw one of the blades.'

'That would have left you vulnerable, Master Poppleton?'

'Yes, Master Urswicke, it certainly would have done. Anyway,
I remembered the walking canes, simple but sturdy rods, just
inside the entrance near the jakes cupboard. I closed the door,
grasped one of these and made myself ready. When I returned,

Colworth lay sprawled on the ground. The assassin was retreating. I lunged forward but he blocked my parry, forcing me back, with a circle of whirling steel. Master Urswicke, he was a skilled swordsman; there was very little I could do. I knew Chadwick had been alerted but only a fool would run down those tower steps. I did what I could, then the assassin abruptly turned and fled, swift as a shadow under the sun.' Poppleton spread his hands. 'I cannot say who it was, where he came from, or why he should kill poor Colworth.'

'Except,' Urswicke retorted, 'poor Colworth is, or was, a member of a company who formed Warwick's bodyguard. Indeed, your company has suffered grievously, and I do believe,' Urswicke tapped the table, 'Barnet must be the cause of all this.'

Urswicke fell silent, staring down the council chamber. It was time to change direction. 'Achitophel!' he abruptly exclaimed, his voice ringing like a bell through the chamber. 'Is all this the work of Achitophel? I know a little about him but I suspect others, people gathered here, might know a great deal more.' Urswicke's words hung like a raised sword, heavy in the air.

'I have heard of him,' the countess declared, 'but only a little. My late husband, Sir Humphrey Stafford, mentioned the name on more than one occasion. When he did, Humphrey wondered if all the chaos and confusion at Barnet was mainly due to the meddling of that master mummer, Achitophel.'

'He must be responsible,' Chadwick wailed. 'Yes, we don't know who he is or where he lurks. But enough of that! Poppleton and I can't wait here like lambs in the pen marked down for slaughter. Your Grace, whether you are willing or not, I must go, and the sooner the better.'

'Peace, Master Chadwick,' Archbishop George soothed. 'You are safe here and, once the festivities are finished, you will be free to go with both my silver and my most solemn blessing.' The archbishop fell silent. He glanced sharply at his sister, some secret message which she understood, for she nodded imperceptibly. The archbishop rubbed his face with his hands. 'Master Urswicke, I must confess, I know, as my late brother did, about Achitophel and his treacherous ways. He was, he is, a true Judas. During the wars, he moved between the camps selling information and offering assistance.' The archbishop paused. 'I became more aware of Achitophel two years ago, after Lancaster was defeated at Losecote Field, called so because the fleeing Lancastrians tore off their jerkins and tabards. Anyway, York captured their camp. Great plunder was found, including a satchel of documents carried by a mailed clerk who had been trapped and killed. York claimed it was crammed with documents which eloquently portrayed how Achitophel worked. How he could manufacture and spread his malicious mischief. A fine example of this was the confrontation at Ludford Bridge. Do you remember it? York was advancing in battle formation, standards and banners displayed. The Lancastrians marched to confront him. King Henry led a truly powerful phalanx of foot soldiers and archers; he was intent on confronting the power of York. The Lancastrians also plotted a secret strategy. They despatched Achitophel, as one document describes him, with instructions to inform the Yorkists that if they put down their arms, they would be pardoned. Achitophel tricked York's battle commander, Trollope, exaggerating the size and strength of the Lancastrians marching to meet them. Trollope was informed that if he fled, he'd be pardoned. He duly did so. Others soon followed, and the Yorkist phalanx simply disintegrated, melting away like wax under the sun.'

'But how does he manage such treachery?'

'Oh, Master Urswicke, I can answer that. Because I also have done business with Achitophel, I admit I have sat and supped with the devil. I had no choice, did I?'

'My brother speaks the truth.' Lady Grace stretched like a cat, putting out her hands as if admiring the rings on her slender fingers. 'Tell them,' she urged harshly. 'About those hurling Easter days earlier this year, when Edward was marching on London.'

'I was left in charge of both the city and the Tower,' the archbishop began slowly. 'Old King Henry had fallen into one of his witless states and was kept fast in the fortress. He truly was in a piteous way. He insisted on being garbed only in a ragged blue gown, his hair and beard untended. He would have no ornament, be it bracelet or ring.' The archbishop shrugged. 'Nobody really supported him or the House of Lancaster. I realized I could not hold London. I was desperate, determined to avoid violence; vicious street fighting which would cause nothing but cruel slaughter and needless bloodshed. Then Achitophel appeared.'

The archbishop gestured at his steward Maillac. 'Come, my faithful henchman, tell them what happened.'

'As His Grace has intimated,' Maillac moved a candle spigot so that the pool of light was clear about him. 'We were locked in the Tower, wondering what to do. I was returning from the city. I reached the quayside close to the Lion Gate and I was approached by a cowled figure, a visor across his face. He whispered how he had come in peace, and he thrust a seal into my hand, the personal signet of Edward of York. The stranger hissed that the archbishop should make submission to York and declare London to be an open city. He said he would wait in a nearby tavern for an hour and no more. I was to bring the archbishop's reply, as well as a purse of silver, ten pieces in all.'

'Of course, I agreed,' the archbishop replied. 'I made full submission.'

'And Achitophel?'

'I took His Grace's reply and the ten pieces of silver to that tavern. I was about to enter when the same hooded figure came out of an alleyway close by. He was swift and terse. He took the scroll I carried, as well as the purse, and promptly disappeared.'

'A dangerous game,' Poppleton spoke up. 'Achitophel could have been seized.'

'Why?' the archbishop mocked. 'Why should I or York seize someone who was trying to help us both?'

'On reflection, very shrewd,' the countess declared. 'Achitophel approaches one party to see what they want or need, then crosses to another who is only too willing to satisfy that need.'

'I did ask him before he left,' Maillac declared, 'if we could approach him, should we need to. Masked and cowled, he just shook his head. I could only make out his outline, nothing to explain who he might be or where he came from.'

'And your question?' Urswicke demanded.

'Oh, he said we could never approach him. He always chose what enterprise to follow, no one else did it for him.'

Urswicke, listening intently, whistled under his breath. He had learned enough from both his own observations, as well as listening closely to his father, that professional traitors, spies,

'*Proditores Atque Speculatores*', had emerged from the chaos during the long years of conflict. In essence, these were professional Judas men who bought and sold information or proposed a solution to whatever challenge their prospective client faced. So why should anyone abuse a stranger who offered solutions to their problems?

'What does this mean for us?' Poppleton demanded. 'In the end, we seem to be no closer to solving the murder of our comrades, not to mention those of Brasenose and Rutger. So,' Poppleton sneered, 'what will you inform your masters?' He didn't wait for an answer but waved his hand. 'Chadwick and I will soon disappear; we have to.' He sighed noisily. 'We have a killer in our midst. Achitophel, or some other assassin, prowls close by, as dangerous as any ravenous wolf in a sheep pen.'

'If you must go, then you must go,' Urswicke retorted. 'But, and I would go on oath, these horrid murders, Master Poppleton, have their roots in the struggle at Barnet, that's something we all believe, yes?' He was answered with murmurs of agreement. 'The battle at Barnet shrouds this mystery. So, Poppleton, you are a veteran soldier, a member of Warwick's bodyguard and, unlike anybody here, you and yours were actually there during the battle. So, what happened? You have already told us about Warwick, but the rest of the battle? How did it unfurl? What actually happened?'

Urswicke tapped the Book of the Gospels lying on the table beside him before pushing it down for Poppleton to touch before he replied any further. Urswicke watched as Poppleton placed his right hand on the sacred book then pushed it away. A deathly silence gathered. All eyes were on this veteran warrior, who must have been at the eye of a storm which had swept the entire kingdom.

'It was a poor spring,' Poppleton began, 'wasn't it, Mark?'

His comrade nodded.

'A candle consumes itself in its own burning,' Poppleton continued. 'So it was with Warwick. Full of energy, bustling about, not waiting to reflect or to plot. During that fateful Holy Week, he hurried south to confront Edward of York, who had already occupied London: that did not really concern us, except that Edward was able to reprovision his army. No such luxury was available to Warwick. On Holy Saturday night, both armies met close to Barnet. York was cunning. Muffling the clink of armour and harness, he approached Lancaster as close as he could. Edward had divided his army into three battle groups or phalanxes. Imagine it if you can.' Poppleton used his hands to demonstrate. 'Edward held the centre, Hastings the left flank, with Richard of Gloucester on the right. The three phalanxes waited there the entire night. It was freezing, and that thick, deadly fog was already beginning to boil. Warwick then made his first great mistake, an error of judgement; perhaps he was just badly advised. Warwick failed to realize how truly close the Yorkists had crept through the mist-hung darkness. Anyway, his ordnance roared out, bombard, cannon and culverin. They belched shot and powder in thick clouds of black smoke.'

'It was as if the mouth of hell had opened,' Chadwick interjected. 'A rain of fire shot into the air, only to fall on nothing.'

'It's now well known,' Poppleton observed, 'Warwick's hail of fire simply swept over York's men and did little or no damage. Worse followed in the battle. Hastings, on Edward's left flank, was driven back by Oxford, whose men set off in hot pursuit. They left the battlefield and, when they returned, Oxford's insignia, the streaming star, was mistaken for the Yorkist sun with its shooting rays. The Lancastrians, of course, let loose, and Oxford's men believed they were being betrayed. The battle descended into chaos. The Lancastrians turned on each other and their battle line simply buckled and broke.'

'Yes, but what was your role in all this?'

'Master Urswicke, I admit we should have been with our master. However, someone had ill-advised Warwick to fight on foot to encourage the common soldiers. The battle swirled backwards and forwards, phalanxes and groups turning and twisting. We lost sight of him and he became isolated. His banners and standards were hacked down so they could no longer serve as a rallying point. None of us had been to Barnet before. None of us knew the lie of the land. None of us could see through a poor dawn light dimmed even further by the thickest mist. By the time we searched him out, near a copse close to the horse lines, Warwick had been cut down.' Poppleton shrugged. 'So we fled with the rest.'

Urswicke, slouched in his chair, just nodded understandingly. 'So,' he declared, tapping the table, 'Warwick could have been caught up in the haze of bloodlust, the love of killing which shrouds any battlefield. Or,' he shrugged, 'he might have been the victim of deliberate cunning. A plot to isolate and so kill him. What do you think, Master Poppleton?'

'As I have said, we were torn away from him by the fury of the fighting. We scoured the field searching for our master. I admit we kept out of the fray. We did not wish to become embroiled in some bloody useless fight. We were searching for our master . . .' Poppleton paused at sharp raps on the door, which was flung open.

Mauclerc swaggered into the chamber and, uninvited, took a chair at the end of the table facing Urswicke.

'Good day, Master Mauclerc. You are welcome.'

'No, I'm not.'

'That, sir, is probably the truth of the matter. So, why are you here? Surely this does not concern you?'

'No it doesn't, Urswicke. I work solely for the Lord Clarence. My task is the welfare of Henry Tudor and his guardian, Master Patmore.'

'Both liars,' Bray shouted.

'Both directly under my care, sir, so watch your tongue.'

'As I will yours,' Bray yelled back. He would have continued, but the countess gripped him by the arm.

'Mauclerc,' Urswicke declared, 'this is a legal and lawful investigation authorised by Sir Thomas Urswicke, Recorder of the City.'

'I don't answer to him,' Mauclerc rasped.

Urswicke smiled to himself as he ruefully admitted he had committed another mistake. Christopher often forgot that the Yorkists hunted as a pack. Nevertheless, they also distrusted and disliked each other just as ardently as they did their quarry.

'But you do answer to him.' Urswicke lifted his head. 'You have to. In this matter, he is the King's representative. My commission, my warrants, are issued in the name of the Crown.'

Mauclerc simply shrugged.

'So why are you here?' Christopher asked gently.

'I am curious, Urswicke. I understand there has been another

killing. I want to find out what has happened, as well as discover
if there is any danger to me and mine.'

'None that I can see,' Urswicke replied.

'Is it safe,' the countess spoke up, 'for the Brothers York and
their retinues to visit this place of blood?'

'They have visited worse,' Maillac retorted.

'No they must come,' the archbishop asserted. 'They have to.
The House of York and Lancaster meeting for the splendid
Feast of St George, patron saint of this kingdom. Yorkist leaders
meeting those of Lancaster.'

Urswicke turned as the countess, who had been silent and
stony-faced as any statue, abruptly startled, dropping her ave
beads to the ground before picking them up.

'Are you well, my Lady?' he whispered.

'Yes, yes.'

To divert attention away from the countess, Urswicke pointed
at Mauclerc.

'So you are here because you are curious?'

'In a word, yes.'

'And in a word, sir, we are finished here.' Urswicke crossed
himself and rose. He bowed to the Nevilles and ushered the
countess out. Bray, trailing behind them, paused to have words
with Maillac. Once all three had returned to the countess's
chamber, she gestured at her henchmen to stand as close
as possible to her.

'God save us,' she whispered. 'But a thought occurred to me
in that chamber downstairs. I must think, reflect and plot. A most
heinous conjecture has occurred. I cannot tell you now. No, I
cannot, but I do believe we could be ever so gently, ever so
cleverly, ushered into a deadly trap.'

'Mistress?'

'Not here, Reginald.' She plucked at Bray's sleeve. 'What did
Maillac want?'

'He wants to speak to Christopher urgently.'

'So let us set up camp across the great meadow. Dusk is fast
approaching, but so is the unnamed threat we face. Christopher,
deal with Maillac.'

Urswicke said he would, promising to join them as soon as
possible. He left the chamber and, helped by a servitor, found

Maillac in his chancery, seated at a desk covered with parchment and manuscripts. He welcomed Christopher, ushering him to sit on the chair facing him. Once he had, Maillac offered refreshment, which Urswicke courteously declined.

Maillac, his dark face more scowling than ever, made sure both door and shutters were secure before retaking his seat.

'Master Urswicke, thank you for coming,' he began. 'I did not, could not, speak in the council chamber. I hold no brief in these matters as you do, and I don't want Poppleton and Chadwick to think I am spying on them.'

'But you did and you do?'

'Yes, yes, of course. To answer bluntly, I followed the Earl of Warwick to his camp close to Barnet. I arrived late; the battle had begun. I scoured the fringes of the conflict. The fighting was already beginning to subside, men fleeing for their lives. I searched out the earl's horse line and entered a copse, where I glimpsed the Five Wounds gathered in the shadows, staring out to where Warwick's corpse lay sprawled next to his fallen banner. It was clear what had happened.'

'Which was?'

'Warwick had been cut off and then cut down. The Company of the Five Wounds had arrived but too late. I watched them cluster together. They talked then left. I did wonder about Warwick's corpse. I could tell the earl had been killed but, to be honest, Master Urswicke, I was very frightened. I did not wish to be taken by Yorkist marauders prowling the battlefield.'

'So you found Warwick's corpse lying by itself with the earl's bodyguard close by? Didn't you think it suspicious? Your master had been slaughtered, yet not one of his bodyguards suffered the slightest wound?'

'True. At first, I was deeply suspicious. I believed they had deserted Warwick.'

'And now?'

'Master Urswicke, I have waited, I have watched and I have listened. In particular to the likes of Chadwick. He, more than the others, passionately protests his innocence. Of course, I made my own enquiries. I truly believe the Company of the Five Wounds were cut off from Warwick, who had made the dreadful mistake of fighting on foot. The battle storm had turned against him. He had little chance of escaping. For heaven's sake, he was in his middle years, exhausted, garbed in armour as heavy as a sack of rocks. Little wonder he was trapped and brought down. True, I am not a warrior, but I was there, Urswicke. I saw, I personally witnessed, the absolute chaos caused by the damnable mist, thick and cloying, shifting across the battlefield, cutting off friend from friend. Soldiers, with their helmets on and visors down, stumbled about as if they were in some deadly game of hodman.'

'And yet,' Urswicke interrupted, 'that same company who allegedly did nothing wrong, is now being slaughtered. Three of them being killed in a most gruesome fashion. Why?' Urswicke leaned across the desk. 'Why should the Five Wounds be punished so ruthlessly?' he hoarsely whispered.

'Master Urswicke, I cannot answer that. I have no idea who is responsible for these terrible murders. I have cast about for answers and found nothing. Perhaps, in the very near future . . .' He then lapsed into silence.

'In the very near future?' Urswicke queried. 'What do you mean?'

'Oh, just that perhaps time itself will resolve these mysteries.' The steward picked up a quill pen and began to sharpen its point with a chancery knife. 'I can really say no more, Master Urswicke. I have been as helpful as I can.'

Urswicke took the hint. He left and went along the passageway but abruptly stopped when he heard a sound behind him. He turned, hand on his dagger hilt, but relaxed as Callista the maid slipped out of the murk.

'Master,' she whispered, 'you must follow me.'

She led Urswicke further down the gallery, fast filling with smoke and smells from the nearby kitchen. Urswicke could hear the clatter of pots and pans as well as the constant chatter of the kitchen scullions. He followed Callista out into a small vegetable garden with its different plots and raised herb banks. She led Urswicke across to a narrow wooden bench, close to a small fountain shaped in the form of a pelican wounding its breast.

'Mistress?'

Callista glanced coyly at him out of the corner of her eye.

Then she leaned closer, her grey gown straining over her small plump breasts.

'Mistress, I am not here for dalliance.'

'No sir, neither am I. I shall be brief. I went down to the wash sheds earlier today and I remembered the soldier who was found murdered in his chamber. From the chatter amongst the servants, I understand he was naked, his wrists nailed to a table. Is that correct?'

'Forester,' Urswicke declared, 'John Forester. Yes, what about him?'

'Well, I remember him, and so do others. Forester went down quite regularly to wash in the tubs.'

'A clean man?'

'But so often, sir? One of the maids spied on him, curious about such a habit.'

'And?'

'Well, Forester would scrub himself – I mean, really hard – as if to cleanse something from his skin and, whilst he did, he prayed. She was certain of that. Anyway,' Callista rose, flouncing out her smock, 'I would be grateful if you would inform your mistress. I did promise . . .'

'And we promised this.' Urswicke handed across a coin. Callista snatched it and scurried away. Urswicke sat and watched her go as he reflected on his mistress acting so startled in the council chamber. What had Archbishop George said which had surprised her? Urswicke trusted his mistress completely. A woman who had supported Urswicke's beloved mother as she slipped towards death. She had been racked by a malignant disease growing in her womb, heart broken by the constant infidelities of her husband, Christopher's father, whom she loved to distraction. After her death, the countess had counselled and supported Christopher, taking him into her household as her principal chancery clerk. He had learned a great deal from Countess Margaret and utterly trusted her judgement. He did so now. The countess was correct; something truly nasty lurked behind the luxury and grandeur of The Moor. If so, Urswicke was certain its roots lay in the devious, tangled mind of his so-called beloved father.

Urswicke left the manor house and made his way across the great meadow. He could glimpse the lantern Bray must have lit, glowing like a beacon through the gathering dusk. A beautiful late spring evening, the sky already a glorious array of stars, with a full moon rising against the fading glory of the day. Bird chatter echoed, broken by the sharp bark of hunting foxes and the haunting call of owls. He reached the bench. The countess and Bray, deep in conversation, broke off. His mistress gestured at Christopher to sit beside her.

'My Lady?'

'Tell us first what you have learned, Christopher.'

He did, summarising what Maillac had told him.

'Nothing really startling,' he concluded. 'Just that the Company of the Five Wounds were cut off from their master, who paid the price. However, despite that, someone now believes they should pay for what has been depicted as the deepest treachery. As for what Callista told me . . .'

'It's proof,' the countess replied. 'Oh yes, it's proof enough that those warriors of the Five Wounds feel a deep guilt over what has happened. I have heard of other veterans, doing the same. Constantly washing, as if trying to cleanse from their bodies the blood they have spilled. Oh, I know only too well such deceitful tricks of the mind. My own father, he . . .' The countess fell silent.

Urswicke stared across at Bray, who just shook his head. Both men knew about John Beaufort, Duke of Somerset, found dead in his chamber. Some alleged he was poisoned. Others argued that his mind became deeply disturbed and he had taken his own life.

'Like Pontius Pilate,' Margaret whispered, 'they wash their hands, but they really need to wash their souls. But come now, Christopher, I asked our good friend here why he had returned to The Moor. Of course, he was swept aside by the flurry of events. Reginald,' she urged, 'tell Christopher.'

'After the death of Caiaphas, I made swift journey to consult with others of my lady's liege men, messengers and informants. Wolkind, Caiaphas's brother, was one of these. He is now comfortably lodged at The Blossoms of Heaven in Rickmansworth. Anyway, when I arrived yesterday, I found he had company. Jonathan Blunden.'

'Oxford's emissary?'

'The same. He gave me a simple message from the earl to our mistress. How John de Vere, Earl of Oxford, was well, and that he was looking forward to meeting my Lady here at The Moor in the very near future, so as to push the great venture to fruition.'

'Great venture?' Urswicke declared. 'What does that mean?'

'I think I know, or at least suspect.'

'My Lady?'

The countess peered up at the sky. She abruptly shivered and pulled her cloak closer about her.

'Mysteries deeper than the night.' The countess crossed herself. 'Believe me, we have been brought here to be destroyed. Do you remember Archbishop George talking about York and Lancaster meeting at this great manor? A meeting of friends. A time of peace. A celebration of friendship. Rubbish!' Her voice rose. 'Christopher, Reginald, if I ask you to list the real enemies of York, whom would you name?'

'Well, first and foremost, you and your son, Prince Henry.'

'And we are here.'

'No, no,' Bray protested, '*you* are here, but that mammet protected by Mauclerc and Patmore is an Imposter.'

'That's the truth, I agree,' Urswicke declared, trying to control his surge of excitement. 'I understand what you are saying, mistress. To us that young man is an Imposter, but the world, thanks to York, believes him to be Prince Henry, who has made full submission to the House of York.'

'And so, what now?'

'So, what now, Reginald?' The countess drew a deep breath. 'York is gathering us all here . . .'

'To kill us?'

Countess Margaret shook her head. 'No no, Reginald, I am sure the Brothers York would love to see us all buried, like Warwick, in some lonely abbey, and that would be the end of it. No, no. If Edward executed me, he would be ostracised by all the other kingdoms of Christendom. No, something more subtle is being plotted and we have sufficient evidence of matters moving to a full ripeness. Patmore has already arranged his swift departure from this kingdom. Is it because the plot he has been drawn into will come to fruition so there's no need for him any more? And that innocent-sounding message from Oxford's envoy about seeing me soon to push ahead the great venture! So why now? Why is all this happening now? Because we are still here. York has established his power, but my son Henry Tudor grows to maturity in Brittany. In the very near future, I will marry Lord Thomas Stanley. My marriage will bring the protection of a most powerful family, with estates strewn across this kingdom.' She paused at the hooting of an owl deep in its haunt amongst the trees. 'The herald of the night,' Countess Margaret murmured. 'If what I say is true, is that the true reason for Mauclerc being here? Oh, he guards the Imposter, but he watches and waits. For what?' She shook her head. 'We cannot say. And Brasenose and Rutger, were they here to spy out the land?'

'And the Nevilles?' Urswicke pointed across at the magnificent building. 'Lord George Neville and his sister seem to be full of festive joy, planning and preparing for the great celebration of St George.' Urswicke paused, chewing the corner of his mouth. 'Are the Nevilles the lure here? The snare? Are they the candle flame and we the moths? Notice how both Nevilles keep to themselves.'

'They are burying the dead tomorrow,' the countess declared. 'This place has become a battlefield, yet the Nevilles seem impervious to what is happening. I just wonder.'

Urswicke rose and walked a little way to ease the cramp in his legs as he sifted through the possibilities. The countess was here, so was the mammet. Oxford would soon be joining them. He recalled those crudely sketched maps of The Moor and some small priory or church. Such charts were often used in planning an assault. Was that going to happen here? Urswicke whistled under his breath, turned, and came back to stand over the countess.

'What if, my Lady, the Nevilles, dyed-in-the-wool Lancastrians, are involved in some conspiracy against the Brothers York?'

'And they hope to draw us in too?' Bray asked. 'But . . .'

'Even more dangerous,' the countess declared. 'What if this so-called plot is being managed by your father, Christopher? As you said, the Nevilles and The Moor are just a lure. George Neville's madcap schemes are notorious. A straw man indeed, a true weather vane, shifting direction under any breeze. Think of it; Neville draws us in to such foolery and, even if we are not guilty, we will be depicted as if we are. So, in one fell swoop, the Brothers York can gather us up. I will be accused of being involved in treason and lodged in the Tower, where God knows what would happen to me. You too would be arrested as accomplices. Oxford is seized. So is the Imposter. He, like us, is consigned to some prison where he could linger for a while before suffering, as I might, some unfortunate accident, or fall ill of a deadly infection.'

'But,' Bray protested, 'he's an Imposter.'

'No, no.' Urswicke disagreed, taking his seat. 'Can't you see, Reginald? The Imposter dies and lies buried in the Tower. The true Prince Henry in Brittany can protest for all his worth, but Edward has twisted the truth. He will proclaim that the Henry in Brittany is the real Imposter whilst the true prince, unfortunately deceased, lies buried in the Tower. Your son, mistress, would become increasingly bereft of supporters, who would wonder until their dying day about the truth of the matter. We could not do much to help. The countess would be confined to her cell, her ties with supporters in England and abroad severely damaged, her intended marriage annulled.'

'Oh yes,' the countess murmured, 'the land of topsy-turvy, our world turned upside down. We could protest our innocence, but we would at least stand accused of being the special guests of others conspiring against the King.'

'But what would happen to the Nevilles? They would also stand accused.' Bray pointed to the manor house. 'They would lose all this.'

'As we have discussed before,' the countess retorted, 'George Neville betrayed his family and handed old King Henry and London to York. He actually prostrated himself before Edward.'

'He could do the same again,' Urswicke declared. 'Who knows, perhaps he and his sister would be cast as those who had made full confession. They'd throw themselves on the King's mercy, and so on and so on. We all know the hymn they'd sing, both the words and the tune. Our archbishop will emerge—'

'As he has done so many times,' the countess interjected, 'as innocent as a new-born babe. He'll probably depict us as the real conspirators. Can't you see? There will be no truth in this. Edward

and his minions visit The Moor. They expect to meet loyal, dutiful
subjects but lo and behold, they discover a conspiracy against
the King.' She paused, collecting her thoughts. 'Of course,' she
added, 'the question we can't answer as yet is how the King is
going to discover this malignant conspiracy? This is a masque,
a murderous masque, written by your father, Christopher, and
we have yet to play it out.'

'So what do we do?' Bray demanded. 'And do the murders
committed here have any bearing on this supposed plot?'

'Not supposed, my friend,' Urswicke snapped. 'I believe the
plot we have just described, even though we don't know it in its
entirety, is very real. The threat to us is very close and it will
come to full fruition very soon. However,' he added, 'to answer
your question, Reginald, at this moment in time I can detect no
link between the murders and the gathering storm.' He paused.
'Reginald, I cannot answer your question about what we should
do.' Urswicke got to his feet. 'Come, it's turning cold and the
darkness deepens.'

'It certainly does. Now listen . . .' The countess also rose.
'Reginald, prepare to leave at first light, go harnessed and buckled
for war. You must take my letters to Wolkind at The Blossoms
of Heaven. He will know how to field them out. Make sure
Oxford's messenger is informed that his master, the earl, must
not even think of coming here. Oh no, the earl must put out to
sea and stay there until the present business passes. Oxford must
be warned that if he comes here, he would be walking into a
trap from which he'd never escape.'

'And try and discover,' Urswicke urged, 'the true meaning and
significance of those two maps. I shall give them to you before
you leave.'

'Tell Wolkind,' the countess murmured, 'to move swiftly. He
knows my cohort of trusted couriers. The letters you give him
must be delivered. They will be clearly dated before the
twenty-third of this month. I must see to them now!'

'And you, Christopher?' Bray questioned.

'Reginald, my friend, get yourself all harnessed and ready to
leave before dawn. Rest assured I shall give you the maps. I
think it's prudent you break out of here. The countess could try,
but I doubt if the Nevilles would let us go. Moreover, if we try

to leave, it might provoke suspicion that we are aware of the trap closing in around us.'

'We could certainly try,' the countess declared, 'but I do not think it would be wise. Something would happen and it would not be pleasant. Christopher, you must stay here.'

'My Lady, I certainly will. I am going to reflect then go hunting Achitophel. Our Judas man took that name and he can hang for that name.'

'So let us return to our chambers,' the countess declared, 'a little wiser.' She gestured across the grass. 'Believe me, there is more than one maze here at The Moor, and I suggest the one we are about to enter is the more dangerous.'

Urswicke and Bray escorted their mistress to her chamber before adjourning to Christopher's room so Bray could collect certain items, prepare for an early departure, as well as seize a little of the night for rest.

Once he knew his comrade was settled, Christopher returned to the countess's room where, as usual, she signalled him to be discreet before returning to her chancery table, where she sat writing a number of letters. Christopher made himself comfortable, wondering how he could trap the elusive demon Achitophel. Undoubtedly this wraith of hell was a killer, an assassin, a true son of the devil. Apparently skilled in stealth, Achitophel seemed to be able to move undetected, either by his hirers or indeed anyone else. And what conclusions could be drawn from all the gruesome slayings carried out here at The Moor? First, there was no doubt that the murders of the three members of the Company of the Five Wounds were linked to Warwick's death at Barnet, but why? All the evidence indicated that Warwick's bodyguard had been swept away in the fury of battle. On that mist-bound morning, they desperately tried to find their master but arrived too late. Urswicke truly believed that men such as Chadwick rightly protested their innocence of any wrongdoing. Maillac, the steward, who'd also been on the fringes of the battlefield that fateful Easter morning, agreed with that. He had reported how Warwick's bodyguard had failed to protect their master, but this was due to circumstance rather than bad faith or malice. So why were they being slaughtered, and in such a gruesome way, mocking the five wounds of Christ?

Then there were the murders of Brasenose and Rutger, why these two? They were not members of the company; indeed the opposite. Yet they too had been marked down for death and duly executed. Urswicke stared across at the countess. She had positioned the candle spigots closer so as to create a pool of light in which to write. Looking at the parchment sheets laid out for signature and sealing, Urswicke reckoned the countess must have finished at least six missives. He rose, stretched, and crossed to one of the glass-filled windows.

'You should sleep, Christopher.' The countess pointed to her bed. 'Either here or in your own chamber.'

'Bray's resting there, mistress, and my mind is a jumble.' Urswicke opened the door window and stared out into the night. What could he do? Whom could he question further? As if in answer to his prayer, the chapel bell began to peal, marking the end of compline and signalling to the household that it was time to retire. Urswicke smiled to himself. Of course, the palace chaplain, Father Benedict! According to Callista, Chadwick had confided deeply in the priest.

Urswicke fastened on his cloak and left the chamber. He found the chaplain in the small sacristy just off the chapel sanctuary. Father Benedict, garbed in a black, fur-edged gown, was busy trimming the altar candles. He glanced up and smiled as Urswicke came through the doorway.

'Good evening, Master Urswicke. You are the countess's man, yes? I did wonder when you would approach me.'

'Why should I do that?'

'Oh come, Master Urswicke. You are here.' The chaplain put down the paring knife and wiped his hands on a damp napkin. 'Master Urswicke, you hold the Crown's commission. You are in fact a justice in eyre, with the right to summon, question and judge, and that includes myself. I am chaplain here. I knew those who were murdered – well, at least Warwick's men – and I am going to bury all the victims in the very near future.'

'So, my visit isn't such a surprise?' Urswicke declared as he climbed on to a high stool to sit across from the priest. 'You must know I am here to question you?'

'About what?'

'Master Chadwick's meetings with you.'

'Ask him.'

'Well, I would prefer to ask you.'

'Now wait.' The priest held up a vein-streaked hand, his lined, weathered face all puckered in concern. 'You can ask, you can summon me, but that does not mean I will reply. I shall plead canon law. I am a priest. What I hear at the shriving pew is covered by the most solemn sacramental seal. If I divulged it, I would be excommunicated by bell, book and candle. My priestly faculties would be suspended. I would be deprived of my living. My soul would be cursed in this life and the one to come.'

'I am not asking for that, Father.' Urswicke paused to choose his words carefully. 'Surely Chadwick spoke away from the shriving pew?'

'No, he did not. Look,' the chaplain's voice softened, 'all I can say is that Chadwick has, and still does, persist in his conviction that the Company of the Five Wounds did not betray their master. Admittedly,' the priest shrugged, 'he did say on one occasion that he had niggling doubts about certain occurrences during the battle, but look, Master Urswicke, more than that I cannot say. I bid you goodnight.'

Hiding his disappointment, Urswicke rose and picked up a taper. 'I will light this before the Lady Altar.' He bowed towards the priest. 'Father, I thank you, I must go . . .'

'Now isn't that strange?'

'What is, Father?'

'You've jogged my memory, Master Urswicke. Brasenose, your father's henchman. He took to wandering the palace. No, no,' the priest lifted a hand, 'I saw him doing nothing suspicious; he simply walked and stared. However, he and his companion – the one who was found in the jakes closet with his throat cut – well, both of them came here. Brasenose, like you, picked up a taper. He said that he wished to placate the spirits of the dead. He wanted to whisper a requiem for those he had killed in battle. As you know, many veteran soldiers do that. They claim to be haunted by the ghosts of those they killed. In some cases, they lose their wits and become quite mad, believing that a cohort of the dead constantly surrounds them. So, it wasn't such a strange thing to say. Nevertheless, I asked him what he meant and who in particular he had killed in battle? Brasenose confessed that he felt the ghosts close about him here at The Moor, more so than in any other place. Again, I asked him why? He replied that both he and his henchman, Rutger, had been responsible for the slaying of Warwick's brother, John Neville, Marquess of Montagu at Barnet. Brasenose simply wanted to offer a prayer for the spiritual repose of a man whose family home he was now visiting. Brasenose seemed unsettled, and I could understand his attitude. We all find it very difficult to live cheek by jowl with people we were trying to kill only a year ago.'

'But not for you, Father.'

'Master Urswicke, don't judge by appearances. I have served as a chaplain in the royal array. God knows,' he rubbed his face, 'I have seen my share of bloodshed.'

Urswicke stretched out a hand for the chaplain to clasp, which he did.

'Father, I thank you.'

PART FIVE

'For the King said to the said
Archbishop that he would come
and disport himself in his
Manor at The Moor.'

U rswicke left the sacristy and went round to stand before
the Lady Altar. He lit the taper and watched the flame
dance in the breeze seeping through the ancient chapel.
Once back in the countess's chamber, Urswicke served some
light ale to his mistress, now busy signing and sealing the letters
she had written. Immersed in her task, she thanked Urswicke for
the tankard and returned to her work. Urswicke, slumped in a
chair before the fire, silently toasted his own success. He had
learned something new, something most significant. He now
had a common thread linking all the murders. So how was he to
proceed?

Urswicke recalled the murders one by one. Brasenose, a bolt
to the head. Rutger, his throat cut. Simon Fladgate, also a barb to
the head. John Forester, probably drugged then killed, his
wrists pierced by spikes so he bled to death. Finally, Colworth,
mysteriously stabbed outside Angel Tower. Urswicke now had a
deep suspicion of who the assassin might well be. If his theory
was correct, he must concentrate on the last murder, as it contained
one factor different to the others.

'Oh yes,' Urswicke breathed, 'one great difference, and I must
push that to a logical conclusion.' Urswicke continued to sift
what he knew; his eyes grew heavy and eventually he slipped
into the deepest sleep. When he awoke, the darkness was beginning to thin under the strengthening glow in the east. Urswicke
stood for a while at the window, listening to the constant cooing
of the pigeons and the flute-like call of courting blackbirds, what

the countess called the hymn of God's creatures greeting the dawn. Urswicke stared around. The chancery desk was clear except for a leather sack tied and sealed at the neck. The countess lay on the bed, almost hidden by the cloak she had wrapped around her. Urswicke was about to cross to the lavarium when the most hideous scream shrilled up from outside. Urswicke froze. Another scream; he was sure it came from the front of the house. The countess stirred. Christopher leaned over her as further screams cut the air.

'My Lady,' he whispered, 'please stay. Lock and bolt the chamber behind me.' Pulling on his boots, Urswicke collected his cloak and warbelt and hurried out on to the dimly lit gallery. Shadows shifted; different sounds carried as the household stirred, aware that something hideous had taken place. Maillac and Bray were in the spacious entrance hall, other servants thronged near the half-open door. A group of women were trying to comfort Callista, who was sitting on a stool, face in hands.

'You'd best see this, Master Urswicke.' The steward looked pallid and agitated.

Bray, all harnessed and ready to leave, indicated with his head for Urswicke to follow him outside. He did. The morning promised to be beautiful, but the gruesome, blood-soaked corpse sprawled at the foot of the steps transformed everything into a nightmare. Urswicke approached, hand over his mouth and nose. The corpse was Chadwick's, dressed as if ready to leave. Beside him lay two panniers, all clasped and buckled. Urswicke stopped, crossed himself, and stared at the pool of blood on which the corpse seemed to float.

'In sweet heaven's name,' Urswicke murmured. 'He's had his feet hacked off.' He crouched down, pushing back the dead man's hood to reveal a face still shocked in death, eyes popping, lips bared in gaping horror. Urswicke noticed the fresh streaks of blood clotting the dead man's hair. He carefully pushed his hands behind Chadwick's neck, lifting the head slightly forward so he could see and feel more clearly the horrid bruising to the back of the head, caused by a narrow crossbow barb embedded deep in the back of the skull. Satisfied as to the cause of death, Urswicke went swiftly through the dead man's pockets, purse and wallet, as well as the two panniers. He found nothing significant except coins, which he handed to Maillac. The steward continued to stand rigid on the bottom step, staring in horror at the grisly spectacle before him. Urswicke finished his search of the corpse. Chadwick carried nothing else of note except for a small parchment scroll which listed the members of the company, with signs and symbols beside each one. Probably a cipher, Urswicke concluded, which only Chadwick would understand. Nevertheless, Urswicke pocketed the parchment and climbed the steps, but Bray plucked him by the sleeve and led him away.

'Before you ask,' he whispered, 'the corpse was discovered by Callista, who opened the front door to sweep the steps.'

'He was killed with a barb to the back of the head,' Urswicke replied, 'his feet hacked off. The corpse was then dragged here.'

'In which case, Christopher, I shall leave this matter to you. I must leave. I will collect our mistress's letters. I also have the maps you found in Brasenose's saddle. I want to show one of them to someone who may understand and decipher it for me. Anyway, God knows what really happened here. I must go. Stay vigilant, Christopher.'

'Oh, I will. Do not worry about the countess. She has her own secret purposes and she's more than aware that the malignancy lurking here is gathering to fruition.'

'I agree. I left your chamber last night, Christopher, and slipped like a ghost around The Moor. I discovered nothing much.'

'Except?'

'Except for the stables. Maillac and others were preparing horses and sumpter ponies. Heaven knows what that portends. Our mistress is correct. Despite appearances, a storm is brewing.' Bray paused as the main door opened. Poppleton, shrouded in a blanket, came out. He glimpsed the corpse and slumped to his knees, face in his hands as he yelled a litany of curses on those responsible for the murder of his comrade. Archbishop George and his sister emerged. They took one glance at what had happened and hastily retreated back into the house. 'Poor Chadwick,' Bray murmured, leading Christopher away.

'As I said, Reginald, the assassin killed him with a hand-held arbalest; his feet were cut off just above the ankles. A blasphemous parody of the wounds to Christ's feet.' Urswicke swiftly crossed himself. 'Those severed limbs, as well as the cleaver the assassin used, cannot be far away. God rest Chadwick's soul. By the way he was dressed, I suspect he intended to flee this benighted place.'

'Which we should do.'

'As we have discussed, I doubt if we would be given leave,' Urswicke replied. 'We must stay to see this masque through to the end. The countess has made her preparations against the coming storm.'

'And you, Christopher?'

Urswicke grinned. 'Like any good hunting dog, I have raised a scent and I will follow it through. What neither the countess nor I can determine, is what is going to happen here. Oh, they can talk about the revelry in a few days' time, but truly? How can anyone exult and rejoice in this house of sudden slaughter, this mansion of brutal murder? Nobody, let alone the King, will be comfortable here. Nevertheless, the truth will out. Matters are moving swiftly, even as we are driven deeper into the dark.'

Urswicke and Bray clasped hands. Bray murmured that he would use the present confusion to slip away as quietly as possible. Urswicke watched Bray go, then entered the manor by a postern door and returned to the countess, who had now prepared herself for the day. She pointed to the chancery table.

'Reginald informed me about what has happened, then collected everything I have written. I have kept copies. Christopher, we are committed.' The countess sat down in a chair. 'As for the most recent murder, it seems that the killer intends to annihilate the entire Company of the Five Wounds. Sweep them away from the face of God's earth. Now,' the countess adjusted her snow-white linen veil and pulled the dark blue, silver-spangled robe closer about her. Despite working late into the night, the countess looked refreshed, her thin face resolute, ready to confront whatever monster crawled out of the dark. She caught Urswicke's gaze and smiled. 'Let's see,' she murmured, 'let's watch for the next move on the chessboard.'

They didn't have to wait long. Archbishop George convened a meeting in his council chamber. With his sister sitting on his right, Maillac, Countess Margaret and Urswicke on his left, Poppleton and Mauclerc seated at the far end of the table.

'Thank you for coming,' the archbishop began. 'Another death, another murder! Ah well, the requiem mass will be celebrated just after midday, followed by the burial of all the dead in God's Acre.'

'The dead do not concern me, Lord George.' The countess declared. 'Your Grace, I intend to leave this place of blood.'

'No, you cannot. No, you will not.'

'I am of like mind too.' Poppleton protested. 'Why should I tarry here, like some trapped animal waiting for the slaughterer to slice my throat?'

'No, you cannot, you shall not,' the archbishop repeated fiercely. 'You must all stay here until the King makes his pleasure known.' He flicked his fingers in the direction of Maillac. 'I am despatching my steward to London to ascertain the wishes of Sir Thomas Urswicke in this matter.'

'Did he propose the King's visit here?' Christopher abruptly asked.

'Yes, he did. He was, how can I say, the conduit through which the royal visit was proposed and planned.' The archbishop pulled a face. 'I cannot say what will happen now, but I insist that we all remain here.'

'And I would endorse that.' Mauclerc's voice cracked like a whip.

'I thought this business was of no or little interest to you?' Urswicke snapped.

'Now it is,' Mauclerc snapped back. 'I and the prince have been ordered to stay here to welcome the royal party. I am the Crown's servant. I, and others,' he added ominously, 'will enforce the King's wishes. Indeed, I understand my Lord Archbishop,' Mauclerc added with a smirk, 'that Sir Thomas Urswicke will arrive here before any of the royal court make their appearance? So there's no need for anyone to leave.'

The countess put a hand on Urswicke's arm, a warning to hold his peace.

'And poor Chadwick?' Poppleton, bleary eyed, scratched his unshaven face. 'He too will be buried with dignity?'

'Of course.'

'And there's no evidence of who the killer might be or how it was done?'

'It would seem,' Maillac replied, 'that your comrade had packed his panniers, cloaked and armed, and tried to leave during the early hours, perhaps well before dawn. His assassin followed and killed him with a bolt to the back of his head.' Maillac crossed himself. 'The killer, then armed with a cleaver, hacked off the poor man's feet. We have found both cleaver and the severed limbs pushed under an outside hedge of the maze, close to the entrance.'

The meeting ended soon afterwards. Mauclerc, smirking from ear to ear, bowed to the countess as he swaggered by. Urswicke watched him go.

'Stay calm,' the countess whispered. 'We tested our theory and were proved right. We are prisoners here and we must stay until the end of this masque.'

Urswicke promised that he would avoid Mauclerc at all costs. He accompanied the countess to her chamber, then left saying he would return in a while.

Urswicke hurried down to the stable yard. He made enquiries amongst the grooms and discovered the whereabouts of the manor's dung collector, who rejoiced in the name of Blod. Urswicke found Blod, a shabby, bulbous-faced individual, sunning himself against the side of his reeking wheelbarrow. When Christopher produced a silver coin and told him what he wanted, Blod assured him he could help and, pushing his barrow with mattock, hoe and spade clattering inside, they made their way across to Angel Tower.

'What am I looking for?' the dung collector asked.

'Oh, don't you worry.' Urswicke clasped him on the shoulder. 'I assure you of this, you will know it when you find it; so God speed, but first let me look inside the tower.'

Urswicke went into the stairwell, a crumbling, dust-filled enclosure, which reeked of stale air. A filthy place; the haunt of mice and other vermin. Urswicke pulled open the jakes door, looked inside, then left the narrow stairwell to tell Blod to begin.

The dung collector had now emptied his barrow, his face covered with a leather mask. Blod was all eager to clear the cesspit. Urswicke left him to it and cautiously climbed the tower steps. He reached the top and stopped to catch his breath. Once he had, Christopher pushed open the trapdoor and clambered gratefully through to stand on the roof of the tower. He leaned against the grey stone crenellations, staring out across the fields, copses and meadows, revelling in the fresh breeze cooling the sweat on his face. He stood for a while, listening to the sounds of Blod hacking and clattering around the base of the tower as he opened and emptied the cesspit. Once he'd recovered from the climb, Urswicke sat on the same stone bench that Poppleton and Chadwick had used. He stayed for a while; the noise of Blod working was clear enough, so the same would have been true when Colworth had arrived to pound on the door. Christopher had, immediately following Colworth's murder, closely interrogated Poppleton and Chadwick, carefully sifting and analysing their comrade's murder step by step. Two issues still remained and he would clarify them now. Urswicke sighed, rose, and took off his sword belt. He looped this over the peg, then took it down and refastened it around his waist.

'Poppleton didn't do that on the day,' he whispered to himself. 'There was no need.' He sat back down on the bench, listening to Blod before springing to his feet. 'Time to go down,' he murmured. He opened the trapdoor and carefully made his descent. The steps were steep and sheer, the staircase winding. Now and again, Urswicke would pause to study the narrow window embrasures. The light, however, was poor; candle or lantern would be of little help at this time of the day, so he was obliged to depend on the sunshine streaming through the lancet windows. 'Truly a place of dappled shadow,' Urswicke whispered to himself. He continued on, listening to Blod calling for him. At last, he rounded a corner and went down the final flight of steps into the stairwell. The tower door was flung open, as was that to the jakes closet. Urswicke peered inside. Blod was sitting enthroned above the turd hole, holding his long, pointed spade as any prince would his sceptre.

'Master Urswicke, greetings.'

'And the same to you Blod, prince of the barrow. Well, did you discover something amiss?'

Blod got to his feet.

'Master Urswicke, I've got it outside.'

*   *   *

Reginald Bray was determined to find his way through the dense woods which surrounded The Moor. He had left the archbishop's palace, fully harnessed for battle, with the countess's letters safely hidden away. Bray, a veteran of different wars, decided to avoid the coffin paths which snaked through the trees. Bray did not depend on what he saw or heard, but what he smelt, be it the tang of horseflesh, leather, or the different odours of cooking fires. He soon detected these on the strong morning breeze. Undoubtedly there were men, soldiers, in the forest, not many but small groups, probably keeping The Moor under close observation. Bray hadn't detected these on his journey to the palace, so he concluded that the presence of these soldiers must have something to do with events planned at The Moor for the Feast of St George in a few days' time.

Bray dismounted, leading his horse, its hooves muffled so they slipped through the trees, moving from the light into the shade of the green darkness. Bray moved purposefully, keeping the main trackway to Rickmansworth on his left. A broad thoroughfare, so well used that Bray eventually decided to join a group of noisy, chattering pilgrims making their way to the great Marian shrine at Walsingham. They eventually reached Rickmansworth, and the pilgrims immediately wound their way to The Blossoms of Heaven, a fairly stately tavern which dominated the small market square. Bray mingled with the pilgrims as they entered the yard. He gave his horse to the ostlers and entered the taproom, where he had urgent words with Minehost who showed him up to a small chamber. Wolkind and Blunden, Oxford's courier, had already assembled there.

Bray, once the stoups of ale were served, came quickly to the point. He informed Oxford's courier how the earl must not, at any cost, come ashore and approach The Moor, which was only a trap waiting to snap shut. Bray's warning was so earnest and startling, Oxford's messenger hurriedly finished his ale and said he would be gone as swiftly as his horse could take him. Once he had left, Bray handed over the pouch containing the countess's letters, informing the close-faced Wolkind that the matter was most urgent. The courier took the hint. He drained his tankard and said he would journey immediately into London and deliver the countess's secret messages.

Bray emptied the chancery satchel and sifted through the tightly tied scrolls and the small, neatly folded pieces of parchment. They all carried the countess's seals, though he was surprised at the different recipients: the Archbishop of Canterbury, the chancellor, other notables in the city of Westminster including, surprisingly, 'Sir Thomas Urswicke, Recorder of London'. Bray was also intrigued by the brief message written on each scroll; 'To be delivered by hand on the Feast of St George before the Angelus bell'. Bray wondered what the countess intended. Wolkind, however, was anxious to leave. Bray gathered up the scrolls, put them back into the chancery bag and handed it to the courier.

After he had left, Bray drew out the map of that church or small priory. 'If Brasenose carried these,' Bray whispered to himself, 'it must be important to our noble Recorder. But why? What is this place?' Bray decided to eat and drink. He left the chamber and entered the taproom which was beginning to fill as the labourers left their fields and market traders decided to satisfy their hunger and thirst after a brisk day's trading. Bray managed to secure a window seat and stared around the tavern to make sure he was safe. He carefully noted windows and doors in case he had to leave in a hurry, before turning to inspect the different customers. The traders and labourers looked innocent enough, others included itinerant mountebanks and a gaggle of Moon People who had camped on the outskirts of the village. Two travelling troubadours were drinking deeply and offering the other customers a song, ballad or lurid tale. They were brusquely refused. Bray could detect nothing suspicious, though his attention was caught by a figure, stooped over a table, feeding morsels to ferrets in their caged box. Minehost Picard waddled across and whispered that the rat-catcher was a constant visitor to the tavern and Bray need not worry. Bray thanked him and ordered a potage of stew, freshly baked bread and a stoup of ale. Once served, Bray paid the tally, then slipped another coin into the taverner's outstretched calloused hand.

'Sit down, my friend,' Bray murmured. 'I have a favour to ask of you.' The taverner did so and Bray handed over the mysterious map. 'What is this place?' Bray demanded. 'Does it mean anything to you? I have a suspicion that it's a local building.'

The taverner rose, fetched a three-candled spigot and studied the drawing carefully.

'Yes, yes,' he breathed, pushing it back to Bray. 'No less a place than the Holy Blood Priory, a small religious property, or it used to be, till the great pestilence struck the land. Now it lies deserted, the home of wild animals. A haunted place.' The taverner scratched his chin. 'The old priory is a place I'd certainly avoid. A hall of ghosts, Master Reginald. You know the kind.'

Bray nodded in agreement. He and Urswicke were acquainted with such places and sometimes did business there. Villagers and peasants tended to avoid these relics of the past, regarding them as both sacred and ghost-ridden. Wolfsheads, however, the *utlegati*, the outlaws who roamed the shires, did not share such an attitude. They often turned the deserted, derelict buildings into fortified homes, an even more pressing reason to avoid such places.

'Look,' the taverner continued. 'The priory stands deep in the woods and . . .' he paused, 'just be careful, Master Reginald.'

'Why?'

'Oh, Rickmansworth is a small village; chatter and gossip sweep backwards and forwards like the breeze.'

'And?'

'Strangers have been seen entering the forest; verderers, skilled hunters. You can tell that by the way they dress in Lincoln green jackets and earth-brown hose.'

'Do you know who sent them, or why?'

'I did approach one sitting here in this very taproom. A tight-lipped, sharp-eyed riffler. He did not tell me much, even though I gave him a free blackjack of ale. No, he was most reluctant to chatter. However, from his talk, I suspect he hailed from London. I did glimpse an insignia, like a pilgrim's badge pinned to his jerkin. A red insignia against a white background.'

'The Guildhall,' Bray declared. 'He must have been Sir Thomas Urswicke's man.'

'And then there's others,' the taverner continued in a rush. 'Strangers, men harnessed and buckled, armed with war-bow staves and quivers on their back. I've glimpsed the same threading through the trees. Now again there's the occasional cart, horsemen as well. Not a comitatus, but I got the impression of men massing together, not in an open way but like a leaking bucket, drop by drop.'

'And they go into the forest?'

'Oh yes.'

'To where?'

'It must be the Holy Blood Priory,' the taverner replied.

'Do you know the way, Picard?'

'Yes.' The taverner licked his lip. 'But it might be dangerous.'

'This dangerous?' Bray slipped two silver coins on to the grease-laden table-top.

'When?'

Bray closed his eyes then opened them. 'Soon it will be the Feast of St George. Time is passing, we should leave now. We should go before the gathering dark. I'll buy a sack of supplies from you as well: some fresh bread, salted meat and a wineskin.'

The taverner agreed and an hour later Picard led Bray out on to the main street. They went down to the end of the village, before turning on to a broad trackway which disappeared into the trees. Bray had every confidence in the taverner. Reflecting on their recent conversation, Bray believed Minehost was also a poacher who made great profit selling pheasant, venison and rabbit, killed here in these woods without permission from anyone. Indeed, the way Minehost, despite his broad girth, moved along the paths, he seemed well acquainted with the forest. Nevertheless, it was a lonely journey. Picard, walking before Bray who led his horse, hooves still muffled, along the needle-thin woodland paths. Night was falling. The prowlers of the dark were gathering, including the owls, which hooted mournfully as they prepared for a night's hunt.

The bracken either side of the track snapped and crackled as predator and prey raced through the tangled gorse. Thankfully the moon was full; hanging low, it provided some light for their journey. The air turned cold as a breeze sprang up to rattle the branches and send the shadows flitting. Bray, hooded and muffled, could only reflect on what was happening at The Moor. So many unexpected questions to resolve, though the countess seemed to suspect what was coming. Was all this just a mummers' play?

A masque to draw out York's opponents and destroy them? Were the Nevilles party to this, or just the unwitting catspaw of Sir Thomas Urswicke and his coven?

Bray trudged on, lost in thought, now and again pausing to gently rub his horse to soothe its fears about the dark, forbidden world they'd entered. Bray reckoned they must have been travelling for over an hour when they abruptly left the trees, going on to a broad stretch of open heathland which divided the forest from the lofty, grimly crenellated wall of Holy Blood Priory. The taverner beckoned Bray to follow him, then abruptly paused as fire arrows slammed into the sparse grass before them. Bray quietened his horse as the main gate, creaking and scraping, was pushed open. A group of men, some carrying flaring torches, hurried towards them. Their leader stopped and raised the torch he was carrying to illuminate his face.

'Good evening, Master Bray. Well met by moonlight.'

'And you sir,' Bray gestured at the archbishop's principal steward, 'no less a person than Henry Maillac. What are you doing here?'

'For the moment, Bray, just comply with our requests, and that means surrendering your warbelt.'

Bray shrugged, threw back his cloak and unstrapped his warbelt. Maillac snatched it up before turning to the taverner.

'And you, my fat friend, do you want to stay or go back?'

'Oh, I will go back.'

Maillac nodded understandingly. The taverner turned and walked away. The steward watched him go then lifted his hand and let it fall. Arrows winged through the darkness. The first struck the taverner high in the back, the second, a shaft to the heart as the taverner whirled round. He collapsed to the ground, gurgling and frothing on his life blood. Maillac went and stood over the dying man as he jerked and trembled, before sprawling still with spurts of blood trickling out of his mouth and nose. The steward watched Picard die before shouting orders to his companions to carry the corpse to the nearest marsh and bury it deep.

'There was no need for that,' Bray rasped.

'Come, my friend,' Maillac slurred. 'Let's leave the dead to bury their dead. Come and see where we shelter.'

Bray had no choice but to follow, leading his horse. They entered a broad, cobbled yard housing stables and a forge, together with other outhouses and storerooms. An ostler took Bray's horse, assuring its owner that the animal would be well stabled, its saddle and harness safely stowed away.

Bray realized he was a prisoner. He let Maillac chatter as the steward showed him around the priory, which was as well fortified as any castle or donjon, with its soaring crenellated walls, fighting platforms and heavily fortified gateways. Maillac informed him that in former times the priory had been a Templar stronghold. An ideal place to gather men and prepare them for battle.

'What battle?' Bray demanded, when he and Maillac supped together in the bleak buttery adjoining the refectory. Bray quietly conceded to himself that – though he was a prisoner – he would not resist, but simply wait and watch what happened next. The priory was well fortified and garrisoned by at least a hundred bowmen. However, Bray had the impression that they were not prepared to hold this place but had assembled here for business elsewhere, probably The Moor.

'You ask what battle?' Maillac asked, breaking the silence. 'But you must know what we intend?' He turned to face Bray squarely and Bray caught it, that gleam in the eye, the tightened lips of a man lost in a vision, a dream or a nightmare. 'Warwick,' Maillac slurred, 'was the very flower of this kingdom. Cut down, crushed by lies, betrayal, and finally the most heinous treachery. He must be avenged. The Brothers York should all go into the dark as they have despatched so many. I call upon all the furies of the night to help us carry out our vengeance. The Brothers York will arrive at The Moor and we shall close the trap.' The steward fell silent, lost in his own wild dreams.

Bray watched him intently. He had seen the like before. Indeed, he and Urswicke were also closely bonded, totally devoted and loyal to the countess, but nothing like this. Maillac, who'd apparently been drinking heavily, had lost any grip of reality. He had become deeply immersed in some devious, tangled nightmare of his own making.

'What did happen at Barnet?' Bray asked quietly.

'I don't know, except that my master was left exposed and vulnerable to his enemies.'

'Were the Company of the Five Wounds to blame?'

'Yes and no. Yes, they should have stood and died with their liege lord. No, because Barnet proved to be the eeriest of battles: a place blighted by the devil's own dark and hell's deepest mist. In short, Master Bray, cruel circumstance played its part in my master's death.'

'And the Five Wounds?'

'Much suspected, nothing proved. At least they survived. Warwick did not.'

'Are you Achitophel, Maillac?'

'I wish to God I was.'

'Then did you hire Achitophel?'

'I would have done to kill Yorkists, but he is an elusive spirit who prowls deep in the twilight of our world. Apparently, as we have all learnt, he alone chooses his ventures, no one else.'

'And now?'

'We will destroy the power of York.'

'We?'

'Yes, we. The countess, Oxford, the Nevilles, and those gathered here in this priory, led by Robert of Redesdale.'

'A fanciful, mysterious name,' Bray mocked. 'Like that of Robin of Sherwood. A title taken by many who lead revolts against the Crown but,' Bray paused, 'you are mistaken, you know that, don't you?'

'What do you mean?'

'Do you know Brasenose, Sir Thomas Urswicke's henchman, had a map of this place? So, ask yourself why? How does our noble Recorder of London know this is your place of assembly, of mustering your troops?'

Maillac breathed out noisily.

'Do you also know that my mistress has warned Oxford off. John de Vere will not be joining you. Even as I speak, he is probably preparing his cog for sea. The countess will not participate in George Neville's madcap schemes. Don't you understand that? Can't you see?' Bray added heatedly. 'All this is a play; a mummer's game. George Neville, Archbishop of York, has never concocted a successful plot in his entire life. If he is busy now fashioning one, it's because the Nevilles want it, or George and his sister are acting on the orders of York. Whatever, the result will be the same. A plot against the King unravels. Rebels gather in a deserted priory. Leading Lancastrians such as the countess and Oxford and even that Imposter patronised by the Crown, are caught up in it. Leading figures who should have known better.' Bray paused to catch his breath. 'And you must know what York will do to you and all your Robin Goodfellows, or whatever you want to call them. Those who are not hacked down will be stretched out on some gallows, cut and sliced open, then hung like rats for others to view.' Bray could see that his passionate speech had disturbed Maillac, who now seemed not so confident.

'What am I to do?' the steward whispered as if to himself. 'I am here with my company.'

'All doomed!'

'No, the archbishop assured me that the countess and Oxford will join us at the last moment.'

'Nonsense!'

'No, no, Oxford sent messages.'

'That was before he was informed of what was intended.'

'But, our spies in London report that Sir Thomas is about to leave the city with only a small company. Can't you see, Master Bray? All we need are the Brothers York in that hall at The Moor. We will soon overwhelm them and so turn the tide.'

Bray just shook his head.

'I have seen this before, Maillac. You are locked into this enterprise, held fast. You believe it will be successful because matters are moving as you wish. But in truth they are not. You are only a piece in a game certainly not controlled by you. So why not return my warbelt? Let me collect my horse and go whilst you disband your men and flee, swift as a bird, across the Narrow Seas.'

'I am committed, Master Bray. Never again will I have this opportunity to strike at the heart of York, wreak vengeance for the slaughter of my Lord.'

Bray shook his head. 'Believe me,' he urged, 'listen carefully, Maillac. George Neville is a fool and a catspaw. His so-called plot is simply a device to expose others so York can, at last, destroy any remaining opposition. The only thing the Brothers York did not count on was the murder of the members of the

Five Wounds, as well as the killing of Brasenose and Rutger. However, I assure you of this. Anyone caught up in a plot against York will face the most horrific consequences. Tell me, Maillac, one more time I ask: are you Achitophel?'

'No.'

'Did you hire him?'

'No. But I am glad that he punished men who should have done better.' The steward then rose, bade Bray goodnight and left the buttery, saying one of his men would show Bray to the narrow chamber prepared for him.

Bray spent a restless night. The room was cold and grim. So uncomfortable after a poor night's sleep. He rose long before dawn. He went out into the courtyard, where some of the soldiers had started a fire and hung a cauldron of oatmeal above the flames. Bray, head and face hidden by a deep cowl, joined them. He remained quiet as he listened to the chatter. He discovered that most of the men hailed from the northern shires, veterans of the recent wars, who now tramped the roads looking for work, or to be included in some great lord's retinue. They were friendly enough, openly discussing the possibility of plunder as well as reward.

Bray cleared his bowl, got to his feet, and once again walked the priory. Standing on the parapet above the main gate, Bray wondered what Maillac would do next. He beat his hand against the stone and stared into the thinning darkness. 'Rest assured, Reginald,' he spoke to himself, 'something is about to happen and it's not going to be pleasant. The stuff of nightmares.' He thought of those men sitting around the campfire in the stable yard, good men doing the only thing they could: fighting for some lord. Bray, however, had a feeling of real danger. Maillac was a fool. Neville was a fool, and both of them were leading their followers to a most gruesome death.

Callista the maid slipped out of the buttery door and scurried across the small cobbled yard. Night was falling, the shadows lengthening. It was also a night of rich promise. The sky was clear, the moon full, and the stars seemed to hang even lower. The breeze was pleasant and the sounds of dusk echoed clear, the bark of a fox, the hooting of the owls and the last birdsong of the day. A good night, and Callista hoped it would be a prosperous one as well. She would earn fresh coin to hide away for the future. She would leave this place of bloodshed and sudden death on the morning of a beautiful spring day.

Plucking up her serge gown and thanking God for her sturdy sandals, Callista made her silent way across the grounds of The Moor and out on to the meadow land. She lifted her head as she reached Twilight Copse, her place of assignation. She moved into the darkness of the ancient oaks, peered around and made to go forward.

'No further, Callista.'

She stopped and leaned against the trunk of a tree, staring into the darkness, then she glimpsed it: a shape that shifted then stayed still.

'I have come,' Callista gasped, 'as you asked me. I glimpsed the scrap of parchment pushed into that crevice close to the pantry door. I always come when you summon me. Have I not brought morsels of information you've found useful? And I don't even know who you really are. Sometimes I wonder—'

'It's none of your business who I am, where I come from, where I go or what I do. So, we meet again at the usual place. I am very pleased you can read, Callista. You are a clever girl. Watching and waiting like a mouse from its hole.'

Callista shivered. She did not like the tone in what she called her 'stranger's' voice; a harshness she had not encountered before. She rubbed a sweaty hand down her cloak and wondered if she should turn and leave. I mean, after all, she did not know who this stranger truly was. He simply pushed a piece of parchment into a wall crevice and expected her to come here at the time stipulated. She would come, she would talk, she would receive a coin and that was it. Previous meetings had been pleasant, but Callista sensed a sharpness here, a change of mood and attitude.

'You've been watching everybody, haven't you, Callista? As well as taking coin from the countess, and that's why I wanted to see you. So, what have you learned?'

'I don't . . .'

'What have you learned, Callista?'

'Everybody seems to be waiting.'

'For what?'

'I don't know. But there's been more murders. You know that? Colworth was slain outside Angel Tower. I never saw who was responsible, but I glimpsed Poppleton running around with a cane in his hand.'

'Oh, that fool.' The words were spat out. 'He must be approaching his time of reckoning. I mean, all the others have died and I suppose he will too. Let us see if his murder is as gory as Chadwick's. So, what else have you learned? You say everyone is waiting, preparing?'

'Yes the countess is busy in her chamber.'

'Doing what, Callista?'

'Writing letters. The Nevilles are preparing for something but we are not too sure whether the King is coming or not. Master Urswicke wanders the house. Bray has left. Some of the servants who journey to and from Rickmansworth talk of seeing many strangers in the vicinity. Sir, I do hear and see so many things . . .'

'Yes, but can you be trusted, Callista?'

'I have served you well.'

'Who am I, Callista?'

'I don't know. Sometimes I suspect, I mean your voice . . .'

'I am Achitophel.'

'You?'

'Of course. Do you suspect who I really am? Oh dear!'

Callista realized she had made a hideous mistake. She should not have come to Twilight Copse. She should have kept her suspicions to herself. She turned to flee but it was too late. The dark shape she had glimpsed earlier now hurtled towards her. She stumbled on an ancient root, as if it had been thrust up from hell to catch her. Achitophel certainly did, and the knife he carried opened Callista's soft young throat from ear to ear. He let her body slump, shaking and trembling, to the ground. Eventually she lay still, the blood gushing out to soak the ground. Achitophel then grabbed her by the hood and pulled her along the narrow, winding forest path to the thick green morass, a marsh created in a small dell by an underground stream. He lifted the young woman's corpse, small and lithe, and hurled it into the shifting, treacherous morass. He watched it float for a while before it sank and disappeared completely.

*   *   *

It was late afternoon, the sun slipping like a fiery ball above the trees, when the bray of a war horn roused the priory to life. Bray, tending to his horse in the stables, joined Maillac and his henchmen on the main parapet walk above the gateway. Peering through the crenellations, Bray's heart sank; his worst fears had been realized. He quietly cursed Maillac's total lack of experience. A battle group had emerged from the line of trees; a long line of men armoured for war. On the flanks of this battle group, horsemen holding the flapping banners of the Crown, the Guildhall and the personal coat of arms of Sir Thomas Urswicke, Recorder of London. Between these horsemen, a phalanx of archers and men-at-arms, and behind these at least four war carts. Mounted on one of these was a stout battering ram. The battle group just deployed then stood in ominous silence, as if trying to frighten the defenders of the priory with a silent, sinister menace.

'Didn't you despatch spies into the trees?' Bray hissed, coming alongside Maillac.

'I never thought that they would bring such a battle group. I thought Sir Thomas was journeying with a small escort.'

'He did,' Bray retorted. 'But he deceived you. This phalanx probably mustered somewhere to the north, with instructions to move swiftly when summoned into the forest. Don't you realize, Maillac, you've been lied to, cruelly deceived, horribly tricked? Now the game which was planned in the shadows comes out into the light.'

Bray fell silent as a horseman left the right flank of the battle group and cantered to rein in just beyond arrow-shot of the gateway. The messenger carried a lance with a crucifix and a white cloth lashed to it. He waved this as he stood high in the stirrups.

'Your message?' Maillac yelled.

'Surrender or face total annihilation.'

The herald pulled his horse back as a bowman, leaning between the crenellations, loosed a fire arrow to thud in the ground before the envoy. The rider simply turned and cantered back as a line of archers raced from the forest to kneel and loose a whistling arrow storm. The air turned acrid with smoke, whilst the stench of burning pitch and tar rose, to sting both mouth and nostrils. The darkness deepened. Night fell, but the besiegers continued to loose volley after volley of fire arrows. A few casualties occurred. The enemy bowmen retreated. Bray, sheltering behind the parapet wall, thought it was over for the night when a rush of flame erupted from behind the besiegers' line. A column of fire roared up to the dark sky. A war cart emerged from the line of trees, soaked in grease, oil, pitch and tar: it was pushed by hooded figures leaning on poles fixed to either side. The flaming cart, a moving wall of fire, a sheer sheet of flame, was pushed up the small incline then down, aiming for the main gate. The wagon trundled, gathering speed. Those managing it now held back. Two of them were caught by arrow shafts loosed from the walls. The rest swiftly retreated, leaving the cart to rattle, crashing and juddering, to smash into the main gate. The flames eagerly caught the old dried wood of the gateway. Maillac screamed for water to be brought. Bray realised the besiegers were not going to waste the night. This was a fearsome assault to capture the priory and all within it. Bray glanced over the wall, now being stripped of defenders so as to deal with the fire below.

The besiegers were determined not to miss any opportunity. Men were now racing forward with long narrow siege ladders. Some of these collapsed as bowmen on the walls selected their targets, but there were too many of them. The smoke deepened, swirling in thick clouds. War horns brayed. Trumpets shrilled. Bray heard a clatter and glanced up from where he was crouched. A siege ladder had been rammed against the crenellations, its sharp iron hooks biting into the stone. Bray cautiously got to his feet and glanced to his left and right. Men were now pouring through the undefended crenellations and he realised it was over. Some of the attackers carried poles from which red and black banners fluttered in the light of the different fires now burning fiercely. Sir Thomas was sending the enemy a message. He had issued his order. No mercy was to be shown. No quarter offered. No pardon possible.

A figure sprang out of the dark. Bray sidestepped then crashed into his assailant, who toppled from the parapet to the courtyard below. Bray hurried to the steps. The fiery fury of the struggle was spreading. The attackers had now brought up their battering ram, crashing through the burning cart to pound the weakened gate. Corpses lay sprawled in thickening puddles of blood on the cobbles. Cries, screams and curses shrilled in a hellish din. The scrape and clash of steel was constant. The sheer fury of the assault was having its way. Sir Thomas's men could now gather on the parapet to loose more arrows against the defenders grouped around the gate.

Bray picked up a fallen sword, then hurried across into the bleak, grey stone chapel. Before entering the church, he threw the sword down and, once inside, snatched a crucifix from the wall above the baptismal font. Bray cautiously made his way down the nave to sit on the steps leading up through the forbidding rood screen into the sanctuary. Cradling the cross, Bray simply sat and waited.

Time passed. The clamour of battle outside grew like a hell-bent hymn of merciless slaughter in a fight to the death. At last, as with every battle, the clash of steel and the hideous roar of war cries faded into an ominous silence. The chapel door, which Bray had bolted behind him, crashed back on its leather hinges. A group of men, sword and dagger drawn, strode up the nave. Two of these carried spluttering cresset torches, creating a pool of light around their leader, Sir Thomas Urswicke. The Recorder was all harnessed and buckled, the visor of his helmet raised to reveal his sweat-soaked face. The sword and dagger he carried were bloodied to the hilt, both blades still dripping as the Recorder drew closer.

'Who are you?' Sir Thomas moved closer. 'Ah yes, Master Reginald Bray, a man I rarely acknowledge. So, tell me on your life, why do I find you in this nest of treasonable vipers?'

'Oh, quite simple . . .' Bray paused at a hideous scream from outside.

'The enemy wounded.' Sir Thomas took off his helmet, stepping closer, eyes intent on Bray. 'Why is it simple, traitor?'

'I am no traitor,' Bray replied quietly. 'I sit here in church and claim sanctuary. I am innocent of any crime. I am not here by my own wishes and I wish to be gone.'

'So why are you here?'

'Sir Thomas, I had no choice. I was pointed here by no lesser person than your henchman, Brasenose. Or should I say the charts he kept in secret pouches just beneath the horn of his saddle. Your son discovered them and they form part of his investigation; that is why I am here. I have them with me and now I return them to you. Two charts. One of The Moor, which undoubtedly is next on your places to visit, and the second is of Holy Blood Priory.'

Bray dug into his wallet, plucked out the thin scrolls and thrust them into Sir Thomas's gauntleted hand. The Recorder studied them closely before letting them fall to the ground.

'You planned all this from the beginning,' Bray accused. 'You knew what Maillac was going to do, where he would go, and whom he would recruit. It was just a matter of watching and waiting. Robert of Redesdale, or whatever he calls himself, threaded men into this forest, ordering them to muster here in this deserted priory. You kept them under close watch, didn't you, bringing in verderers and huntsmen from the royal household, yes?'

'I hear what you say,' the Recorder replied. 'But I still found you consorting with traitors.'

'I have told you once, I will tell you again,' Bray replied casually. 'I was curious, and I am working on behalf of your son who holds a royal commission to investigate certain matters at The Moor. I knew nothing of Maillac's plans. As I said, I was curious about the map and reports of armed men entering the forest, so I hired a local man to guide me here. Maillac had him killed.'

'I know. We passed his corpse bobbing on the edge of a marsh.'

'I was detained here against my will. See, I have no warbelt; that was taken from me when I arrived. I had no hand in that fighting except to protect myself.'

'Yes, we saw that too.'

'I am a loyal subject of the Crown. The henchman of the countess of Richmond, whose loyalty to the King cannot be questioned.'

'Enough,' Sir Thomas snapped. 'Find your warbelt, resaddle your horse and join me outside the main gate.'

Bray did so, moving around the slaughter house with corpses sprawled everywhere. Sir Thomas's men were now only concerned with plunder. They made sure their victim was truly dead before helping themselves to coins, belts, personal jewellery, even a stout set of boots. Bray found his own property on a chair just inside the refectory and, as he did, he heard the most heart-chilling screams from the stable yard. Bray left the refectory and went into the yard. No mercy had been shown. The ground was strewn with cadavers, blood trickling between the stones to form thick, glinting puddles. This was an execution ground. Those defenders who had surrendered had been forced to their knees and summarily decapitated. Their corpses still spouted blood, the severed heads rolling backwards and forwards like gore-soaked balls. A fire had been built up beneath a door taken from somewhere in the priory. Spreadeagled across this lay Maillac, naked as he was born, jerking against the ropes which held him fast. The fire was growing in strength, the tortured steward turned his bloodied face towards Bray.

'In God's name!' he begged, then screamed as the bolts hammered into the door, grew red hot to burn the prisoner's already bruised body.

'Step closer,' Sir Thomas taunted. 'See what happens to traitors.'

Bray did so, wrinkling his nose at the gruesome stench of burning human flesh.

'Like a rabbit on a skillet,' Sir Thomas declared.

'Please Bray!' Maillac turned his head, mouth gaping in suffocation. Bray could take no more. He drew his sword and in one stroke sliced Maillac's throat. The prisoner coughed, shuddered then hung still. Bray stepped back, as Sir Thomas came alongside him.

'Executed! A true traitor. He not only confessed to being in arms against the King but claimed he and his coven were marching on The Moor to seize, attack and murder our noble Lord and his principal henchmen.' Sir Thomas smiled. 'He claimed he was going to meet up with other traitors residing there. He could have told me more but you, Master Bray, silenced him. I understand that you too are travelling to The Moor so as to meet your countess, who also resides there.'

PART SIX

'Many other diverse gentlemen and yeomen were sent to that Manor of The Moor.'

Christopher Urswicke was dreaming about his father on that morning before the eve of the Feast of St George. A pleasant enough dream of the golden time before the shadows closed in. He was roused from his sleep by an insistent rapping on the door and, when he answered it, exclaimed in surprise. Mauclerc, all dressed and armed, stood there, a strange look on his face. Behind him Poppleton, similarly attired.

'Gentlemen?'

'We have news,' Mauclerc grated. 'Sir Thomas and his host, a large comitatus are making their way here. Messengers have arrived to inform His Grace the Archbishop as well as share the news of a fierce ambuscade at Holy Blood Priory.'

Urswicke kept his face impassive. 'In which case, gentlemen, I will welcome my esteemed father. Yet, I am mystified why you have roused me at such an early hour with such news.'

'There's more.' Poppleton came out of the shadows. Urswicke caught the smell of leather, sweat and horse dung.

'Patmore,' Mauclerc declared. 'He has locked himself in his chamber and we cannot rouse him.'

'So why did you rouse me?'

'You hold a royal commission,' Mauclerc replied, 'to investigate happenings here at The Moor. You know you do.'

'And you think this is a "happening"?'

'I suspect that something is very wrong. When an able-bodied man does not answer loud and insistent knocking on his chamber door, something's amiss, surely? You are a royal commissioner, Master Urswicke. You, rather than His Grace, have the right to force that door. It needs to be done.'

Urswicke agreed, going back into his room. The two men
waited for Urswicke to hastily dress. Once completed, he strapped
on his warbelt and followed them down the gallery. Despite the
early hour, the household had been roused, as if the servants
suspected that something unwholesome had occurred. Retainers
fluttered like ghosts. A few carried tapers to light lanterns and a
host of capped candles. Others were opening windows and doors
or preparing to sweep, clean and polish. Mauclerc led them to
the guest chambers at the rear of the manor. Two labourers, armed
with mallets, were waiting outside one room. Urswicke was about
to order the door to be pounded open when he heard the archbishop's voice raised in protest, followed by that of his sister.
Both Nevilles swept up on to the gallery, loudly demanding what
was happening? Urswicke hastily informed them, Mauclerc
adding that it was the only way. The archbishop and his sister
shrugged and mumbled their agreement.

'Good,' Urswicke declared. 'That's how I want it. Gentlemen,'
he gestured at the labourers and pointed at the door 'smash that
down. I suspect it has bolts, one at the top, the other at the bottom.'

'Yes, and a lock, a simple device with a tooth-edged key,'
Mauclerc declared. 'I have been in that chamber a number of
times, I remember it well.'

'Break it down,' Urswicke repeated. 'We'd best stand aside.'

They let the labourers do their hammering; sharp, cracking
blows which snapped both lock and bolt. The door fell back,
crashing down like a drawbridge. Urswicke walked across it into
the gloomy chamber, the only light being a sliver of sunbeam
which seemed to point at the corpse, neck all twisted, turning
and creaking as it hung on the rope lashed around one of
the roof beams. A macabre sight, rendered even more so by the
reeking stench in the chamber and the squeak and squeal of
rodents and other vermin busy in the room's murky corners.

Urswicke asked for a lantern. One was swiftly produced and
Urswicke held it up so he could clearly see Patmore's thin,
scrawny face, full of the shock of sudden, violent death. His eyes
popping to burst, his mouth half open, the swollen tongue
held fast between yellowing teeth, the bloodless lips slightly
rolled back. The hanged man's belly, bowels and bladder had
emptied; the stench was so offensive that Urswicke gagged as

he drew his dagger and sawed at the rope. Once he had cut clear, Poppleton helped him lay the corpse out on a stretch of clear floor near the doorway. Urswicke went through the dead man's pockets and wallets, handing the paltry findings to Mauclerc. He found nothing significant. Trying not to stare at the victim's gruesome face, Urswicke turned the dead man's neck so he could slice the noose. He first stared hard, hiding his surprise, before he cut the rope just above the knot and threw it to one side. Ignoring the gasps and croaks of gas escaping from Patmore's stomach, Urswicke examined the victim's wrists for any sign of ligature or binding, but there was none. Urswicke turned to the others.

'In my humble view,' he declared, 'Patmore apparently committed suicide.' He stared round the narrow, fetid-smelling chamber and glimpsed the pewter goblet lying next to the stool which Patmore must have stood on before stepping off into eternity.

'What is that?' Urswicke went to grab the goblet but Mauclerc was nearer. He picked up the wine cup, sniffed and shook it before handing it to Urswicke.

'It smells all right,' Mauclerc declared.

Urswicke carefully examined the cup but could detect nothing amiss.

'So.' Urswicke put the goblet down. 'Patmore came in here. He bolted and locked the door, drank a cup of wine, then prepared to hang himself.' Urswicke walked back to the stool and calculated the distance between that and the rafter from which part of the rope still dangled. He stood on the stool, steadying himself, and realized Patmore would have had little difficulty in fastening the noose. He got down and gestured at the corpse. 'Who will . . .'

'I will,' Mauclerc declared. 'I will see to Patmore's swift burial. In the meantime,' Mauclerc's voice rose, 'you must know Sir Thomas is approaching with all haste and will be here soon.'

'Of course he will be,' Urswicke retorted. 'But let's keep to the matter in hand. Why should Patmore commit suicide?'

'You're not going to question me, are you?' Mauclerc laughed. 'Do you think I know what went on in Patmore's mind?'

'What about that young man? Would he know?'

'Oh for heaven's sake, Urswicke. Look around you. Is there any indication whatsoever that Patmore was murdered? The door was locked and bolted. There is no sign of any disturbance in the chamber. Nothing to indicate that Patmore was forced. He's dead and I neither smile nor weep. Patmore alive meant nothing to me and now he's gone . . .' Mauclerc pulled a face. 'He was a failed teacher, a failed lawyer; maybe he just felt that he had failed once too often. I'll have the corpse removed and I repeat, your father, the esteemed Recorder of London, will soon be with us.'

Sir Thomas Urswicke and his comitatus swept into The Moor just before the Angelus bell. A posse of mounted archers, with little ceremony or concern, dismounted and stormed through the palatial manor house, securing doors, windows and gates. Sir Thomas set up camp in the Great Hall. He commandeered the banqueting table on the dais at the far end to display his commission and warrants, along with his unsheathed sword and a book of the Gospels, snatched from a startled Father Benedict sheltering in the sacristy.

Bray arrived with the Recorder. The countess's henchman was tired, dusty and saddle-sore. He slipped away from Sir Thomas's retainers and joined the countess in her private chamber.

'The King's justiciar, the Lord High Recorder, has arrived as if he's God Almighty on horseback,' Bray declared, sinking into a cushioned chair and gratefully accepting the goblet of wine that Urswicke pushed into his hand. He toasted both the countess and Urswicke. 'And this,' he sighed, 'is what I know.'

Bray then gave a terse, pithy account of what had happened since he had left them. The countess assured him in a loud voice that she did not care who heard them, though in fact she gestured at both her henchmen to keep their voices low. Bray did as he recounted what had happened at Holy Blood Priory, and how Sir Thomas was determined to lay a charge of treason against all those sheltering at The Moor. Once he had finished, the countess and Urswicke described what they had done to defend themselves. They were still discussing this when they were summoned down to meet with Sir Thomas.

In the Great Hall, two benches had been placed before the dais. The Nevilles were already seated, both highly agitated, together with Poppleton, Mauclerc and the Imposter, who looked as pale faced and taciturn as ever. Urswicke noticed how he edged closer to Mauclerc, as if desperately seeking greater protection. Sir Thomas's archers ringed the room, guarding doors and windows.

They stood, bows strung, arrows notched. The Recorder himself sat behind the banqueting table, with a mailed clerk to his right and left, quill pens at the ready. Sir Thomas peremptorily directed the countess and her henchmen to the second bench. Once settled, Sir Thomas banged the table with the pommel of his dagger before rising to his feet and stepping off the dais to stand over the Nevilles.

'Maillac is dead,' he began, stooping down to glare in their faces. 'Your so-called steward, the foul traitor Maillac, is dead, as is the villain calling himself Robin of Redesdale. They and all their company; their bodies lie rotting at Holy Blood Priory, the fodder of birds and wild animals. Now listen. Maillac was questioned and, with witnesses present, confessed to devious, diabolic treasons. How you, my Lord Archbishop, together with others, including your sister, Maillac himself, de Vere of Oxford and the Countess of Richmond, were conspiring to seize and take prisoner our noble Lord King, together with whatever entourage he brought here. You invited the King to participate in the so-called festivities of the Feast of St George. An outrageous lie, as it masked a most treasonable plot. The threads are now clear. The Nevilles, the Countess of Richmond, Robert of Redesdale and John de Vere, Earl of Oxford. So,' the Recorder stepped back, hands clasped as if in prayer, 'what do you say my Lord Archbishop? How do you plead?'

'Mercy.' George Neville lurched forwards to prostrate himself at the Recorder's feet. His sister did likewise.

'Mercy, pardon,' she pleaded. 'We were misled. We were used, tricked and deceived by others.'

Her brother took up the same refrain until Sir Thomas stepped forward, pressing his boot firmly on the prostrate archbishop's shoulder, telling them to get up. Both Nevilles, still moaning and pleading, scrabbled back into their chairs. Sir Thomas was clearly enjoying himself.

'I shall,' he poked a finger at the accused, 'refer you to the King's pleasure and, whilst we wait, you will be securely lodged in the Tower so you can pray, fast and reflect on your crass stupidity. Now . . .' Sir Thomas turned, preening himself like a peacock strutting through the grass. 'Now, my Lady,' he pointed at the countess.

'Wait.' Christopher sprang to his feet. 'Can I remind you,

esteemed father, that I too hold the King's commission, a royal warrant and licence to investigate certain matters here at The Moor.' He paused and watched his father's face. Christopher had struck home, shifting himself – and by implication the countess – on to a more legal basis.

'And?' his father stuttered.

'I, as the King's justiciar, holding a commission which has not been revoked by the Crown, have a great deal to say. But first, the stupid and empty-headed allegations levelled against the Countess of Richmond must be dealt with. I have here, esteemed father . . .' Urswicke picked up the chancery satchel he'd brought down from the countess's chamber.

'What is this?' Sir Thomas murmured, the good humour draining from his face.

'Esteemed father, I have a number of letters signed, sealed and dated by my lady and despatched at least two days ago to the King, the council, the Mayor of London, the Archbishop of Canterbury, the Speaker of the Commons, the sheriffs of London, the Lord Chancellor and last, but certainly not least, my esteemed father, no lesser a person than yourself.'

'What letters?' Sir Thomas's face had turned slightly red. 'I received no such—'

'That's because, Sir Thomas,' the countess declared, 'you had probably left the Guildhall to attend to business here. I am sure my letters will be waiting for you on your return there. In the meantime, Christopher, give your father a copy of the missive I sent.'

Urswicke opened the satchel and took out a scroll tied with a red cord and embossed with the countess's seal; he handed this to his father. By now the Nevilles, startled by the sharp turn of events, had stopped their blubbering and sat, mouths gaping. Mauclerc, secretly enjoying the abrupt turn of events, held a hand to his face to hide his amusement. Now and again, he'd turn to give the Imposter a hug or touch him gently on the head. Poppleton just sat deep in the shadows at the end of the bench, watching warily.

'The letters,' the countess now rose to her feet, 'reveal my deep suspicions about a treasonable plot being formed here at The Moor, to do great damage to both Crown and court. How John de Vere, Earl of Oxford, and other rebels were to come here to meet fellow conspirators.'

'And how did you get to know all this?'

'By the same means as you, Sir Thomas. Logic, deduction, reflection, rumours, gossip, as well as the indefatigable work of Master Bray and the sharp enquiries of the King's justiciar, your son, Christopher Urswicke.' The countess waved a hand. 'And so on and so on. I was determined to discover more, hence my despatch of Master Bray, whom you met at the priory. Indeed, Sir Thomas, our deductions were proved correct.' The countess used her fingers to emphasise her argument. 'We learned that Oxford was going to land and come here. We guessed that a comitatus would be raised, a posse of men. We suspected the Nevilles. We collected the scraps of information like pieces of a tapestry and stitched them together to form a clearer picture. I was determined not to be drawn into anything treasonable, or what might even appear to be treasonable. We were forced to stay here. I tried to distance myself but this was vetoed, hence my letters protesting my innocence, and you must agree with them, yes Sir Thomas?'

The Recorder clicked his tongue, tapping a booted foot against the floor. Lady Grace began to whimper until the Recorder snarled at her to be quiet.

'Esteemed father.' Urswicke decided to make his move across this deadly chessboard.

'Yes, my son.' The Recorder smiled at Christopher, a genuine, gentle gesture, as if acknowledging his son's sharp wit.

'A word with you,' Christopher offered. 'We are two royal commissioners desperately seeking a way forward.'

Sir Thomas caught the sarcasm in his son's voice. He fluttered his fingers at Christopher, a sign to follow him down the long, cavernous hall to a corner where they could quietly converse.

'Right, esteemed father,' Christopher began, 'what is the real source of all this nonsense, this farrago of lies? You know the Nevilles as do I. You're also acquainted with that popular rhyme: "with the Nevilles all truth is gone, as they betray their allies one by one". In short, there is not a shred of evidence to indict my mistress.'

'Maillac's confession?'

'Oh come, come father! The testimony of a man being grilled alive over a roaring fire.'

'Then how did the countess learn what she did?'

'Rumour, gossip, and the good services of both myself and Master Bray and, above all, the countess's keen wits and sharp mind. Father, look at the alternative.' Christopher glanced over his shoulder; the others gathered in the hall sat silent spectators to this masque which threatened all kinds of danger.

'The alternative?'

'Yes, esteemed father, the Nevilles are treacherous. Oxford is desperate to intervene. Maillac was fanatically loyal to the Earl of Warwick. Robin of Redesdale and his ilk are, like the poor, always with us.' Christopher scratched his face. 'Father, it's like preparing ingredients for cooking. Why was my mistress invited here? Why should she be chosen to participate in the royal revelry? Why is it so important for Edward of England to honour the Feast of St George here at The Moor? Why not at Windsor, in the royal chapel dedicated to his name?' Christopher half laughed. 'My mistress sensed mischief was being planned. It wasn't hard to speculate, to suspect, what might truly happen, and of course it really did. But that does not mean my mistress is implicated. Now it has collapsed, face the reality. How would it look to the Lords Temporal and the Lords Spiritual, not to mention Lord Stanley, who is about to enter marriage negotiations with my mistress? What would all these people think of a dastardly, treacherous attempt to implicate a most revered and learned lady in a so-called plot against the Crown? The countess is also the mother of a claimant to the English Crown. There is no wrong in her being that. She is his mother, and he does have a claim to the throne.'

'Not in my eyes.'

'But, esteemed father, that is exactly my point. Politics divides. People have different opinions, it doesn't mean they are guilty of any crime. Moreover, her son Prince Henry, and I am talking about the true Prince Henry, shelters deep in Brittany. He does not interfere in this kingdom's affairs.'

'His mother certainly does.'

'She has every right to do what she has to, but may I refresh your memory, esteemed father. You created the Imposter. You brought him here to cause confusion as well as play a role in what has happened here. Would he also have been depicted as a traitor sheltering with his mother who was deeply implicated in some treasonable design? Well father, that has not happened. So, what will happen to him now?'

'He has served his purpose,' Sir Thomas retorted. 'I understand Patmore has taken his own life. Well, he can be buried at some crossroads with a stake driven through his heart. He has passed all usefulness. But, to return to the living, without Patmore to verify matters, there is, as I have said, little further use for our princeling. I will leave him to the tender mercies of Mauclerc. He seems to relate well to our young claimant.' Sir Thomas gave a lopsided smile. 'Whoever he might be.'

'So, beloved father, we now have the truth though, as St Paul said, we see it darkly as if through a glass. My Lady will be exonerated of even the slightest suspicion. The Imposter will fade away. Oxford will be sailing his ship as far out to sea as possible. Robin of Redesdale and his comitatus lie rotting in Holy Blood Priory, whilst the Nevilles will be referred to the King for his decision.' Christopher paused. 'Father, I warn you; I advise you that is the truth of the situation. Anything else could cause danger to us and, I believe, to you.'

'In what way?'

'As you well know. You failed to seize Oxford and my mistress emerges from all this as innocent as a newborn babe. True you have the Nevilles but, let's be honest, you had them already. There is nothing new in their treachery.'

'So it would seem. So it would seem.' Sir Thomas breathed, scratching the back of his head. 'But look at it this way, beloved son. Your mistress was put to the test and not found wanting and that's all we wanted to establish. The same cannot be said of others, but let's leave that for a while.' The Recorder took a step closer. 'Christopher, surely you have other business? You made great play about being the royal commissioner, the King's justiciar here, so what have you discovered?'

'A dark soul. Achitophel. Are you him?'

'Nonsense, my son.'

'But you have used him, father, you have sat and made compacts with this wraith of the night. But now it's all finished. The game is nearly over. The dice are being shaken; the throw is imminent. However, to ensure all is as it should be, I have one question for you. Only one, and I plead with you for the truth.'

'My son, what is it?'

'Did you hire Achitophel to bring about the destruction of Richard Neville, Earl of Warwick at Barnet?'

Sir Thomas glanced back down the hall.

'Please father, even though I suspect your answer, as I do the identity of Achitophel.'

'Yes,' Sir Thomas answered in a rush, 'when Edward occupied London and was preparing to march against Warwick.'

'How did Achitophel approach you?'

'He didn't. He approached Brasenose, my henchman, as he left a tavern, The Paradise of Night, close to the Guildhall. A meeting held in the deep dark, no more than whispered conversations. Achitophel declared who he was and that he could, for a price, ensure Warwick be left vulnerable during the coming conflict. He informed Brasenose he would return in an hour to the same place to collect what he called his fee.'

'But didn't you suspect this could have been trickery? Some ploy by a cunning man?'

'No, no.' Sir Thomas shook his head. 'Brasenose had heard of Achitophel as had I. Certainly it could have been some subtle trick. However, if that was the case, Achitophel, whoever he may be, would have been marked down by York. My son, as you may appreciate, you can play such a trick once, but it would be highly dangerous to try it a second time. So yes, we hired Achitophel and, in the end, Warwick was isolated and slain. Finally, beloved son, do trust me on this.'

'Yes father?'

Sir Thomas leaned so close, Christopher could smell the rose-water he'd washed his hands and face in.

'Never, ever,' Sir Thomas hissed, 'believe the story that King Edward wanted his old friend Warwick to be spared. No, Edward of York, and never forget this,' the Recorder's voice sank to a whisper, 'is ruthlessly determined to destroy the House of Lancaster, root and branch, both below and above ground.' The Recorder stepped back. 'Never forget that.' He grinned. 'Or that your mistress, on this occasion, was tried and not found wanting.'

'As she will ever be, esteemed father. But enough of threats and menacing hints. Let us finish this present business.'

PART SEVEN

'As soon as he came, the Archbishop was arrested and impeached of high treason.'

They returned to the dais. Christopher took one of the high, leather-backed chairs and placed it just before what Sir Thomas called his judgement table.

'Sir Thomas,' Christopher called out, 'I need two of your retainers to accompany Master Bray to one of the guest chambers.'

'Which one?'

'Oh, that of Master Matthew Poppleton who, indeed, as a royal commissioner, I order to bring himself to sit on this chair and so listen to the indictment I will place against him.'

'Nonsense!' Poppleton roared as he sprang to his feet.

The Recorder rapped out an order for two of his archers to accompany Bray from the hall. Four more gathered around Poppleton, who tried to resist, but he was pinioned, his warbelt removed and pushed across to the chair Urswicke had chosen. He was made to sit and, at the Recorder's behest, lashed with ropes to the chair.

'This is a nonsense,' the prisoner shouted. 'Sir Thomas, my Lord Archbishop . . .'

'No, no listen well, Master Poppleton.' Urswicke folded back the sleeves of his gown. 'You are a mercenary, a man who sells his soul as well as his sword to the highest bidder. You enjoy, no you actually revel in the war which has ravaged this kingdom. Over the years, you have learnt how to move like a shadow, slipping between the different factions. For you are Achitophel, a true son of Judas.'

'I am nothing but a simple soldier.'

'That is not true. You were in fact the captain of the Five

Wounds, Warwick's personal bodyguard, a small battle group dedicated to protecting your master.'

'We have touched on this before; we have explained what we did.'

'No, you confessed to doing nothing; nothing wrong but nothing right. You had already sold your master after you had entered into a compact with Sir Thomas Urswicke. Barnet provided the ideal opportunity. The faded dawn light, the dense, swirling mist. Did you also advise your master to fight on foot, making him more vulnerable? The battle swirled backwards and forwards, and you led your company a merry dance along the outskirts of that blood-spattered skirmish. You did what any professional assassin would have done. You withdrew the guard. No one would suspect that – either then or later. Except,' Urswicke raised a hand, 'perhaps Mark Chadwick, and that was the one great flaw in your treacherous design. Time! Months would pass into years and perhaps your comrades would begin to reflect, to recall, to remember, and perhaps to wonder what truly happened on that gore-strewn battlefield.'

'Who would care?' Mauclerc jibed. 'Warwick was another Lancastrian bastard sent into the dark.'

'I would care,' Lady Grace abruptly asserted, drawing herself up in the chair. She no longer acted the broken, tearful lady. She glared at Mauclerc then pointed dramatically at Poppleton. 'Traitor!' she spat out.

'Traitor indeed, my Lady.' Urswicke moved to stand over her. 'You mistress,' he leaned slightly forward, 'you know the truth of all this. Oh yes, you trip trip trip after your twin brother and support his madcap schemes. He can hide behind his sacred orders and plead he is a cleric whilst you can act the distracted demoiselle, not really aware of what is happening. Oh but you are.' Urswicke held Lady Grace's stare. 'Hard of heart and hard of mind, but here is an opportunity to redeem yourself. He,' Urswicke pointed at Poppleton, 'played a most decisive part in the disaster at Barnet where two of your brothers were slain. Indeed,' Urswicke tapped his foot against the floor, 'because John and Richard Neville fell, others did.'

'I don't—' Poppleton protested.

'Oh shut up,' Lady Grace snarled. Her voice, sharp as a lash, silenced Poppleton. 'I was approached by Achitophel. A message through one of our retainers: how a mysterious stranger, cloaked in darkness, was waiting for me amongst the ancient oaks of Twilight Copse, a clump of trees, their branches interwoven to cut out the light. He claimed to have news about my two brothers killed at Barnet.'

'Weren't you suspicious?'

'Of course not, Master Urswicke. The battles of Barnet and Tewkesbury were disastrous to the House of Lancaster. We have many visitors; men who fled for their lives, who pass through here. Sometimes they bring scraps of information about the battle or about this person or that. Sometimes they just want help; some coins, food and drink, or a stable loft to sleep in.'

'And you would go out all alone?'

'Twilight Copse lies just over the border of our estate, a mere stroll on a warm, sunny afternoon. Maillac came with me, though I told him to hang back and only intervene if I called. In the end there was no need. The stranger, cloaked and hooded, his voice no more than a whisper, informed me that the Company of the Five Wounds, under that creature,' she flicked her fingers at Poppleton, 'had deliberately deserted my brother. They had betrayed him, left him vulnerable by wandering the edge of the battlefield. Of course, he depicted Poppleton as the moving spirit behind such treason.'

'Of course, of course,' Urswicke interjected. 'Suspicion was cleverly diverted, Poppleton being held up as the real traitor.' Urswicke smiled thinly. 'He actually offered himself up as the perpetrator. A very cunning move.'

'Yes, yes,' Lady Grace agreed. 'The stranger, who I now realize is Poppleton, said he had the truth of the matter. He offered, for a very steep price, not only to kill each and every one of them, but to do so in a manner which mocked their hypocritical name, the Company of the Five Wounds. I agreed. The price was very high but what he offered was sweet revenge. Justice for my two brothers.'

'And there was more on offer?'

'Oh yes.' Lady Grace's face was now slightly red, her breathing short and sharp. 'Oh yes,' she repeated, 'by the time I met Achitophel, news had reached us of the impending arrival of two of Sir Thomas's henchmen, Brasenose and Rutger. Achitophel gave me a detailed account of how Brasenose received the injuries to his face at Barnet, a life and death struggle between him, Rutger and my brother John. I had heard rumours, gossip and chatter from a number of sources which alleged the same. Anyway,' she waved a hand, 'Achitophel said if I would double the fee, he would take care of both miscreants.' Lady Grace ignored Sir Thomas's spluttered curse. 'I asked him how could I trust him? Achitophel told me not to pay a coin until both henchmen and the first of the Company of the Five Wounds were slain. I waited. I did not betray to anyone, not even my brother, what I intended. All I knew was that I could strike back.' Her voice quavered. 'My two beautiful brothers. You know I went to St Paul's and I saw their corpses in that arrow box, naked and wounded. I went back in time to when we were children running naked through a field to splash and swim in some mere or pond. They were just lying there in the cold embrace of death, pieces of meat, flung there for strangers to gape and wonder at. Oh yes, I accepted Achitophel's offer,' she pointed at Poppleton, 'you know that and I don't deny it. I'd do the same again.' She paused to catch her breath. 'Once Brasenose and Rutger were dead and the first of the Company of the Five Wounds, I was to leave good, freshly minted gold coins in a purse pinned to the very oak I was standing by.' Lady Grace fell silent as the Recorder, still cursing, rose to his feet, scraping back his chair.

'Esteemed father, Sir Thomas,' Urswicke called, 'please wait until my indictment ends.'

Breathing heavily, the Recorder swallowed hard, nodded and retook his seat. Urswicke glanced quickly around. The countess sat, face impassive, threading her ave beads through mittened fingers. Mauclerc, hands cupping his face, looked as though he was thoroughly enjoying himself. George Neville just slumped, a broken man, though his sister sat upright, smiling to herself at a deed well done.

'The killings began,' she declared, 'and I left the gold.'

'They certainly did, yes Poppleton?' Urswicke accused. 'Because you are Achitophel, a veteran soldier, a silent, skilled assassin, who could slip like a shadow around this palace. You followed Brasenose into that maze. He was your first victim. He was not a member of the Company of the Five Wounds, though you made reference to that in the way you slaughtered him. A crossbow bolt, high in his back just beneath the neck. You then stabbed the corpse four times, a reference to the Five Wounds; people could draw what conclusions they wanted. Rutger was next. He may have died a drunkard, but Rutger was sharp. For God knows what reason, he immediately began to wonder if Brasenose's death, here in this Neville stronghold, was connected somehow to the death of the Neville brothers at Barnet in which he and Brasenose had been so deeply involved. I suspect that might explain his enigmatic remark about what we do is more important than who we are. Was he referring to John Neville's death at the hands of his master? We shall never know because his murder followed swiftly. Rutger, sorrowing over Brasenose, drank to forget. He staggered out to that latrine. You followed. Once Rutger was settled inside, you crept across and pulled open the door to the closet. Rutger, all confused and bleary-eyed, glanced up, exposing his throat to your dagger gashing him from ear to ear.'

Christopher ignored the whispered curses of his father. 'Afterwards, armed with a crossbow, you stayed in that yard. You were waiting to see if anyone else – needing the jakes or curious about the night light burning there – came into the enclosure. You were rewarded. Fladgate comes out and crosses to the jakes. Silent as moonlight, you follow and deliver a bolt to the poor man's head, the first of the Five Wounds to die.' Urswicke walked slowly away and stood head down, wondering if Bray would discover anything incriminating. Christopher prayed that he would. Bray had a unique talent for probing the secrets of others.

He walked back to stand over the accused, bound securely to the chair by Sir Thomas's archers. 'Poor Forester was next, full of guilt about what happened at Barnet, so much so that he frequently indulged in bathing from head to toe. I can understand why. And do you know, Poppleton, I am certain you have studied the human heart. As I have said before, your companions failed their master and, rightly or wrongly, they were blamed. You played on that when you pinned those doggerel verses to the chapel door here: that was your handiwork. Now, sometimes, thoughts turn and turn again. People become lost in a maze of

their own making and they try to find their way out. I just wonder
if Forester, like Chadwick, had begun to wonder about the truth
of what happened at Barnet. I mention this,' Urswicke gestured
at the accused, 'because Lady Grace, although you hired
Achitophel, Poppleton here, to carry out revenge on your behalf,
I believe he would have done so anyway, just to silence burgeoning
suspicions. Surely one of the Five Wounds would have begun to
wonder why they wandered backwards and forwards across that
battlefield. But all of this is conjecture. I have no real proof.
Suffice to say that Forester was the next to die. He was getting
ready to bathe when Poppleton knocked on his door with a goblet
of wine. Forester would not be embarrassed at the arrival of an
old comrade, in fact his captain. He would throw a robe around
himself, take the goblet of wine and drink deeply, listening to
Poppleton's empty chatter about some matter or other. The wine
undoubtedly contained some dream powder. Forester fell into a
deep sleep. You gagged him and drove those spikes through his
wrists at a point where the blood flows strong. Forester could
not save himself. He died almost instantly, the injuries on his
corpse a blasphemous mockery of the cult of our Saviour's
wounds.' Urswicke leaned down. 'How say you, sir?'

'How say I?' Poppleton spat back, his eyes full of fury, lips
curled like a snarling dog.

'Oh, I am sure you would kill me, Poppleton. I had to be very
careful that you never suspected that I was hunting your soul. I
am hunting it, God wants to meet you. You are a true killer,
Poppleton, aren't you? A doom-laden shadow, responsible for so
many slayings in this cause or that. You rejoice like a farmer at
harvest time. You revel in the blood of the slaughter house.'
Poppleton just glared back, eyes all fierce. 'An assassin to the
very marrow. You showed no mercy for the likes of poor
Chadwick. Now there's another man torn by guilt with scruples
and doubts. I suspect he was beginning to question the accepted
story about Warwick's death and the failure of the Five Wounds
to protect him. A curdling suspicion, a deepening unease. I found
a scrap of parchment on his corpse: a list of the Five Wounds,
and beside each name strange symbols; some kind of secret
cipher containing what? Information about who was where at
Barnet? Or was it a record of how each of his comrades died?

We will never know. Oh yes,' Urswicke sipped from his goblet, 'Chadwick was troubled. He certainly wanted to escape from this House of the Red Slayer, he said as much to Father Benedict at the mercy pew. Perhaps he felt that not only would he be safe in some refuge, but he would be free to reflect and recall events on that battlefield. You watched, Master Poppleton! You waited then you struck! You followed Chadwick out into the dark. He intended to flee; you were determined he would not. You loosed a crossbow bolt to the back of his head, then you hacked off his feet, a sacrilegious, blasphemous parody of the title you all shared.'

'You haven't mentioned Colworth,' Mauclerc demanded. 'The one slain outside Angel Tower.'

'Ah yes. Poor Colworth! Now there's one soldier who didn't die in vain, because,' Urswicke jabbed a finger at Poppleton, 'this is where you made a truly fatal mistake. All the others died in the dark, sudden and silent. One minute living, the next cruelly slain. You had become immersed in the game, hadn't you? You were thoroughly enjoying yourself. At the same time you needed to create the illusion that the killer was someone else here at The Moor. After all, so you would argue, if the finger of suspicion was ever raised, you were with Chadwick when Colworth was slain. You could act the innocent, the comrade who came running down those steps to confront Colworth's killer. However, because you were not properly armed, you could only use a walking pole and then the assassin fled. All a silly nonsense. So arrogant, you never reflected.'

'Explain.' Sir Thomas's voice was almost a shout.

'Yes, what do you mean?' The accused pressed against the cords restraining him. 'What do you mean?' he repeated, snarling like the animal he was.

'I mean this.' Urswicke went and opened the chancery satchel and took out a small leather sack. He opened this carefully and plucked out the dagger, placing it on the table. 'You forgot about this, didn't you?' Urswicke taunted. 'You should have been more careful. You see, I went out to Angel Tower. I climbed the steps, noticing all those little recesses and shadowy corners. I scrutinised the pegs driven into the wall on the tower platform. Then I came down and inspected that rarely used jakes closet.' Urswicke paused. 'From the very beginning,' he continued, 'I was intrigued by your account of what had happened. Apparently, you and Chadwick met at the tower and climbed to the top. A pleasant day, you could enjoy the breezes, have a sip of wine, look out over the countryside and, above all, discuss what was happening at The Moor. You and Chadwick took off your sword belts and looped them over those pegs I have just described. Colworth arrives and knocks on the door leading into the tower. You rise, you consider strapping on your warbelt but then changed your mind. After all, you are going down to meet a comrade, aren't you? That's what happened, yes?'

'Of course.' Poppleton gasped as he tried to ease the cramps of his bonds.

'Now what really happened,' Urswicke continued, 'is that you stretched out and, unbeknown to Chadwick, you not only put your sword belt back on the peg, but created a tangle with that of your comrade's. It's easily done when more than one item hangs from a peg, be it a cloak or sword belt. You act calmly and assuredly, telling Chadwick to stay whilst you go down to unlock the door.'

'That's the truth,' Poppleton replied

'Oh yes it is. The lie began when you opened the door. There was no one there but Colworth, all expectant. You swiftly lunged forward with that dagger.'

'I had no warbelt.'

'Of course you didn't.' Urswicke picked up the dagger he had placed on the table; a long, thin, wicked-looking blade with the sharpest point and a serrated edge, the horn handle easy to grip. 'You had certainly prepared well. You had hidden this dagger in one of the many dusty, shadow-filled recesses along the tower steps. You take it on the way down and hurry on to meet your comrade. Colworth is totally unprepared. You close quickly with him and stab deep, a deadly thrust to the left side, straight to the heart. A mockery of that wound suffered by Christ. Colworth collapses. You seize one of those walking canes and create your own tumult at the foot of those steps before throwing the dagger down that jakes hole, where Blod the dung collector later found it.'

'No, the assailant could have . . .'

'Nonsense, you yourself described the so-called attacker: how he was weaponed with both sword and dagger, so how could he hold a third? Anyway, why should he throw his blade away? Now, to return to my indictment. Chadwick, at the top of the tower, is roused by all the noise and clamour. Like the soldier he is, he immediately seizes his warbelt but he has to deal with the tangle you have deliberately created. A clever ploy to provide you with more time in carrying out Colworth's murder. Eventually, Chadwick untangles his belt from yours and goes cautiously down. You know, as we all do, never to hurry down such steep, winding, sharp steps. Despite the noise of the affray, Chadwick would be cautious, giving you even more time. He eventually reaches the stairwell and the rest we all know. You describe yourself as gallantly wielding a walking cane, a tale of closing with the assassin who apparently turned and fled. You pursued him with no success and returned to ensure that Colworth was truly dead. You planned his murder . . .'

Urswicke broke off as Bray and the two archers came back into the hall. Bray carried a small, reinforced coffer and placed it on the table. He then pulled back the concave lid and took out a few small treasury sacks. Once it was empty, Bray tugged hard, lifting the false bottom of the casket and plucked out two bulging, brocaded pouches, which clinked as Bray dropped them on to the table. Lady Grace, who sat face in her hands, stood up and immediately yelled that those purses were the same as the ones she'd given Achitophel. Poppleton sighed noisily, head bowed, as he realized his life was about to be torn away. Christopher confronted him. 'It's finished,' he murmured, leaning down, 'the case weighs heavily against you. You are Achitophel, a master of murder, the cause of all the deaths here.'

'Except Patmore's.' The archbishop, who had sat silent as a statue, made to rise, but an archer standing close by pressed him on the shoulder to sit.

'What about Patmore, my Lord Archbishop?' Urswicke replied, staring at the prisoner. 'Though it's true,' he added softly, 'that is one death that cannot be placed at your door. So, let me return to my indictment. Chadwick's death was meant to seal the past. Once he was gone, the Company of the Five Wounds no longer existed. Not one of them would survive to reflect on days past;

on what really happened on that mist-bound Easter Sunday morning when Richard Neville, the great Earl of Warwick, stumbled to his death.'

'All of them?' Mauclerc bawled. 'Poppleton would have survived!'

'Oh yes,' Urswicke agreed. 'With the death of his four companions, it was time for Matthew Poppleton, not to mention Achitophel, to disappear. After all, the war has finished. York reigns supreme.'

'He certainly does,' Sir Thomas yelled.

'And may Heaven bless him,' Urswicke replied gently. 'But, be that as it may,' he hurried on, 'Achitophel's services would no longer be needed. It was time for him to collect his earnings, the blood money he had garnered over the years, and disappear to emerge as a completely different person.' Urswicke paused then began to walk up and down. He stopped before the accused. 'Who are you?' he demanded. 'I mean the truth. I doubt very much whether you are Matthew Poppleton. I don't think those were the names given when you were held over the baptismal font in some lonely parish church. No, no,' Urswicke shook his head, 'I wager you are someone completely different. You are as clever and as skilled as any mailed clerk, yet you are also a soldier. Perhaps a defrocked priest or some sort of cleric? What exists behind that mask? The way you present yourself. Well?' Poppleton simply glared back. 'Whatever,' Urswicke accused. 'Years ago, when civil strife tore this kingdom apart and the Lord Almighty went to war, you seized your opportunity. You became Achitophel, a professional Judas man, moving between the warring camps, selling information, offering possibilities. A most lucrative trade. You honed your skills. You became as adept and as skilled as any actor in a masque. You could play your part and move between enemies without any hindrance or hesitation, but then the times began to change. They always do, whether you like it or not. Edward of York is now master of his own house; he will crush all opposition.'

'Amen to that,' Sir Thomas and Mauclerc chorused together.

'Oh yes,' Urswicke echoed back. 'Amen to that and farewell to Matthew Poppleton. He in fact was going to be your last victim. He would cease to exist.'

'Don't be . . .'

'Stupid? No no. Master Poppleton's corpse, its face severely disfigured would, before summer's end, be found in some country ditch. He'd be wearing your clothes and have enough on his person for the local coroner or beadle to conclude that Matthew Poppleton, veteran soldier in the late wars, had either been attacked or had fallen ill of some infection. The corpse would be swiftly buried and that would be the end of Matthew Poppleton. In truth, the true soul or spirit of Achitophel would, like a fresh, poisonous plant, survive to flourish again. You are well garnished with good coin. You would assume a new name, title and trade. You would alter your appearance; the way you walk, the way you spoke, as you merged into some thriving village community as a successful trader. They would accept you. They would be grateful for your generosity. You would attend church on Sunday and holy days. You would pay court to the daughter of some prosperous yeoman, even becoming a member of the parish council. You would certainly have enough wealth to live high on the hog.' Urswicke walked to a side table where he swiftly drank some ale before walking back. 'Of course,' he continued, 'this will not happen. Prepare yourself well, Achitophel, the ghosts of all your victims are beginning to gather. They have come for you and they will not be refused.'

'They certainly are.' Sir Thomas came around the table and, before anyone could intervene, lunged at Poppleton, his gauntleted fist smashing time and again into the prisoner's face. Despite his son's shouted warnings, the rain of blows continued. At last, the Recorder, face twisted in anger, staggered back, catching his breath whilst Poppleton's cries sank to a pathetic whimper. Christopher swiftly intervened.

'If you confess . . .' he declared, staring at Poppleton's bloodied face.

'If he confesses,' Sir Thomas yelled, 'he'll have a swift death. But if not,' he pointed a finger at Poppleton, 'you'll die the death of a traitor. You will be torn apart by the executioner over Tyburn stream.'

'Do you?' Christopher insisted. 'Do you want to leave life in such a bloody manner?'

'Oh, by the way,' Sir Thomas yelled, still incandescent with fury. He pointed at the treasure casket Bray had brought down. 'That, and everything in it, is mine. Indeed,' Sir Thomas walked up and down, as if inspecting the tapestries and other treasures hanging on the wall, 'all of this is mine. Well, the King's, but it's mine to give him.'

'Take it all, esteemed father.'

'Very good, very good.' Sir Thomas pointed at the prisoner. 'And you Master Poppleton, what say ye?'

'It is,' the prisoner slurred, straining against his bonds, 'it is as you say.' His mouth bubbled blood and spittle.

'Louder!' Sir Thomas yelled. The prisoner complied, with a blood-splattering shout. 'Good.' The Recorder snapped his fingers at the archers standing close by. 'Take him out, find a priest to shrive him. What's his name?' He turned to his son.

'Chaplain Benedict, esteemed father.'

'That's right, take him to the priest. You two,' the Recorder jabbed a finger at the Nevilles, 'both of you stay here or I'll hang you as well. Beloved son,' he continued, 'as you have said so often, you are the royal commissioner here in this place. I ask you and the lady countess to remain. Mauclerc, see to the hanging!'

'I am not—'

'You will do what you are told.' The Recorder clapped his hands. 'Come, come now, you have your orders.'

The archers seized the prisoner and bundled him out of the room. The two Nevilles sat in petrified silence whilst Mauclerc openly sulked as he slouched in one of the window seats. Sir Thomas left for a while, shouting orders at his captain of archers. Once the Recorder had left, Christopher approached the Nevilles.

'What will happen to us?' the archbishop whined.

'My Lord, you are in a most perilous position.' Urswicke paused at the sound of crashing and clattering on the gallery outside. He walked to a window, stared out and noticed the servants, most of them carrying bundles, hurry out of the manor, desperate to escape. He walked back to the Nevilles. 'You know,' he declared, 'Sir Thomas will plunder this palace. He will leave not one stone upon another. He will strip it to the very bone and load his booty on to carts, some of which might reach Westminster.'

'That's what he wanted from the beginning,' the archbishop replied. 'They want the treasures kept here.'

'And they want more,' his sister sharply intervened, her beautiful face now pale and tear-streaked, though her eyes remained hard. Urswicke realized that beneath the mask of a courtly lady, Grace Neville was as hard and ruthless as her elder brother, Richard of Warwick.

'What do you mean, my Lady?'

'Not now,' she whispered quickly. 'But I and my brother need to have urgent words with you, Master Urswicke.'

'Why with me?'

'Because you are a man of integrity. I think you live in the truth.' She gave a half smile. 'Unlike most of us. I want to bargain for our lives. We will need your help and that of your mistress.'

Urswicke stared at this precious pair who had been party to a most deadly threat against the countess.

'So, you wish to have words with me later.'

'Yes, Master Urswicke, if that's possible, certainly before we leave here.'

'And I have questions for you,' Urswicke replied, 'but let them wait.' Christopher rose and took the chair next to the countess.

'My Lady,' he whispered, 'you did very well. Cunning and sharp! No wonder my esteemed father is beside himself with rage.'

'Well of course. He gathered us here to destroy us.' She paused as Bray who, at Sir Thomas's insistence, had taken the coffer out of the hall, came and sat with them. 'What now?' the countess murmured. 'What do we have here?'

'We still have to deal with Mauclerc and the Imposter,' Urswicke retorted. 'God knows what is going to happen there. Patmore is dead but, unfortunately, Mauclerc is very much alive.'

'And I have some questions for Poppleton before he dies,' the countess replied.

'Mistress?'

'Callista,' the countess answered. 'I enquired amongst the servants: I kept my eye sharp as I moved around The Moor. I cannot find her, nor does anyone else have news about Callista or where she may be. But let's wait and see.'

'And I have unfinished business.' Bray declared. 'It's wonderful what you notice as you carry this or that here and there. The Moor is now full of Sir Thomas's men and there's more arriving.' He fell silent as the door to the hall was flung open.

Sir Thomas strode in, Poppleton dragged behind him. The Recorder shouted his orders. Poppleton was made to stand on a stool. An archer looped a hanging rope across one of the ceiling beams. Sir Thomas snapped his fingers at Mauclerc who then took over, fastening the slip knot so the rope hung secure. He then fashioned the noose which he put over the condemned man's head, placing the knot just behind the prisoner's right ear. Poppleton, tightly bound, could do nothing but stagger, gasping on the stool.

'One word.' The countess rose to her feet and walked towards Poppleton. Sir Thomas made as if to interfere but then thought better of it. The countess got as close as she could to the condemned man. 'In a few heartbeats,' she declared, 'you will meet your judgement. So tell me now: the young maid, the girl Callista? Do you know anything about her, of her whereabouts, or what might have happened to her?'

Poppleton simply closed his eyes, lips moving soundlessly.

'What is this, what is this?' Sir Thomas barked, drawing closer.

'There was a maid,' the countess replied. 'A sweet young woman. I was much taken by her. This house is now a sinister place of violence and sudden death. I have sent for her this morning. I have enquired. I cannot find her. I want this man to answer if he knows anything of her whereabouts.'

'In God's name leave me alone,' Poppleton grated. 'I have confessed my sins; I have nothing for you, Richmond. If I am to die, then let's do it swiftly. I am tired of answering to people I have no care for.'

The countess withdrew. The hall fell chillingly silent, except for Lady Grace's sobbing and the eerie heavy breathing of the prisoner.

'Good riddance,' Sir Thomas bawled. He then strode across and kicked the stool away.

Poppleton, neck tightly strung, began his deadly dance in the air. Bray watched. Urswicke turned away, facing his mistress as she whispered the words of the requiem. The Nevilles clung to each other, the archbishop trying to soothe his sister. Sir Thomas and Mauclerc simply stood and watched the macabre scene. At last, it was over. Poppleton's soaked, self-fouled corpse was cut down and laid on the floor.

Urswicke hastily drew his dagger and went to crouch beside the corpse. He swiftly cut the noose from around the dead man's throat. It was what he expected. There was one last gasp of trapped air. The cadaver trembled then lay still. Carefully pocketing the noose, Urswicke rejoined his mistress. Sir Thomas ordered the dead man to be removed and given swift burial in God's Acre. Once the archers had left with their gruesome burden, Sir Thomas became as calm and as charming as if he'd just strolled through a garden on a bright summer's day. He bowed at the countess.

'My Lady, you are now free to leave. As for you,' the Recorder gestured menacingly at the Nevilles, 'when I am ready and when I have finished here, you are for the Tower. You can both lodge there until the King decides your fate.' The Recorder bowed cursorily at his son then left. The countess, accompanied by Urswicke and Bray, left the hall to Sir Thomas's archers and returned to her chamber.

'Sir Thomas,' the countess declared, taking her chair before the hearth, 'is now no longer concerned with us. We are safe here. But Christopher, Reginald, there is unfinished business.'

'Oh yes, my Lady.'

'With Mauclerc?'

'One item amongst a few, my Lady. Whilst we were in the hall, I had words with him. He and the Imposter should be joining us shortly. In the meantime . . .' Urswicke filled three goblets from a jug of the finest Alsace, but only after Bray had insisted on ensuring it wasn't tainted. 'One of the disadvantages of Bordeaux,' he murmured, 'is its deep blood-red colour which can conceal a venom. This, thank God, cannot. Heaven's own nectar!' he exclaimed, lifting his glass in toast. They had taken their first sip when a sharp knock on the door stilled all conversation. It opened and Mauclerc, one hand on the Imposter's shoulder, slipped into the chamber. Clarence's henchman looked wary and watchful. His protégé, garbed like a forester in a dark green jerkin, earth-coloured hose and black boots was equally watchful, as if ready to flee. Urswicke ushered them to chairs around the table then stopped, listening to the growing clamour echoing through the house.

'It's your father,' Mauclerc slurred, his face flushed with wine.

'He has seized every barrow and cart and is intent on looting the entire manor from cellar to garret. The stock has already been driven away. Now he is seizing anything which can be moved from this house. Indeed, he is so zealous, I do wonder if he is searching for something in particular.'

'Such as?'

'Master Urswicke, I do not know.'

'Which room did he pillage first?' Bray asked.

'The Nevilles' chancery chamber. All manuscripts have been seized and sealed ready for Westminster.'

'God help anybody,' the countess declared, 'caught up in this sordid tale.'

'True, true,' Mauclerc agreed.

'Were you party to all of this?' Urswicke asked.

'Master Urswicke, like you I take orders, but if the truth be known, your father was the moving spirit behind this enterprise. I know he had the support of my master, George of Clarence, but also the King and that of Richard of Gloucester. So,' Mauclerc forced a smile, 'what do you want with us?'

'What,' Urswicke demanded, pointing at the Imposter, 'will happen to him now that Patmore is no longer with us?'

'The boy is left in my charge,' Mauclerc smirked. 'As for my good friend's claim – well, time will tell.'

'No, I don't think so.' Urswicke disagreed. 'Patmore's suicide has finished this farce; that young man becomes one Imposter amongst many.'

'If you say so.' Mauclerc shrugged.

'But he has,' Urswicke insisted, 'the potential to be used again.'

'Perhaps.'

'And perhaps not,' Urswicke snapped.

'What do you mean?'

'I mean this.' Urswicke opened the chancery satchel lying on the table beside him and took out three coarse-haired knots. He held each one up. 'Caiaphas,' he declared, 'Poppleton and this is Patmore's. All three are tied with a distinctive noose knot fashioned by you, Mauclerc. We know why Caiaphas and Poppleton were hanged; you acted as executioner for both, whilst this third knot proves you did the same for Patmore. You know I speak the truth. All three knots are fairly unique. All are your work. A knot learned, perhaps, when you served at sea on some royal cog?' Urswicke smiled thinly. 'Isn't it strange, Mauclerc, all three knots could hang you.' He fell silent as the Imposter, even more pale-faced, gave a deep moan before glancing fearfully at Urswicke then back to his protector.

'I can prove what I say,' Urswicke declared. 'And my father, Sir Thomas, would be deeply interested. He would not be too happy losing Patmore because of the interference by one of Clarence's henchmen.'

'You have no real evidence,' Mauclerc retorted.

'Oh uncle, yes he has.' The Imposter sang out in that lilt of his native tongue.

'Yes I have, boy,' Urswicke declared, turning to the Imposter. 'I have all the evidence I need. However, what I should do with it very much depends on what is decided here today. So,' Urswicke gathered all three knots together and put them back in the chancery satchel. 'Young man,' he leaned across the table, 'who are you really? No Mauclerc,' Christopher held up a warning hand, 'I want no more nonsense, no lies. We are not going to sit here and listen to some tale which is nothing but a tapestry of lies.'

'It's best, uncle.' The Imposter turned all pleading to Mauclerc. 'I am tired. We cannot go on like this. I was promised comfortable quarters, good food, my safety guaranteed. But men have been cut down or hanged in the hall below. I'm weary of the fable. I want the truth.'

Mauclerc sagged in the chair. He closed his eyes, tapping his fingers on the table-top.

'It's best,' the Imposter pleaded.

Mauclerc opened his eyes.

'I will not wait,' the Imposter blurted out. 'I will wait no longer. I am Owain of Neath. I am Owain,' he repeated swiftly, fearful that Mauclerc might interfere again. 'I don't know my father, whilst my mother entrusted me as a babe to the nuns of Valle Crucis who, in turn, when I was a young boy, handed me over to the good monks of Neath Abbey. I was truly happy there. I attended the cloisters school and I excelled.' He blinked and smiled. 'They said I was a scholar, skilled in writing, learned in my horn book. They wanted me to become one of them and I thought I would. I planned to enter the novitiate, then Patmore arrived a few years ago.'

'Why did he come to Neath Abbey?' the countess asked.

'Mistress, I don't know. All he said was that he'd been searching for me as if he knew about my existence before he came. He promised me riches and a splendid life outside the abbey. He claimed to be struck by my appearance and said I had a close likeness to Henry Tudor, the son of Lord Edmund and the Lady Margaret Beaufort. He asked me questions about my life. They were easy to answer, living with the nuns before arriving at Neath Abbey. He talked about the future and what I wanted in life. He said if he had his way, he would take me to London and Oxford. I would enter the Inns of Court, study at the schools of Oxford and Cambridge and I could become a lawyer, a powerful clerk, and have a soft and comfortable life in the service of the Crown. Of course, I was impressed. I was fascinated. But then he left. I was disappointed but, after a while, thought no more of it.'

'Patmore came to us in London, just after the Battle of Tewkesbury,' Mauclerc declared. 'He informed the Secret Chancery of what he had found and the possibilities it offered.' He took a deep breath. 'The King and his brothers warmly supported the emergence of Owain as Henry Tudor. Patmore was summoned before the Secret Council and given very precise instructions about what he should do.'

'He returned to Neath Abbey,' Owain declared. 'He came well furnished with silver and gold and so we began our life together. He explained how he had once been the tutor to your son, mistress, and that he knew everything. I was to be instructed, guided, to become your son. I have a good memory and I learn very swiftly. Day in, day out, Patmore instructed me as if I was a scholar in the schools. I learned how to walk like him, talk like him, even eat my food and drink from a tankard like him. He described Henry's mannerisms and taught me how to imitate them in every detail. I had to dress a certain way; he even dictated how I should wash my face at the lavarium. I had the same likes and dislikes.' Owain smiled. 'Patmore said I was perfect, a true imitation, an accurate reflection.'

'The more we learned about your son,' Mauclerc declared,

'the more the King and his brothers pressed for the emergence of Owain as Henry Tudor.' He smiled wryly. 'I am sure, indeed certain, that you did your own investigation and found the tale Patmore spun was most convincing.'

'So why murder him?' Urswicke demanded. 'That's what you did, Mauclerc, you murdered Patmore. Why?'

'Because he abused me.' Owain's voice rose to a shout. 'He hurt me. He treated me like a girl. He'd crawl like some monster into my bed. Patmore with his stubby fingers and slobbery lips.' Owain fell silent as Mauclerc leaned sideways to embrace him, hugging him gently around the shoulders.

Urswicke, the countess and Bray just gaped in surprise. Mauclerc, a true wolf of a man, seemed to have become another being: fatherly, gentle; even his pock-marked face lost that ravenous, predatory look. Clarence's henchman leaned down and kissed Owain on the top of his head. He then stared at Urswicke who glimpsed the tears in his opponent's eyes.

'Master Urswicke, you must in your searches have found out about Patmore. He loved to play with young men, mere striplings. He tried the same with young Owain here and persisted in it even when he came here. Patmore was cunning. He realised his secret life could betray him. He also had the wit to realise that one day Sir Thomas might not need him, and what then? Through my spies and searches,' Mauclerc continued, 'I learned about Patmore's plans and plots to escape this kingdom for some place across the Narrow Seas. Indeed,' he half smiled to himself, 'I suspected he would travel to Ghent in Flanders.' Mauclerc suddenly paused, closing his eyes as if he was about to say something but then thought better of it.

'Mauclerc, do you know more?'

'I have told you what I can. I will not say more. I don't want to. Owain may be my friend, my closest friend, but you are not. So, Master Urswicke, what do you and your mistress want of me? My death? Will you betray me to your father? You know how that wolfpack at the court swirls and curls. Sir Thomas Urswicke would only be too pleased to learn what you have. He would certainly use me to attack my Lord of Clarence, and your revelations would be the vice he'd clamp around Clarence's neck. Patmore alive was dangerous. Now he's gone he is not. But,'

Mauclerc forced a smile, 'I concede the manner of his passing would, if it became known, pose a real danger to me and, to be fair, to the boy here.'

'Yet you killed Patmore. You murdered him?'

'No, I gave him a choice. Public arrest, public shame, and the most gruesome death; being cut and hacked open on the gallows at Smithfield.'

'Was Patmore that frightened?' Bray demanded. 'So frightened he took his own life?'

'To answer you bluntly, Master Bray, yes. People like Patmore constantly live under the shadow of the axe. It was only a matter of time before he was betrayed. He was a broken man. I fastened the noose. I provided a goblet of the best Bordeaux. I told him to lock and bolt the door behind him.' He shrugged. 'The rest you already know, and again I ask you, what now?'

'Come here, boy.' The countess waved at Owain, who rose, came down the table and stood beside the countess; she took his hand and gently pulled him closer. He did not resist. 'You have a look of my beloved Edmund,' she breathed, 'oh yes, but that's not for now. Christopher,' she smiled at her henchman, 'give Mauclerc our offer.'

'Certainly.' Urswicke took a chair directly opposite Clarence's henchman. 'You and I,' he began, 'are the same. I called you friend but, of course, you are not. You are my adversary and yet, whatever our differences, you, Bray and myself are men of blood, squires of the night, doers in the dark. You know that. We work in the twilight where all kinds of monsters lurk and prowl. Death can happen like that.' Urswicke abruptly clapped his hands but Mauclerc did not even startle or flinch. 'So it will be,' Urswicke continued. 'You sir, like me, despatch people into the dark. Some day, some time, somewhere, the same will happen to you and to me. And then, what would happen to the boy?'

Mauclerc did not answer but stared stonily at a point above Urswicke's head. He then blinked and gave a thin smile.

'You have a proposal, Master Urswicke?'

'Give the boy to us. No, no, he will be safe.'

'He will be safe.' The countess echoed Urswicke's words. 'I'll take a solemn oath.' She moved Owain aside so she had a clear view of Mauclerc. 'I'll send him as a companion, a body squire to my son in Rennes. He will be safe there. I will give you licence to visit him under very strict conditions. Moreover, if Fickle Fortune spins her wheel and the power of York is no more, perhaps then Owain can rejoin you to walk whatever path you choose.'

'Think man,' Bray urged. 'Reflect on what has been said. Owain will be safe and so will you. York no longer needs him. Tell the Secret Chancery that it would be better for them if Owain just disappeared into the Tudor household. The game has been played and it's over. What else can they do with the lad? Better for them to show mercy than have it proclaimed abroad that they used an innocent child then mercilessly disposed of him.'

'You know,' Urswicke declared, 'how to compose the words for such a hymn. Add whatever you want. Emphasise that Patmore's suicide has brought the matter to an end.' Urswicke waved a hand. 'And so you have it!'

'Your offer is most gracious and generous,' Mauclerc replied slowly. 'And so, I will tell you more. First you should really thank me for executing Patmore. Believe me, he was planning more mischief.' He fell silent, head down. Owain tapped him on the back of the hand.

'Tell them,' the boy urged. 'Tell them what was plotted. How Patmore's death brought it to nothing.'

'Very good.' Mauclerc rubbed his face. 'To the world and his wife, there are two Henry Tudors. The first shelters in Brittany. The second is now a member of your household, mistress. This has caused you and yours a great deal of chaos, as was intended from the start. However, as I have already hinted, there is more. My Lady, do the names Eleanor and Matilda Patmore mean anything to you?'

'Why yes,' the countess replied slowly, 'two Welsh ladies who served in my household when Edmund and I were together,' she glanced up. 'My apologies,' she murmured. 'My mind is in such a whirl, I didn't make the connection. I never thought of them as "Patmore", just Eleanor and Matilda.'

'And they looked after you when you gave birth to your son Henry?'

'Oh yes they were present in the birthing chamber, helping the wise woman with the birth, both before and afterwards.'

'And your brother-in-law Lord Jasper was also present?'

'Yes, he certainly was, though outside the chamber.' She paused, fingers to her lips. 'Oh yes, I do remember Eleanor and Matilda.'

'Were they well disposed towards you?'

'Sometimes I detected a resentment. Women who envied what I was and what I had. They left my service soon after the birth. Both women were widows. Eleanor is, or was, the mother of Thomas Patmore, yes?'

Mauclerc nodded in agreement.

'That's right,' the countess continued, 'it was because of Eleanor, in order to help her, that we later hired her son Thomas to be tutor to Prince Henry. At the time, Thomas Patmore had a reputation for being a scholar, a man who had attended the Inns of Court and the halls of Oxford and Cambridge. I was never really sure about what he actually achieved, but he was an excellent teacher. He entered my household and signed the usual indentures for service.'

'And his mother and aunt?'

'If my memory serves me right, they were widows. They left our service because we no longer needed them. I gave them dowries so they could enter the nunnery in Valle Crucis. They took simple vows and became members of that community.'

'And that's the same convent which took young Owain in,' Urswicke interjected.

'True,' Mauclerc agreed, but he couldn't quite hide the amusement in his voice. 'Let me take you through a veritable tangle of intrigue. As you all know, our King's spies beyond the Narrow Seas are as many as bees on a honeypot.'

'Or flies on a turd,' Bray retorted.

'Be that as it may, the King's agents in Ghent garnered evidence of a new tale being spun.'

'Mauclerc,' Urswicke snapped, 'tell us what you want to.'

'To cut to the quick: Eleanor Patmore and her sister Matilda left the nunnery in Valle Crucis and moved to a house of the same order in Ghent, Flanders. Their story began as a wave of whispers, but allegations were made which the King's agents traced back to this precious pair.' He paused. 'They allege that after you gave birth my Lady, Lord Jasper changed your baby for young Owain here.'

'Nonsense!' the countess cried. 'Nonsense indeed! Henry's birth was very simple: plucked out, plucked up and wrapped in swaddling. The wise woman pronounced him a hale and hearty boy.' She paused. 'Stories about changelings are common enough. We can easily counter such a lie.'

'Can you, mistress? The wise woman is now dead, we know that.'

'And why should Lord Jasper do such a thing?' Bray asked.

'Oh, I can see what tune they are singing,' Urswicke declared.

'You probably have the truth of it already, Urswicke. These two ladies claim that Lord Jasper was deeply fearful about what was coming. York and Lancaster were embroiled in a fight to the death. Whatever our differences, my Lady, I am for York, you are for Lancaster. Your son, Prince Henry, has royal blood in his veins. To the Brothers York, he has been – and he always will be – a serious threat to their rule. These two ladies are simply adding fuel to a fire already burning merrily. They will maintain that young Owain here is the genuine Prince Henry and the one sheltering in Brittany, the changeling.'

'And Patmore?' Urswicke asked. 'Were his preparations to flee connected to this?'

'Patmore,' Owain spoke up, 'was steeped in villainy. He knew what he was as well as what he tried to do to me. He was very fearful. He wanted to rejoin his mother for many reasons.'

'He was also very cunning,' Mauclerc declared. 'I believe he was determined to join his mother and aunt in that nunnery in Ghent where all three of them could peddle their story.'

'Why should they do that?' Bray demanded.

'Oh, I can see what they were plotting,' the countess answered heatedly. 'They shelter in a House of God in Ghent where no one can really touch them. They will set up shop within the sacred precincts, offering their filthy lies to anyone who wishes to buy. Patmore was intent on joining them so he could sit on the same table and sup from the fruits of their wickedness. Patmore, helped by those two crones, could write his chronicle, his broadsheet, his proclamation about the Tudors; a salacious story, a titillating tale. Oh yes, and he would boast that his sources were impeccable, two holy nuns, the only surviving witnesses from the birthing chamber. Matilda and Eleanor saw what happened and I, to silence them, showed great generosity in arranging their admission to the convent, as well as hiring their son as Prince Henry's personal tutor. They would use whatever information they had, including my generosity, to peddle their lies.'

'But not now,' Owain declared. 'Not now, mistress, which is why I want to join your son in Brittany. Thomas Patmore is dead and I will proclaim the truth about myself.'

'Yes, yes,' the countess agreed. 'That will put an end to the lies, though the Brothers York will not be pleased.'

'True, my Lady,' Mauclerc replied. 'The King wanted to use Owain to counter your claims and those of your son. York is not interested in two old ladies hiding in a convent in Ghent, chomping on their gums as they spin some ridiculous tale. Anyway, are we finished here?'

'If you are,' the countess retorted, 'then so are we.'

Mauclerc nodded, scraped back his chair and sat staring at the floor.

'It's what I want!'

Mauclerc raised his head at Owain's singsong declaration.

'Uncle, it's what we both want!'

Mauclerc smiled, ruffled Owain's hair, and once again Urswicke wondered what was going on in this wolfman's soul.

'Very well, Owain.' Mauclerc got to his feet, beckoning at the boy. 'Come, we will talk for a while. And then my Lady, Master Urswicke, we will reach an agreement. I shall bring Owain back.'

Once again Mauclerc ruffled Owain's hair and, placing one arm across the young man's shoulder, led him to the door.

'Mauclerc?'

'Yes?'

Christopher pointed at Owain. 'Why? Why are you so close? How did it come to this?'

'Old memories, Urswicke. Memories of my own childhood.' Mauclerc couldn't keep the bitterness out of his voice. 'Yearnings for a son I never had. For a family I would have craved. Of times lost and opportunities missed. We seek redemption through many ways; I am no different. I bid you good day.'

PART EIGHT

'The King broke the said Archbishop's mitre in which were many rich stones . . . And made a crown for himself.'

'I do wonder . . .' Urswicke murmured as Mauclerc closed the door behind him.

'Christopher,' the countess replied, 'the human heart is strange. It yearns for those things which could be and mourns for what could have been.'

'It might all be a trap.' Bray's harsh words rang through the chamber.

'Ever the pragmatist,' Urswicke retorted.

'You know he'll be their spy? The likes of Clarence will have a spy close to your son, mistress.'

'Oh Reginald, we will see.'

'And we should do something about those two witches at the convent in Ghent. They are a festering wound: their clacking tongues should be silenced. It's time I made my own enquiries and arranged a visit. Yes, my Lady? It won't be difficult to find the convent and identify our two hags. Accidents can happen. They could eat tainted food or drink a subtle poison. Whatever . . .'

'They certainly deserve to die, Reginald,' the countess replied. 'But let's leave it. Time will take care of them. Do they pose any real danger? After all, they have lost Thomas Patmore.'

'No,' Urswicke replied. 'The threat has diminished but it has not disappeared. Those two ladies are self-proclaimed witnesses; the only surviving ones who were present in the birthing chamber when Prince Henry was born. True, they are not York's creatures, but they might attract others to them. We really should bring such malicious mischief to an end once and for all.'

'No, no.' The countess shook her head. 'I will not have their deaths laid at my door. God will take care of them.'

'Sometimes God needs a helping hand,' Bray added. He glanced quickly at Urswicke who nodded silently in agreement. Urswicke knew that Bray would never let the matter rest. He would either visit that convent or arrange for one of his many friends to do so and those two mischievous women would be silenced for ever.

'Strange, isn't it?' the countess mused. 'How the ghosts of the past come back to haunt you. I was only fourteen when I gave birth to Henry. Edmund died two months before his birth. Strange, clashing times! On the one hand, great joy at the birth of my son, on the other deep sorrow and mourning at the loss of my beloved husband. Yes, yes.' She closed her eyes for a moment then opened them. 'A time of confusion and women like Eleanor and Matilda would use such confusion. God have mercy on them. God forgive them. Anyway,' she pulled herself up in the chair, 'we still have business here, questions to be asked. I can tell that from the expression on both of your faces.'

'We certainly have unfinished business here,' Urswicke agreed, then paused at a knock on the door. Mauclerc strode back into the chamber.

'Mistress, Archbishop George and Lady Grace have petitioned Sir Thomas to have words with you. They wish to purge themselves and give solemn assurances to you that they intended you no harm.'

'Do they now?' Bray sneered. 'I am sure they regret what they have done. Mistress, they are a waste of time. They are nonentities, souls of straw, soon to be dispersed by the wind.'

'Bring them here,' the countess declared. 'There's nothing wrong, Reginald, with a little courtesy. After all, both of them will soon be carted away and buried deep in the Tower. They have lost their liberty and they may soon forfeit their lives in some hideous, "*casus fatalis*", a terrible accident which no one can really explain. So let them come.'

'I agree,' Urswicke declared. 'I need to have words with those souls of deceit.'

'As you wish,' Mauclerc replied and left the chamber.

Bray got to his feet.

'Reginald?'

'My Lady, I think it's best if we are armed. You brought weapons, yes?'

'I have a small hand-held arbalest in my chamber,' Urswicke offered. 'You will find it in the clothes chest at the foot of the bed.'

Bray murmured his thanks and left. He returned a short time later and carefully hid the arbalest, and its small quiver of bolts, beneath a blanket on the bed.

'You distrust Archbishop George so much?' Urswicke teased. 'He and his sister will offer no violence. They can't stand the sight of blood.'

'Oh, it's not for the Nevilles, Christopher. I saw something downstairs which deeply intrigued me and I mean . . .' He fell silent at a knock on the door; this was flung open and Archbishop George and Lady Grace were pushed roughly into the room. The four archers guarding them shoved the two prisoners towards the countess.

'Do you want us to stay, my Lady?' one of them asked.

The countess gestured at Urswicke and Bray. 'I have protection enough.'

Once the archers left, their leader adding that they would stand on guard outside, the countess indicated that her two guests should sit at the table with her. Despite what had happened, Urswicke felt sorry for them; both had lost their poise and inborn self-assurance. They looked dishevelled and tired, and Urswicke noticed the bruise high on the archbishop's cheek.

'Would you like some wine?'

Both prisoners said they would. Urswicke filled two goblets of Alsace and pushed the cups into their hands.

'You wanted to see me?' the countess demanded. 'To purge yourself? But of course you don't. There's another reason, isn't there? After all, the damage has been done. Too late to go back now, whilst any regret would only sound hollow.'

'True,' Lady Grace replied. 'Look, Countess Margaret, my brother and I are for the dark. York will never forgive us unless . . .'

'Unless what?'

'Hear me out,' Lady Grace replied. 'You've heard about the Secretum?'

'I've heard rumours,' the countess replied.

'A document drawn up by the late Earl of Warwick, which records in great detail the treachery of several lords, in particular the King's brother, George of Clarence, that prince of broken promises.'

'What about it? Some people claim it's just an empty rumour.'

'Oh no,' Lady Grace replied. 'It does indeed exist and we have it.'

'Where?' Urswicke demanded.

'Time is passing,' Lady Grace replied. 'The candle flame burns quickly and I have chosen to play this game of hazard. In short, I am going to trust you completely. If you want the Secretum, go to the Creeping Cross at the centre of the maze. There are a number of steps up to it. Dig beneath the first and you will find a copper tube sealed at the top. Open it and you will have the Secretum.'

'You went there the day Brasenose was murdered, didn't you?' Urswicke demanded. 'You were going to check that all was well with what was hidden there. It was you Brasenose glimpsed entering the maze?'

'That is true.'

'So why are you telling us this, and why now?'

'Master Urswicke, as I have said, at this moment in time we are finished. We are giving you this because we trust you, Countess Margaret. You and yours enjoy a reputation for integrity which cannot be found elsewhere.'

'And in return?' Bray demanded. 'You want something, don't you?'

'Yes, we want a great favour. We ask you, we plead with you, to go on your knees before the King and beg for our lives. If you are successful, Edward of York would not dare kill us. Locked away in some manor house or castle, true, but we'll escape that fatal accident which is undoubtedly being prepared for us.'

'We could just take the Secretum,' Bray declared, 'and do nothing. After all, it's a great favour you ask. Margaret Beaufort, of royal blood, the renowned Countess of Richmond,' Bray's voice sank to a whisper, 'and mother of the rightful King of this country, should kneel before York, the usurper, who has slaughtered so many of her family.'

'Murdered!' the countess interjected. 'York murdered my kin. Put them to death on public scaffolds without any vestige of a trial. Bray is correct. I could seize the Secretum and ride out of here without any thought for you.'

'You won't do that,' Lady Grace replied. 'I know that and so do you. But I tell you this. If you take the Secretum, it will give you considerable power. A hidden weapon which you could later use to your own advantage.'

The countess rose and walked to stare out of the window, as if drawn by the clash, clatter and cries from below.

'They are looting my palace,' the archbishop wailed. 'They have seized my golden mitre so as to smash it to pieces. They have taken my tapestries, my furnishings, even the chamber pot from my jakes closet.'

Urswicke stared hard at the archbishop; this once proud prelate was truly broken. Archbishop George just sat slouched with a vacant look in his eyes, bruised lips parted, unshaven chin stained with dribble. Lady Grace, however, still possessed that hidden strength, the urge to strike back even if she was sorely wounded.

The countess turned and came back from the window.

'Oh yes, York would love that,' the countess declared, clasping her hands as if in prayer. 'He would love to see a Beaufort kneel before him and beg for the life of two Nevilles. But, I say this George, Duke of Clarence, as far as York is concerned, truly is the enemy within. One day he will make his move. George of Clarence thinks he should be King. Oh, he's muffled and muzzled for the moment, but he's still as treacherous as ever.' She paused. 'Yes, it would be good to own a record of his previous treasons.' The countess stood for a while in silence. She then abruptly took her seat. 'I will do it,' she declared. 'I will do it because of my veneration and respect for your late brother the Earl of Warwick. He fought for my house and he died for it. God knows there has been enough Lancastrian blood spilled, never mind the present circumstances. Both of you,' she gestured at the Nevilles, 'are Lancastrian. I shall also do it, for pity's sake, as repentance for my many sins against other Lancastrians. Finally, and most importantly, I am to be given the Secretum. Now I know,' she moved in her chair, an impish smile on her face, 'I know that Richard, Earl of Warwick, was a man who attracted others like candlelight does moths. He suborned many of York's adherents. Now earlier I mentioned Clarence. I am sure the Secretum will contain tasty morsels of his treachery and of others, and that is a weapon I would love because one day I shall certainly use it. So yes, I will make my plea at Westminster and, if I know Edward correctly, he will grant it and keep his word.'

'And there's more.' Urswicke abruptly rapped the top of the table.

'Christopher?'

'Listen well,' Urswicke declared, 'you can hear the clamour. Satan's ruffians – or my father's, to be more precise – are pillaging your house from cellar to loft. They will strip you of everything, seize all your treasures whilst you are completely disgraced. So, my question to you is this. I laid an indictment earlier about the plot and counter-plot here at The Moor but I never really got an answer to this question.'

'Ask it!' Lady Grace demanded.

'How in God's name did you ever get involved in such a madcap scheme, my Lord Archbishop? Lured, tricked and trapped!'

George Neville, however, mouth dribbling, could only sit shaking his head, quietly mumbling some prayer in Latin. Urswicke listened intently and recognised the words of the Mercy Psalm.

'I shall answer that.' Lady Grace declared. 'We were lured and trapped because we were seriously misled. Maillac, our steward, was Lancastrian to his very marrow. He was totally devoted to the memory of the Earl of Warwick. He would never accept York's ascendancy.'

'One man!' Bray scoffed. 'You were led into this by your steward?'

'No sir, we were not. Oh yes, we were zealous and keen, but what was presented to us seemed real enough. Maillac would meet us in the dead of night. He was often accompanied at such midnight meetings by Robin of Redesdale, a most eloquent and very persuasive speaker. He assured us that he had been in communication with the Earl of Oxford. How de Vere would soon gather more war cogs and land troops, both adherents of Lancaster and mercenaries. Redesdale also assured us that he would raise thousands of men in the shires. He showed us proclamations that he and his comrades had nailed to church doors in villages across the shires.'

'Sweet Lord!' Urswicke breathed. 'And you believed him?'

'Master Urswicke, he brought written messages from de Vere and those he called his "captains in the shires", who assured us of support. He described in great detail how, once the Brothers York journeyed here, they would be surrounded by a veritable army. Justice would be swift. The Yorkist victory at Barnet totally reversed. Sometimes Redesdale brought others with him, mailed clerks, veteran bowmen from the wars.'

'I am sure he did,' Bray declared. 'It would have been simple and easy, to prepare the plot here at The Moor. I mean until Brasenose and Rutger arrived, I doubt if York had any spy here. No, no, this would be an ideal place for plots and schemes. The likes of Robin of Redesdale and his so-called comrades could easily slip in and out of here at the dead of night and no one would be the wiser.'

'Yet all a lie.' Lady Grace's eyes filled with tears. 'We were cruelly tricked and trapped. We were assured of victory but their pledges were simply straw upon the water, dust in the breeze.' She crossed herself. 'And now our ruin is complete. Mistress, will you do as I ask?'

'I shall.'

'Is there anything more?' Urswicke demanded. 'Do you know anything about Warwick's death at Barnet?'

'No, Master Urswicke. You know as much as we do, that he fought on foot, became isolated and was cut down.'

'God rest him,' the countess whispered.

'And God bless us,' Lady Grace retorted. 'My Lady, after you have pleaded for us, please visit us wherever we are to ensure that York keeps his promises.'

Countess Margaret agreed. She wished both Nevilles God's grace, and asked Bray and Urswicke to take them out on to the gallery and the waiting archers. Once they had, both henchmen returned to the countess, Bray murmuring they had other business to do. The countess nodded absentmindedly and picked up her psalter from the table.

'Do what you have to,' she declared. 'George Neville was

reciting the Mercy Psalm. I will do the same and so give thanks to God for his protection.'

Once they were out of the chamber, Bray plucked Urswicke's sleeve and led him further along the gallery. He then paused and pushed open a door window, staring down at the confusion and chaos in the great bailey. Urswicke did likewise and realized that George Neville was correct. Sir Thomas Urswicke was fully intent on plundering The Moor. Huge war carts now thronged the bailey. Soldiers stumbled around carrying chests, coffers, caskets, bundles of tapestries, drapes, pictures and statues, weapons and clothing, all to be piled high in the waiting barrows. The bailey was protected by Tower bowmen, bows strung, arrows notched, watching intently for any attempt by the soldiers to filch or steal. One had already been caught red-handed and summarily hanged from a makeshift gibbet. The corpse, its neck gruesomely twisted, swayed in the breeze, a dire warning to any would-be thief. For a while, Bray and Urswicke just watched the commotion below.

'Reginald, why are we here?'

'Christopher, I will tell you. However, for the moment it is best if you acted as if you really didn't know the person I want you to meet.'

'What on earth . . .?'

'Just for the moment, Christopher.' Bray pushed the window open a little further. 'Ah yes, Heaven be thanked,' he prayed, 'Sir Thomas is not here.'

'Of course he's not. My esteemed father will be busy in the treasure chamber. He will be as happy as a boy who has found a large jar of sweetmeats.'

'I am sure he will be, Christopher, but look down in the yard. There!' Urswicke followed Bray's direction. 'Do you see that sharp-featured rogue standing near the well? He's pulled up his deep green hood and he is loading a box of silver goblets into that cart?'

'Yes, yes, I see him.'

'Very well. I want you to go down and ask him his name, then bring him, with as little show and fuss as possible, out of the bailey and into the maze. Make some excuse but do enter and follow the guide rope to the centre.'

'And?'

'I will be waiting for you.'

'And you cannot tell me what this is all about?'

'For the moment I cannot. Just stand here for the space of ten aves, then go down and engage with that man of blood. Oh, by the way Christopher, now I have you alone and the countess cannot hear. Those two bitches in Ghent must be silenced. The countess has demurred, but it has to be done. I don't know how old they are or how long they have to live. They will soon receive news about Patmore's suicide. They may well suspect the truth and make one last stab at the countess, peddling whatever treacherous tale they can concoct. They will be a sore, a constant sore, to the countess.'

'Reginald, I leave that to you.' Urswicke half smiled. 'I know you of old. What you promise, you will do but, for the moment,' his smile widened, 'I will begin those aves.'

Bray left whilst Urswicke stood by the window, reflecting on all that had happened. At least he had established why the Nevilles had been trapped and what had caused their downfall. He quietly marvelled at how his father had turned and twisted, building traps to enmesh the countess, the Nevilles, and anyone else opposed to the power of York.

'And it's not finished,' he whispered to himself. 'Let us see what Reginald intends. God knows what information the Secretum holds. Ah well, time to go.'

He fastened his warbelt tighter and went along the gallery, down the stairs and out into the great bailey. The dusty air reeked of wine, ale and the fragrances of spice jars, which the clumsy soldiers had dropped. The great bailey truly was a place of frenetic confusion. The stables had been opened and the horses led out to be assessed for their worth. A war dog that had escaped from its kennel had been killed by a crossbow bolt, and now lay sprawled in a widening pool of blood. The looters had also helped themselves to both kitchen and manor livestock: ducks, swans and even a partridge had been killed, their necks wrung, plucked clean and gutted to be roasted over makeshift fires. Soldiers staggered about but, as long as they threw the plunder into the carts, their captains and the Tower archers did not interfere. Urswicke, his cowl pulled close, stared around and glimpsed the soldier with the green hood. He walked across and waited until the man had finished drinking from his wineskin before plucking at his sleeve.

'Yes?' the fellow growled, his thin, bony face twisted into a scowl. 'What do you want?'

'My name is Christopher Urswicke, I am Sir Thomas's son.'

The man forced a smile, desperate to conceal his former hostility.

'I am sorry sir,' he slurred, 'what do you want?'

'My father truly trusts you. What is your full name?'

'John Saltburn.'

'Ah yes, Saltburn. Now look, I am carrying out a special task for Sir Thomas. He told me to order you to help me. I will then give you some coins and send you on your way.' Urswicke dug into his purse and took out one of his father's seals, which he always carried with him. He showed this to Saltburn then leaned closer. 'John,' he whispered, 'this is an important task. Just follow me out of the bailey, we have to enter the maze.'

'What?'

'Yes, it's that secretive. But don't worry, the guide rope is sound and I know my way. Come, come!'

They left the bailey, crossed gardens and stretches of grass which wound around to the front of the house. Once there, they followed the path leading to the maze. Urswicke walked quickly. Saltburn tried to engage him in conversation but Christopher simply shook his head.

'Wait and see,' he said, 'that's all I can tell you for the moment.'

The entered the maze. Saltburn grew anxious, fearful of the walls of thick greenery which rose on either side, the snaking paths which seemed to lead nowhere as they twisted and turned. Nothing seemed to change. No break in the enclosing greenery. Urswicke felt as if the hedges were living things, watching and waiting for the unwary. Once again, Christopher wondered what Bray intended. At last, they reached the centre, a pebble-dashed circle around the Creeping Cross on its broad, stone plinth. Bray was waiting there, sitting on the top step, head down, cowl pulled forward. The bottom half of his face was hidden by the muffler of his cloak. Saltburn became visibly agitated. He would have turned and fled but Urswicke grabbed him by the arm.

'Where are you going, my friend,' he warned, 'do you want to run away? Do you think you'd ever find your way out of this maze? I doubt it very much. For a start, you would need to know which of these paths leading off from here has the guide rope.' Saltburn, looking startled, said nothing.

Bray got to his feet, glanced quickly at Urswicke then pointed at Saltburn.

'You were not killed at Holy Blood Priory, but you certainly deserve to die,' Bray accused. 'You are responsible for the deaths of so many.'

'No, no.' Urswicke intervened. 'Let us hasten slowly; let us take each step at a time.'

'Sit down,' Bray ordered, pulling back his hood and lowering the muffler. He threw his cloak back and unhooked the small arbalest from his warbelt. He placed a thin, wicked-looking barb in the groove and tightened the cord. Saltburn could only stand moaning to himself. 'Don't you recognise me?' Bray demanded. 'Sit down and look at me.'

Saltburn did so.

'Oh, sweet God.' Saltburn's fingers flew to his lips. 'You are Bray, you were at Holy Blood Priory.'

'Very good,' Bray answered. 'Very good indeed, my friend. So, you gleefully admit you were at the priory. So my next question is very simple. Why did all the others die, whilst you survived to help Sir Thomas plunder this magnificent palace?'

'I-I-I . . .' Saltburn stammered.

Urswicke sat down beside the prisoner and drew his dagger. 'Are you John Saltburn?' Urswicke demanded

'No, he isn't,' Bray declared. 'He is Robin of Redesdale, the one who misled the Nevilles; who promised them a great array of men. In truth, he is a liar and a murderer.'

Urswicke paused as if listening to the clear, fluted call of the blackbird in the hedge behind him. This died away and the strong breeze carried the discordant sound of looting and pillaging. Urswicke pointed at Saltburn. 'You caused all that. Now, is your real name John Saltburn?'

'Yes.'

'And you are,' Urswicke pointed to the man's forefingers and wrists, badly marked by callouses. 'Yes, you must be a master archer, a skilled bowman and a capable leader of men.'

'I was and I am,' the prisoner replied and Urswicke caught the intonation in his voice.

'You were educated, yes? You studied your horn book. You are skilled with a quill pen. You have learned your alphabet and can calculate to a hundred. You attended some village school which met in the aisle of its parish church, yes?'

'I did, yes. I became a mailed clerk. I left my village in Teesdale and fought in the retinue of Duke Richard, the present King's father.'

'So, you are a Yorkist through and through. You must be my father's sworn man. He enticed you into his company. You became a trusted retainer. The wars ended but certain problems remained, so my father persuaded you to adopt a new guise, that of Robert of Redesdale, a title taken by others who've led uprisings against the Crown. He used you to lure the Nevilles into a trap. You suborned their steward Maillac. That poor soul was a fool, blinded by his grief for the Earl of Warwick and his desire to seek revenge. You promised him and the Nevilles a splendid array of fighting men. In truth, all you did raise was a few score, whom you enticed to their deaths at Holy Blood Priory. So yes,' Urswicke gestured at Bray, 'my friend is correct. You certainly deserve to die.'

'As will you.' Saltburn's voice rang clear.

'Do you threaten us?'

'No, your father does.'

Bray winched back the crossbow cord and held the weapon down, waiting for Urswicke's signal. Christopher glanced up at the sky. He instinctively felt that Saltburn was telling the truth. His esteemed father was plotting something nasty and dangerous: his deadly game of hazard was not yet over.

'It never will be,' he muttered to himself.

'What is that?' Bray asked.

'Nothing, my friend. So, Saltburn, tell us the truth.' He turned and tapped Saltburn on the shoulder with the blade of his dagger.

'It is as you say. We gathered at Holy Blood Priory. Sir Thomas stormed the place.' Saltburn nodded at Bray. 'He saw what happened. Sir Thomas gave the order; no prisoners.'

'We know what happened there. What else?'

'We were to sweep on to The Moor; we would occupy it easily and arrest everyone there, including the countess and your good selves.'

'We know that too.'

'What you don't know is that Sir Thomas Urswicke was to allow you and the countess to travel back to London.'

'Without a guard? You said that we would be arrested? I cannot understand Sir Thomas seizing someone like the countess and then turning her away. Are you sure? Without any guard or escort?'

'Well, that was part of the plot. I would attack the countess on her journey back to London. Sir Thomas was very blunt and precise. I was to kill the countess, you Master Bray, and anyone else who might be with you. But not his beloved son. Christopher Urswicke,' he added slyly, 'was to be spared.'

'And how would my father explain all this to the world?'

'Oh quite easily. He would proclaim that the countess and her two henchmen, faced with charges of high treason, decided to escape from The Moor. They eluded the guards placed on them and fled. Unfortunately, on their journey through the lonely countryside, they encountered outlaws, survivors perhaps from the battles at Holy Blood Priory. These would attack, hooded and visored, speaking in a tongue you would not understand. We'd give no hint of who we were or portray the truth of the situation.'

'And me?' Urswicke demanded.

'As I said, you would never know who attacked you. You'd get a knock on the head and be left to your own devices. You might suspect what had happened but there would be no proof.'

'How do we know you are speaking the truth?'

'Promise me my life and I will show you. To kill a countess on the King's highway, especially one such as Margaret of Richmond, with royal blood in her veins, is not a crime to be taken lightly. So, promise me my life and I will prove it.'

Urswicke rose to his feet and walked to stand beside Bray.

'What do you think?' he murmured.

'He's telling the truth. Such a plot, ruthless in intent, could only be concocted by your father. You know that, Christopher. Let the bastard live. He probably saved all our lives.'

Urswicke walked back, making sure he did not come between Bray or Saltburn.

'You have your life,' he declared.

'And I will leave here sound of limb?'

'You will leave here as hale and hearty as you are now but you must flee. My father will wonder what happened.'

'Have no worries, Master Urswicke. By the time the compline bell rings, I will be riding fast to the coast and some cog to take me further north.'

'Then prove to me what you have alleged.'

Saltburn opened his wallet. He took out a seal which Christopher immediately recognized as his father's, followed by a small scroll of parchment. He handed this to Urswicke who unrolled it. The seal and signature at the bottom were certainly his father's, the message it contained stark and simple. Urswicke read the words aloud so that Bray could hear them. '"What the bearer of this letter has done is spared by a royal pardon and should not be held against him in any court of law." The seal is fresh and valid,' Urswicke commented. 'As is the signature. It is dated six days ago in my father's chancery chamber at the Guildhall.' Urswicke passed it to Bray. 'It's an absolution for all sins,' Urswicke commented, 'a general pardon for any crime committed or about to be committed. Of course,' he walked closer to Saltburn and raised his dagger to prick the man just beneath the chin. 'Of course,' he repeated, 'no crime is going to be committed. I tell you this, sir, and I speak for my comrade here. You have one hour to disappear. If either of us sees you again, we will kill you.' Urswicke pointed to one of the entrances back into the maze. 'There is your way out. Use the guide rope but hasten, don't delay!'

Saltburn nodded and, as swift as any lurcher, ran and disappeared into the darkness of the path.

'If my father ever finds out, John Saltburn will receive his just reward.'

'What concerns me,' Bray retorted, 'is the danger now confronting the countess. Ah well, we came here to confront that killer but also to collect the Secretum. Come, let's do it.'

Both men crouched before the first step leading up to the Creeping Cross. They hacked with their daggers at the thick wedge of scrawny grass and coarse weeds which flourished there. Abruptly this wedge fell away to reveal a gap large enough for Urswicke to put his hand through. He felt around and his fingers brushed soft leather. He pulled at this and brought out a dirt-stained chancery pouch tied securely at the neck. Urswicke cut the twine and gently shook the gleaming copper scroll container out of the bag. It weighed heavily and was sealed around its rim with chancery wax bearing the imprint of a signet, though this had begun to fade.

'Let us go,' Urswicke urged. 'We must return to the countess.' He slipped the copper container back into the sack, opened his jerkin and pushed it inside. They rose and left the maze.

When they reached the great bailey, the sound of revelry was deafening. Most of the war carts and barrows were crammed to overflowing with treasures and precious items from the house, the soldiers now busy feasting and celebrating. The crowd milling there were lost in their carousing, and Urswicke and Bray were hardly given a second glance. Both men hastened into the house where the countess was waiting for them in her chamber. Urswicke and Bray washed their hands and faces at the lavarium, then joined their mistress at the small chancery table. Urswicke, with Bray adding details, gave a brief account of their confrontation with Saltburn and the threat he revealed. Countess Margaret just sat and listened, only showing her anger by a tightening of the lips and the occasional whispered imprecation.

'Give me the copper container.'

Urswicke took it from his jerkin, undid the sack and handed it to his mistress, who used a chancery knife to slice the copper tube's seals and loosen the lid. Once she had, she shook the parchment scroll out on to the table, tapping it with the blade of the knife.

'I will come to that in a moment,' she declared, 'but the threat you described, Christopher, is certainly real. We must counter it.'

'It was also real to others.'

'Christopher?'

'Remember, my Lady, who was to accompany us back to London? Young Owain, now a member of your household. He'd be slain as well.' Christopher paused, eyes closed; he wondered what his father really intended.

'If Owain died,' the countess declared, 'Sir Thomas would use that when he published his farrago of nonsense. How the countess of Richmond and her beloved son were killed and the young man sheltering in Brittany remains a fraud. Oh, I am sure your father would twist it any way he wanted. All this is his device. The plots and counter-plots here at The Moor were an attempt by your father to clear the board. Patmore's arrival, along with the Imposter, was to create confusion and chaos in my party, and it certainly did. Your father intended the total destruction of the Nevilles and the seizure of all they own. He has achieved that. He also wanted the removal of my good self once and for all. For the moment he has failed, but he still persists in trying. I strongly suspect that this is Sir Thomas's doing rather than the King's. The Brothers York, apart from Clarence, would never be party to plotting such a murder.' She smiled wryly. 'However, if it happened and they were presented with a fait accompli, Edward and Richard would shrug and express their sorrow with false grieving and hypocritical tears. In a word, they would be joyful.'

'So, what do we do?'

'Oh Christopher, I know exactly what we will do. One of the letters I despatched was to my betrothed, Lord Thomas Stanley. I understand he is on his way here with a strong comitatus. I will now announce that I am most unwell and have decided to stay here until my dearly betrothed arrives to escort me back to the city. Your father will not wish to cross swords with Lord Thomas. Now, as for the Secretum.' Lady Margaret opened the scroll, telling her henchmen to sit and relax whilst she gave it swift perusal. Before she did, she showed it to Urswicke. 'See, Christopher, the cramped hand, the small letters, now I know it was written by no lesser person than the Earl of Warwick himself. So, what does this treasure chest contain?'

Urswicke and Bray made themselves comfortable, openly intrigued by their mistress, who now and then would pause in her study to exclaim in surprise at what she was reading. The scroll was of the finest vellum, sheets of costly parchment, stitched expertly together. The ink was pitch-black, so the words clearly stood out despite the cramped style of writing.

'Oh good Lord,' she exclaimed, rolling the manuscript up and putting it back in the copper tube.

'My Lady?'

'Christopher, Reginald, you can both read this on our return to London but, I assure you, the Secretum truly is a bowl of the juiciest morsels. The manuscript reveals secrets and scandals and, Christopher, on this be sure, clear mention is made of your father.' She tapped the manuscript. 'He is the individual who appears here as 'T.U. of the Secret Chancery': it must be no lesser a person than your father.'

'Of course, you must remember,' Urswicke declared, 'that the Secretum was drawn up long before my father received his knighthood and became the Recorder of the City, the champion of the Brothers York.'

'Well, Christopher, let me inform you. If Edward of England had read this manuscript, your father would certainly not have been knighted. Let me explain. Cast your mind back to three or four years ago when Richard Neville, Earl of Warwick, violently quarrelled with Edward of York. Once bosom comrades, they clashed over matters politic.'

'Yes, that's right.'

'The cause of the quarrel,' Margaret declared, 'was marriage. Warwick was trying to arrange a marriage between Edward of York and some princess abroad. All of this was completely overturned by Edward falling in love with – and secretly marrying – Elizabeth Woodville. The split between Warwick and Edward was bitter, most rancorous. People took sides. New alliances were forged, even in York's own family, where George of Clarence sided with the Nevilles. All kinds of dirt and mud floated to the surface; it truly was the season of intrigue. Whispering campaigns became the order of the day. Amongst these were the constant rumours that Edward of England was not Richard of York's true son. Consequently, he should be excluded from the succession in favour of his brother, George of Clarence, who, of course, had sided with Warwick. As I said, everyone took sides and your father was no different. According to the Secretum, Thomas Urswicke wrote to Warwick, and later visited him, to offer assistance and support. Of course, intrigue is like a fast-flowing river: nothing stands still; everything moves on. For reasons best known to himself, your father decided to stop currying favour with Warwick and sheltered deep in the Yorkist camp. Nevertheless, evidence now exists that your good father wavered and, for the likes of Richard of Gloucester, the King's brother, that is enough for anyone to be rejected. So—'

'So what?' Bray demanded.

'Reginald, Christopher, I think it's time we informed Sir Thomas Urswicke that at the present moment I am indisposed. So, I will await my betrothed, Lord Thomas Stanley, before taking to the roads.' She sipped from her goblet. 'It will be strange to leave The Moor, but one day, gentlemen, when my family have come into their own, I will return here. I want to walk these corridors and galleries again. I want to visit that maze and, above all, I want to go out across the meadow to sit where we met with Callista.'

'The maid?'

'The same, Christopher. You've heard my question to Poppleton, the bastard! Callista was a busy little thing. She probably sold information to anyone who asked. But I liked her; she had courage, a keenness of wit, yet I have a nightmare . . .'

'My Lady?'

'I suspect Achitophel invited her out to a meeting in some lonely, desolate place where he killed her. A brutal murder to silence her for good, then he disposed of her corpse. Once I have returned to London, I want you, Christopher, to visit a chantry priest in St Paul's. I would like masses offered for the repose of her soul. In addition, I make this vow. Once I and my family have come into their own, I shall return. I will have a thorough search made until we find that poor girl's remains, and give them honourable burial.'

'But in the meantime?'

'Oh, in the meantime, Christopher, tell your father that I have the Secretum and that I have studied it closely. So, please reassure him that he will never be far from my thoughts!'

AUTHOR'S NOTE

*D*ark Queen Wary is of course a work of fiction, but it is based on sound historical facts. Many of its strands, I believe, accurately reflect the spirit of the age, with all its eerie occurrences. The emergence of imposters was not as rare as some people might believe. Indeed Henry Tudor, after he had seized the Crown, had to face two sinister threats with the emergence of Lambert Simnel and Perkin Warbeck, both of whom claimed to be Yorkist princes. The danger of imposters was that they became a beacon light for all those unhappy with the political status quo: those who wished to challenge the Crown and searched desperately for a pretext to do so. Imposters provided them with this.

Lambert Simnel, for example, was only crushed after a bitter and savage battle at East Stoke. Warbeck, imprisoned in the Tower, resolutely refused to give up his intriguing against Henry VII. These pretenders plagued Henry Tudor for years. This phenomenon also explains why, after many battles, the victorious generals displayed the corpses of their dead rivals. For example, as described in this novel, after the Battle of Barnet, the mortal remains of Warwick and Montagu were displayed in an open arrow chest before the rood screen of St Paul's. This macabre ritual proclaimed that both Neville brothers were dead and would remain so!

The published broadsheets mentioned in the novel were also rising to prominence as a device to be used against political opponents. Printing and publishing were becoming easier. Garish proclamations were used to launch political attacks, which in turn attracted the close attention and sharp interference of the Crown and its ministers. Richard III, after his seizure of the throne from his two nephews, became the subject of such cruel, anonymous threats. A series of attacks which continued even to the very evening of the fatal Battle of Bosworth, where Richard was killed. On the morning of that conflict a proclamation was found pinned to the tent of Richard's principal commander, John Howard, Duke of Norfolk, warning him that his royal master was riding to destruction, the hapless victim of a most deadly conspiracy.

The Battle of Barnet was one of the most intriguing conflicts of the era. Commentators truly believed that the thick mist which swept the battlefield came directly from Hell. It certainly created hideous confusion, as described in this novel, with Lancastrian turning on Lancastrian in the firm belief that they were the enemy. The Earl of Warwick was caught up in all of this and came to regret his order to fight on foot. In the end his battle line broke, Warwick became isolated and was easily cut down. Matters were not helped by the treason and treachery which plagued both York and Lancaster. Individuals changed sides with the speed of a spinning top. George of Clarence is a fine example of this, but so is George Neville, Archbishop of York. (Please note that Lady Grace Neville is a figment of my imagination, though she represents the Neville clan in general.) Archbishop George, a leading prelate of this kingdom, proved to be one of the greatest turncoats of the era, a priest given to constant intrigue, who took to treachery and betrayal as a bird to flying. There is no doubt, as this novel describes, that in the late spring of 1473, George Neville once again decided to meddle in politics. There is considerable evidence that he was in communication with John de Vere, Earl of Oxford, who used as his emissary a former soldier called John Bank. George Neville definitely became involved in treasonable mischief. On one occasion, George was busy hunting with the King, next he was attending treasonable meetings in the dead of night. Edward of York learned all about this and struck with his usual speed. George Neville was arrested in the spring of 1473, carted off to the Tower, before being shipped out to Hammes Castle in Calais. Neville's beautiful palace of The Moor was ruthlessly plundered by Edward's agents. The archbishop's proud possession, a golden mitre, was seized and smashed to pieces.

George Neville, Archbishop of York, truly represents the spirit of the age which reached its climax with the Battle of Bosworth (1485). Richard marched out to meet Henry Tudor, fully believing that Percy of Northumberland was coming to assist him. The

Northern Earl however, had other ideas, moving south so slowly that Richard was dead before he ever reached the battlefield. The same is true of Lord Thomas Stanley, Margaret Beaufort's third husband. He took up position at Bosworth, where Richard gave him firm instructions about when to attack. Lord Thomas did lead his troops into the battle, not to assist Richard but to attack him. This was the moment Richard fell and the Yorkist cause collapsed. Countess Margaret's dream was realized!